PRAISE FOR
HELEN HARDT

"I'm dead from the strongest book hangover ever. Helen exceeded every expectation I had for this book. It was heart pounding, heartbreaking, intense, full throttle genius."
~ Tina at Bookalicious Babes Blog

"Proving the masterful writer she is, Ms. Hardt continues to weave her beautifully constructed web of deceit, terror, disappointment, passion, love, and hope as if there was never a pause between releases. A true artist never reveals their secrets, and Ms. Hardt is definitely a true artist."
~ Bare Naked Words

"The love scenes are beautifully written and so scorching hot I'm fanning my face just thinking about them."
~ The Book Sirens

Shattered

**STEEL BROTHERS SAGA
BOOK SEVEN**

This book is an original publication of Helen Hardt

This is a work of fiction. Names, characters, places, and incidents either are the product of the author's imagination or are used fictitiously, and any resemblance to actual persons, living or dead, business establishments, events, or locales is entirely coincidental. The publisher does not assume any responsibility for third-party websites or their content.

Copyright © 2017 Waterhouse Press, LLC
Cover Design by Waterhouse Press, LLC
Cover Photographs: Shutterstock

All Rights Reserved
No part of this book may be reproduced, scanned, or distributed in any printed or electronic format without permission. Please do not participate in or encourage piracy of copyrighted materials in violation of the author's rights. Purchase only authorized editions.

Paperback ISBN: 978-1-943893-23-2

Shattered

**STEEL BROTHERS SAGA
BOOK SEVEN**

WATERHOUSE PRESS

For all survivors of childhood abuse

WARNING

This book contains adult language and scenes, including flashbacks of child physical and sexual abuse, which may cause trigger reactions. This story is meant only for adults as defined by the laws of the country where you made your purchase. Store your books and e-books carefully where they cannot be accessed by younger readers.

PROLOGUE

RYAN

The last barrel of wine had been sent to bottling, and my busy season was finally over. I knew I had been neglecting my family, and it wasn't fair to them, with both Talon and Jonah going through so much.

Now that Jonah was back, the woman who had been stalking him was safely behind bars in a mental institution, and two of Talon's abductors had been taken care of, life was finally getting good for my family.

Jade and Talon and Jonah and Melanie were planning weddings. Well, actually, Marjorie was planning everything. Soon we'd all be en route to Jamaica for the celebration. And Melanie was pregnant. I would be an uncle in several months. I couldn't help smiling. It would be good for Joe. That man was a born father. He had taken good care of us when we were little, though of course he would deny that. But Melanie had been so good for him. Finally, he was letting go of the guilt that had consumed him for so long. He had been through so much during the last month. He deserved all the happiness in the world. He and Talon both did.

I was heading over to the main house now, to have dinner with my family. From now on, I was going to take an active role in finding Talon's last abductor. We had a name and several aliases. We would find him. My brothers and I were that determined. But first, I was going to get my two brothers married off.

As I stepped into my truck, my cell phone buzzed in my pocket. It was a number from Grand Junction I didn't recognize.

"Ryan Steel," I said.

"Ryan Steel? Ryan Warren Steel?"

"Yep, you got him. Who is this, please?"

A soft whimper came through the phone.

"Hello?" I said.

"Ryan," the female voice said. "Ryan, my darling. This is your mother."

CHAPTER ONE

RUBY

"Tom Simpson is dead."

I dropped my cell phone, and it clattered onto my kitchen table. I quickly picked it up. "Sorry," I said to Melanie Carmichael. "And...what?"

"He's dead. He killed himself. Jonah saw the whole thing. The police were there too."

My heart beat rapidly. "Oh my God. Is Jonah all right?"

"Yeah. He's fine, thank God. I begged him not to go over there. Our PIs found Simpson at his house in Snow Creek. Jonah went over to confront him, and Simpson ended up killing himself."

Despite the twinge of nausea that crept up my throat, I felt no remorse that a human being was dead. I only wished I could have shot the fateful bullet. I didn't know Tom Simpson personally, but I did know he was a criminally insane psychopath. Jonah Steel referred to him as an ice man, according to Melanie. The world was better off without him. The only other thing I knew about him was that he'd clearly been working with my father for decades.

My father.

Theodore Mathias. Known by many other names.

My father, who had raped my cousin, Gina. Who had

raped and tortured a ten-year-old Talon Steel. Who had killed and mutilated ten-year-old Luke Walker. Who had attempted to rape me.

And God only knew what other heinous things he'd done, though I had my theories.

Just thinking about Simpson and my father was reason enough for my queasiness, but another reason existed.

If Simpson was dead, I wouldn't be able to question him.

I'd gone to see Larry Wade, their third partner, a few times and peppered him with questions. I hadn't told Melanie or the Steel brothers. Didn't matter anyway. Larry wouldn't roll over. I'd tried everything. Deals, money, a conjugal visit, you name it. The dude just wouldn't talk.

Most of the dumb fucks sang like a canary when I offered them women. Of course, I wasn't able to offer Larry any young boys, which seemed to be his preference.

Maybe now that one of his partners in crime was dead, he'd start talking.

I doubted it.

I eyed my phone in my hand. Shit. Melanie. "Sorry. Are you still there?"

"Yeah. Are you okay?"

"Sort of. It's all surreal. Now we won't be able to get any information out of him. Since he's dead and all."

"I know. Jonah said the same thing. But at least he can't hurt anyone else."

I inhaled. "Amen to that. When did this all happen?"

"Earlier tonight. I figured you hadn't heard yet, since the Snow Creek police handled it."

"No, I hadn't. Thanks for letting me know."

"There is another reason I called, Ruby."

"Yeah?"

She cleared her throat. "How would you like a vacation?"

A vacation? I hadn't had a vacation in... Well, since never. I'd been working my ass off since I was fifteen. Work was my refuge, my solace. If I was working, my mind was occupied, and things I didn't want to think about couldn't creep in. A vacation? Nope. Not for me.

"I'm not sure what you're getting at, but I'm pretty busy at work."

"I know. Cops always are." She sighed. "This may seem like a crazy time to bring up a vacation."

"Kind of," I said.

Silence for what seemed like a small eternity.

"You still there?" I asked.

"Yeah. It's just..."

"What?"

"Jonah and I are getting married."

So that's what this was about. I couldn't begrudge her some happiness in this sea of misery and psychopathy we were both embroiled in. "Congratulations!"

"Yeah. Thanks. And I'm...pregnant."

I jolted a bit. "Oh? So..."

"That's not why we're getting married."

"Oh. Good. I guess."

"Anyway, we're going to Jamaica. Talon and Jade are getting married too. A double wedding."

"How nice." I wasn't sure what to say. I knew nothing about weddings. Nothing about men. Nothing about...any of it.

"Anyway, the reason I was asking if you wanted a vacation is that...I don't really have any close friends. I've been a workaholic my whole life."

"I hear you." Seemed we were two peas in a pod as far as work was concerned.

"I don't have any family members I'm close to, so I was hoping that you might..."

Was she saying what I thought she was? Was she about to ask me to stand up for her at her wedding?

We hardly knew each other.

Yet...Melanie Carmichael knew more about me than anyone else in the world. She knew about my past as well as my present. My coworkers knew only my present. My father and uncle knew only my past.

Melanie was about the closest thing I had to a friend.

She was probably thinking the same about me.

And while I didn't really relish a vacation, time spent with Melanie and the Steels would give me a great chance to question them about...things. Though they probably wouldn't want to talk about that kind of stuff in the middle of a wedding. A wedding was a happy time.

Happy.

Now there was a word I wasn't very familiar with.

I'd grown content with my life. Content with my work.

Content.

But never happy.

Never full of joy.

Never flying to the fucking moon.

Nope, not in the cards for me.

"...come along and be my maid of honor?"

Yep, there it was.

"I don't know..."

"Look, I know we don't know each other very well, but you're honestly the first person I thought to ask. I understand if you can't make it, but I'd love it if you could come."

For a minute I let myself think about it.

Jamaica.

Beach. Sand. Sun. Swimming.

Relaxation.

Another word I wasn't very familiar with.

Of course, the Steels wouldn't do anything halfway, and I could never afford to do it their way.

"That's really nice of you to ask. I'm honestly flattered." And I was. "But there's no way I'd be able to afford to go, Melanie."

She laughed. "It's all on me. Seriously."

"I couldn't let you do that. We don't know each other well enough for me to let you treat me."

"Please. I want to. I have some savings, and the Steels are paying for the big stuff. The wedding and all. I have a feeling no one has offered to do anything for you in a long time, Ruby. Let me. Please."

She had the truth of that. A vacation... Suddenly the idea didn't seem so scary.

"That's really generous of you, but I can pay my own way. I mean, as long as you're not staying at the Ritz Carlton or anything."

"No," she laughed. "We'll be spending a week at this all-inclusive resort in Negril. All of the rooms are the same price, and Jonah's sister was able to book us all in one bungalow. But I really wish you'd let me—"

"No. I've managed to save a few bucks over the years." That was no lie, either. I lived well beneath my means. Not that I made a lot as a cop, and now a detective, but I spent little on clothes. Little on luxuries. My gym membership was my big expense. I needed to be able to work out, stay in shape. It was a great way to work off steam, and I also wanted my body in the best condition possible. Just in case.

"Then are you saying you'll go?"

I smiled into the phone. *Was I?* "Yeah, Melanie. I guess I'll go."

"That's so great!"

She actually sounded happy that I was going. I hadn't known Melanie Carmichael for that long, but I did know she was a genuine person. A caring person. Maybe we could both use a friend.

"There is something I should warn you about."

"Oh?"

"There's a nude beach on the resort."

My stomach dropped. "Is the resort *all* nude?"

She laughed. "Oh, no. Of course not. There's a regular beach too, and several pools. Then there's a nude beach and a clothing-optional pool as well. All other areas, like the restaurants, are clothing required."

"Okay..."

"You don't have to go near the nude beach. I promise you. I already made Jonah promise that we weren't having a nude wedding."

Before I could stop it, a guffaw emerged from my throat. I wasn't ashamed of my body. Hell, no. I was in great shape. I looked better naked than clothed. But no one, other than physicians, had ever seen me naked. Not since that fateful day when my father had tried to...

But I really didn't want to go there now.

"That's good. I'm not sure I want to participate in a nude wedding."

She laughed. "Believe me, neither do I."

"Still, I need to see if I can get off work. When is the event?"

"Next week."

Next week? Shit. I had plenty of vacation time to spare. I rarely used it. Even when I was off the clock I was working. I had spent a lot of time investigating my cousin Gina's death with Melanie, all off the clock. Of course, I had only just made detective a few weeks earlier. I didn't know if my boss would be amenable to me taking a week off already.

"I can't make any promises. I have the vacation time, but I have to clear it with my boss."

"Great. Let me know what he says."

"I will." I cleared my throat. "Melanie?"

"Yeah?"

"Thanks for inviting me. I mean really. Thank you."

CHAPTER TWO

RYAN

"Who the fuck is this?"

"I told you, dear. Your mother."

"Look, I don't know who the hell you are, but my mother's been dead for decades." I ended the call and promptly blocked the number from my phone.

My heart pounded for a moment. I had been nine years old when my mother died. She killed herself in her bathroom in the main ranch house.

My father had gutted that room afterward and then nearly rebuilt the house from the ground up. Talon and Jade lived there today. I lived in the guest house.

I hadn't seen my mother's body. My father hadn't let us. He'd thought it would be too traumatizing. After what we'd been through two years before with Talon's abduction, I doubted we could have been more traumatized, but I was the youngest, and I never questioned my father.

None of us did.

I'd resented him for years because he wouldn't let us see her, but I eventually got over it. Still, it had affected us—so much so that none of us had looked at our father's dead body when he passed.

My sister, Marjorie, didn't even remember our mother.

That was a shame, because she was the only one of us who actually looked anything like her. The three of us boys all favored our father. Jonah the most. There didn't seem to be a speck of our mother in any one of us. Especially not in me.

My memories were sparse, but at least I *had* some memories. She had been a good mother. A loving mother. I hadn't been as close to her as Jonah was. I always thought he was her favorite. Then, once Talon returned, she had a hard time with all of us, Marjorie especially. Marjorie was a brand-new baby and needed her mother, but I never felt that my mother connected with her. She had a hard time connecting with all four of us once Talon returned.

Talon's abduction changed my mother.

We had found two of his abductors. Larry Wade, our mother's half brother, was in prison awaiting trial. Tom Simpson, the mayor of Snow Creek and Joe's best friend's father, had killed himself rather than face the music. Only one was left. Theodore Mathias, the father of a Grand Junction detective who was a friend of Melanie's.

He was the one who had been the most elusive throughout our entire investigation.

According to Talon, Mathias was the worst of all three.

I shook my head to clear it. Why was I thinking about all this shit because of some stupid prank phone call? My brothers were getting married next week. In sunny Jamaica. We were going to have a fucking blast. We hadn't had a vacation in so long.

Marjorie was making all the arrangements. She had booked us into an all-inclusive resort in Negril called Destination Desire. It was an all-adult resort, complete with a nude beach and clothing-optional pools. Thankfully, it also had another beach and other pools where clothing was required. I wasn't sure how I felt about walking around naked in front of my brothers' two fiancées and my sister. Or my brothers, for that matter. It was the only resort where Marj could get reservations on such short notice, so we'd agreed to turn a blind eye to the nude side of the resort.

However, I planned to sneak over...by myself.

Knowing Marj, it would be first class all the way. Jonah had asked me to be his best man, which was nice of him, since Talon had wanted Joe to be his. I was a little disappointed that Talon hadn't chosen me. I loved both of my brothers equally, but Talon... Talon was my hero.

Because of Talon, I had been spared the torture that he endured for two months. He and I had been walking together that day, trying to dig up clues about the disappearance of his friend Luke Walker.

When the two men attacked us, Talon had gotten me free and yelled at me to run.

And damn, I had run.

I'd run like my life depended on it, which it most likely had.

That was the day. The terrible day. The day that had brought us to where we were now.

Talon was finally getting the help he needed and was healing. He was better each day. Now he was strong enough to take the plunge with Jade and get married.

I was ecstatic for him. And I was honored to be Jonah's best man. Still, Talon meant so much to me.

No matter.

This was going to be a great vacation for all of us. And I was just as happy for Jonah and his new bride, Melanie. Melanie had worked miracles as Talon's therapist and was now working more miracles with Joe. She was pregnant, too. I would be an uncle.

Watching my brothers fall in love and prepare to get married made me happy. But it was all just a little bittersweet. I wasn't sure anything like that was in the cards for me. Oddly, I was the only one of the three of us who had ever had a serious relationship. I had been in a relationship with Anna Shane, a woman from a neighboring ranch, for several years. We were comfortable together, we'd thought we were in love with each other, but now, seeing what Jonah and Talon had with their women, I knew Anna and I had made the right choice not to continue. We'd had a lot in common. But that fire? That fire that I witnessed between Talon and Jade, and Jonah and Melanie? That had been missing.

I kept busy at the ranch. We all did. But winemaking was especially tedious in the summer and fall. I had been working twenty hours a day the last three months, and I was looking forward to a break.

So I wasn't getting married. So I wasn't Talon's best man. So what? I was Ryan Steel, and Ryan Steel had fun no matter what he did.

I was known around town as being the most jovial and having the best personality of all three Steel brothers. I wasn't sure if that was true, but I did like to have a good time.

And next week in Jamaica? I was going to party it up, Ryan Steel style.

Rum punch, beach bunnies, a little boating, a little surfing.

And, I hoped, a whole lot of fucking.

Quite a while had passed since I'd had a woman. I planned on taking a case of condoms with me to Jamaica. And even that might not be enough.

★ ★ ★

We were situated on the plane, all of us in first class except for Melanie's friend, a mousy detective named Ruby Lee, who just happened to be the daughter of Theodore Mathias. I'd given her a once-over at the gate. Her nearly black hair was pulled back in a schoolteacher style, and she wore no makeup that I could see—although her face didn't seem to need it. Her cheeks had a natural rosy glow. She wore a white button-down shirt and green Dockers. What might that body look like under those boyish clothes?

One thing I didn't lack was imagination. My imagination was what made me a good winemaker. It was also what allowed me to envision the curves hidden underneath Ruby Lee's garments.

Very nice.

Jonah and Melanie had tried to persuade Ruby to join us in first class, but she'd been determined to pay her own way and simply didn't want to spend extra to upgrade.

The seat next to me was empty, as were several other first class seats. I flagged down a flight attendant as soon as the captain had turned off the seat belt signs.

"Yes?" she said.

"There's a woman in coach I'd like to have join us."

"You can certainly do so. She'll need to pay the upgrade fee."

I whipped my wallet out of my back pocket, took out a credit card, and handed it to her. "That's on me."

"How generous of you. Which passenger do you want to

upgrade?"

"Ruby Lee. She's near the middle of the plane."

"Of course. Give me a moment."

She returned with my card a few minutes later. "All taken care of. I'll tell Ms. Lee that she's been upgraded."

I put my card away. "No, that's okay. I'll tell her."

She nodded and walked toward the front of the plane.

One thing I wasn't was shy. I got up, walked through first class and back into coach, found Ruby sitting in an aisle seat, and touched her shoulder.

She looked up at me, her cheeks reddening. "Yes?"

"Come with me," I said.

Her cheeks reddened even further. "You mean me?"

"You've been upgraded. To first class. With the rest of us."

"I already told Melanie. I'm paying my way."

"Melanie has nothing to do with this."

"Then what's going on?"

I smiled. Women always said they couldn't resist my smile. And while I had no physical interest in Ruby Lee—though she did look amazing naked in my imagination—I did want to do something nice for her. After all, she was in a similar boat as the rest of us. Her father was the last of Talon's abductors and was still at large. Her life couldn't have been easy.

"I upgraded you."

She arched her eyebrows. "You? Why?"

"Because you're one of our party. Because it was a nice thing to do. Because I have the money. Because there are vacancies in first class. You want me to continue listing more reasons?"

"Look, it's decent of you, but I couldn't possibly—"

"Say no. That's what you were about to say, right?" I

smiled again.

"Well...no, actually."

"Come on. I've already spent the money to upgrade you. The flight attendant took my credit card and everything. So if you stay back here, you're just wasting my money."

That seemed to get to her. She twisted her lips. "I never asked you to do this."

"I know you didn't. I did it because I wanted to."

"Why would you want to?"

"Look, why don't we continue this conversation up in first class, where it's more comfortable? Once you settle in there, I'll be happy to regale you with tales of why I made the offer."

That got a smile out of her. Well, only a half smile, but I could tell she was holding back.

"I've never sat in first class before."

"Then you're in for a treat." I opened the overhead bin. "Which one is your bag?"

"The plain black one."

There were several plain black ones, but I quickly found the one with her name on it and grabbed it. "Get your other stuff and follow me." I moved toward first class.

When I got back to my seat, I stowed her bag in the overhead bin and then looked behind me. She was holding her laptop case. I took it from her and put it in the overhead bin as well.

"I'll keep that," she said. "I thought I might do some work."

"Nope. No work. Part of my treat. You're going to sit in first class, let the airline staff pamper you, have a mimosa or martini or whatever your drink of choice is."

"Red wine," she said.

I arched my eyebrows. "Really? I love red wine too. In

fact, it's what I do for a living."

She smiled shyly. "Yes, I know. Melanie says you're a genius."

"Melanie is overstating my prowess, I'm afraid." Though my winemaking skills were well documented by the array of awards my wines had won. But I didn't need to blab about that right now.

"That's not what I hear. She said I definitely need to try your wine."

"Unfortunately, I doubt my wines are stocked at the resort in Jamaica. When we get back, I'll make sure you get a case of my finest."

"You don't need to do that."

"Of course I do. If you like red wine, I have to see if you like mine."

"That's very generous of you. In fact, all of this is generous of you. I'm afraid I don't understand why—"

I placed two fingers over her lips, which were surprisingly soft. "I've already explained that. Then again, we did agree to continue the conversation about why."

Her rosy cheeks pinked up a bit more. "I'm just...not used to people being so nice to me."

"Get used to it. We Steels try to be nice to everyone. Everyone who's nice to us, that is."

"I hear that," she said. "I've been crossed myself."

Something in me wanted to ask more. To find out exactly what she'd been through. But damn it, we were on our way to Jamaica. For a relaxing vacation. A happy vacation. To watch my brothers get married.

Still, something about her... I couldn't help myself.

"What do you mean?" I asked.

CHAPTER THREE

RUBY

How I wished I could take back that statement. Now was certainly not the time to get into my life. This was Ryan Steel, a man I hardly knew.

And the best-looking man I had ever laid my eyes on.

God, it was true what the gossipers said. Ryan was the most handsome of all the Steel brothers. Having seen only Talon and Jonah before now, I'd had a hard time imagining that anyone could be better looking than those two.

But Ryan was. Where Jonah and Talon were rugged and handsome with dark hair, dark eyes, a couple days' worth of stubble on their cheeks, Ryan Steel was Greek god gorgeous. He had a sculpted jawline, a chin with just the right amount of prominence, a perfect Grecian nose, and lips... Was it possible for a man's lips to be beautiful? It was now. His were full, and pink, and... *Dare I think it?* Kissable.

Kissing was something I knew nothing about. Hell, I knew nothing about men, period. Men didn't pay much attention to me, which was how I preferred it. I was often mistaken for a lesbian, no doubt because of the way I dressed in mostly masculine clothing. I rarely wore makeup, and I pulled my long hair back in a tight bun most of the time. I'd considered cutting it off more than once, but I couldn't. It was my one link to my mother. She'd had long, lustrous hair, though lighter than mine.

Being a lesbian might've made my life easier. But no, I was attracted to men. I just didn't act on it. I kept myself under the radar, tried to keep myself from being attractive. The truth was, I was scared shitless of men.

I had often thought about going to therapy. I was smart enough to know that my fear of men stemmed from being attacked at the age of fifteen by my own father. But I was so consumed by my work and my fear of delving inside myself that I'd never bothered to get any help.

My new friend, Melanie Carmichael, was a renowned psychotherapist. She was currently on a leave of absence because of my cousin's suicide and my shithead uncle's malpractice suit against her, but I was hoping that maybe she and I could do a little talking during vacation.

That was selfish of me. This was her wedding. I couldn't saddle her with my problems. Nope, there'd be no free therapy for me during this trip. In fact, there'd be no free therapy for me at all. Once Melanie went back to her practice, I'd pay her. I had insurance.

I always paid my own way. Had since I was fifteen. Until now.

I looked around at the wide comfortable seat I sat in, the leg room, the menu of fine spirits...

This wasn't paying my way.

"Earth to Ruby."

I turned my head toward Ryan. I'd nearly forgotten he had asked me a question. What was it again? Right. I'd said that I'd been crossed before, and he'd asked what I meant.

"Nothing," I said.

Nothing. So far from the truth. But I wouldn't saddle any of the Steels or their brides with my issues. Not now. Perhaps not ever. Already I was having second thoughts about seeing Melanie for therapy.

Was it possible for me to relax during this vacation?

I had to try. I *had* to.

"Nothing?" Ryan said.

"Yes. Nothing."

"You said you'd been crossed before. That's not nothing."

I sighed. "You know who I am. Who my father is. You know my whole story."

He nodded. "I wouldn't say I know your whole story. Tell me about you."

Why in the world would this western god be interested in me? "It's a long, boring tale."

"I'll be the judge of that." He called the flight attendant and then perused the wines available on the menu. "Not a great selection..."

The flight attendant approached. "Yes, sir?"

"Two glasses of the Sioux Valley Meritage red, please."

"Right away."

He turned to me. "Not great, but passable."

"I don't usually drink before five."

"We're in the air! It's five o'clock somewhere. Besides, this is vacation."

I turned to him and smiled. Or tried to. "Right. Vacation. Which means I don't want to talk about how I've been crossed. I'd much rather talk about something a little less...intense."

He laughed. "I hear that. Good enough for me."

The flight attendant returned with our wine. "Thanks, sweetheart," Ryan said.

Something niggled in my stomach. I wasn't sure what it was, except that Ryan calling the attractive blond stewardess "sweetheart" kind of hit me the wrong way.

The very wrong way.

Get over yourself, Ruby. Someone like Ryan Steel would never look twice at you. And even if he did? You wouldn't know what to do with him.

My lot in life was to stay single. To take care of myself. I'd been doing it for seventeen years. I didn't need to change my way of life now.

Truthfully, I was scared to change. Scared of men. Scared of feeling anything for a man.

Ryan interrupted my thoughts. "So what do you want to talk about?"

Good question. He was a winemaker, and I was interested in wine. "Wine?"

"I do know something about that."

He swirled the wine around and then stuck his nose into the glass and inhaled. His nose was so far in I thought he might have wine dripping from it when he pulled it out. But he didn't.

"Nice nose."

I touched my nose. "Huh?"

He laughed. "I mean the nose of the wine. Its fragrance. But your nose is nice too."

Oh. My. God. Embarrassment swept through me. What a moron I was. And here I'd thought I knew a few things about wine. "Of course."

"What do you smell on the nose?"

I stuck my nose into the glass.

"Swirl it around first," he said. "To release the aroma."

"Sure. Right." I swirled the wine and then sniffed it. "I

don't know. Red plum, I think. Maybe a little vanilla?"

"Good! I got those too. Also some tobacco. A little shitake mushroom."

Shitake mushroom? Was he serious? "Okay."

"You don't seem to believe me."

"I'm not even sure what shitake mushrooms smell like. Do mushrooms even have a smell? I mean, outside of soup."

"It's kind of a savory, funky odor. Go ahead and taste. Tell me what you think."

"Okay." I swirled the wine in the glass again, took a sip, trickled it along my tongue, and swallowed. "Definitely plum, but some earthy tones too. It's kind of dry on my tongue. I don't mean not sweet."

"Those are the tannins. Common in Bordeaux blends." He took a sip. "I taste the plum and the earth. A little vanilla, a little chocolate. A lot of tannin. I like tannin, but this is a little much." He took another sip. "Not a bad blend, but overrated based on the awards it's received. In my opinion, anyway."

I took another sip. I liked it. "What are the grapes in this blend?"

"I'm not exactly sure. It's a Meritage, so it's made with Bordeaux grapes. Mostly cabernet sauvignon, I'd say. Some merlot and malbec as well. But I'm getting mostly cab."

The flight attendant returned. "We'll be serving dinner soon. We have two choices today. *Boeuf bourguignon aux champignons* or chicken cacciatore."

"The lady and I will have the beef," Ryan said.

Why was he ordering for me? "I'd prefer the chicken," I said. "I'm not really a beef person."

"Not a beef person?" Ryan clutched his heart. "When I'm part owner of the greatest beef ranch in the world?"

"I thought you were the winemaker."

"I am. But beef is the biggest part of our enterprise." He held up two fingers to the flight attendant while still looking at me. "Two chickens."

She smiled and hurried away, while my skin warmed me in a cocoon. He was looking at me. *Me.* Instead of the pretty stewardess.

"I'm used to prime beef," he continued, smiling, "and I doubt the airline has access to that."

I returned his smile. How could I not? Ryan Steel wasn't just gorgeous. He was a damned nice guy. I liked him.

God help me.

CHAPTER FOUR

RYAN

After I settled in to my room at the resort, I changed into board shorts and a muscle shirt and decided to look around. No one would miss me. I had promised to meet up with the rest of the clan for a late dinner at ten, but for now I was going to check out the place...and possibly wander onto the nude beach. I knew there was zero chance of encountering anyone in my family there.

I walked along the beach and found the nude section. Bodies of all shapes and sizes greeted me, and before I knew it, I had walked off of the sand and found a nude swimming pool. I stripped off my shorts and shirt, entered, and swam to the pool bar.

"What'll it be, mon?" the bartender said in his Jamaican accent.

"Rum punch."

He handed me my drink with a toothy smile. "Enjoy."

I took a sip of what I expected to be refreshing and sparkling. Instead, it was cloyingly sweet.

What was the big deal about rum punch anyway? Give me a good red wine any day. I drank the rest down and then turned around. Naked bodies were everywhere, including a luscious-looking blonde on the other side of the pool who was checking me out. I gave her a smile.

She swam toward the bar and then stood next to me, her full breasts bobbing on the surface of the water.

"Can I get you a drink?" I asked.

"Sure. I'll have a Bahama Mama."

I got the drink from the bartender and handed it to her. "I'm Ryan."

"I'm Juliet. Where are you from, Ryan?"

"Colorado."

"Cool. I'm from Cali."

The blond hair could've told me that. "Whereabouts?" I asked.

"LA. I'm an actress."

"Oh?"

She nodded. "Actually a waitress, but I go on lots of auditions. One day I'll get my big break."

I nodded. Girls like her were probably a dime a dozen in California. Though she was pretty cute, I'd never been much for blondes. My only serious relationship had had brown hair. Still, Juliet wasn't bad to look at.

"So what do you do in Colorado?"

"I make wine."

"Wine? That seems more like California."

"Colorado has a pretty good winemaking industry. Ever hear of Steel Acres Vineyards?"

"No. I'm sorry."

I wasn't surprised. Juliet didn't really look like a wine lover. Anybody who drank Bahama Mamas the way she was sucking it down no doubt preferred something sweet.

"That's my vineyard. I'm the winemaker there. It's part of the Steel ranch. My brothers and sister and I all own it together."

"Ranchers? Wow. I've never met someone from a ranch before."

I wasn't sure why she was surprised. California had plenty of ranches. Of course, the only ranches she was probably familiar with were the old *Bonanza* sets. She'd probably never stepped foot outside LA.

I was quickly becoming bored. Funny, I'd talked to Ruby Lee for hours on the plane ride, and I hadn't been bored once. Now, when I was trying to pick up a woman—and Juliet was *all* woman—I was bored out of my mind.

"So are you here with anyone?" I asked.

She shook her head. "I'm traveling with a couple girlfriends. One of them is out to dinner right now. I'm not sure where the other is. She probably picked someone up." Juliet giggled. "We have a system. If one of us is in the room with a guy, we put a sock on the doorknob."

For the first time, I wondered how old Juliet was. She was acting like a sorority chick. "Do you mind if I ask how old you are?"

"I'm legal, if that's what you mean."

That could mean as young as eighteen. Being thirty-two, I wasn't really interested in hooking up with a teen. Of course, that was all it would be. A hookup.

"Who are you with?" she asked.

"I'm here with my brothers. And my sister. My two brothers are getting married. We're having a big wedding here in a couple days."

"Oh," she gushed. "How romantic. But are you here with a...girlfriend?"

I smiled. "Nope. I'm free as a bird."

She lit up like a Christmas tree, the softness of the pool lights landing on her luminescent skin. It was nearing November, and even though it was still hot enough here in Jamaica to be in the pool, darkness had set in.

"I assume you have your own room?"

"I do."

She moved forward and touched my shoulder. No sparks. Not that I expected there to be. If this would be anything at all, it would be a one-nighter. Actually, more like a one-hour-er. She was certainly pretty enough. But man... She was so young.

"Tell me how old you are."

"I told you. I'm legal."

"Does that mean eighteen or twenty-one?"

"Silly. The resort doesn't allow anyone under twenty-one, with the nude beach and all."

I hadn't thought of that. "So how much older than twenty-one?"

She giggled. "About three months."

Just a baby. A baby who shared a room with two others and left a sock on the door when it was occupied. This was sorority central.

To my surprise, I wasn't interested.

"I think you're too young for me, Juliet."

"Why? How old are you?"

"I'm thirty-two. Pretty close to thirty-three, actually."

"Wow, an older man." She widened her eyes. "Shay and Lisa will absolutely be green with envy if I bring you to our room."

Just what I needed. A couple of other teenyboppers jealous over me. "I don't think so."

"But you bought me a drink."

"Correction. I *ordered* you a drink. This is all-inclusive, remember?"

She turned her lips down into a pouty frown. "What if I got you another? What do you like to drink?"

"Wine. Good wine."

"Hmm. I don't know anything about wine. I don't like it much."

This was so not happening. Not that I couldn't handle a woman not liking wine. She was just too young. I held out my hand. "It was great to meet you. I'm sure we'll see each other around."

"I hope so. My friends and I are here for a few more days. How long are you here for?"

"A week."

She smiled sweetly. "Are you sure I can't convince you? You'll have fun with me. I promise." She winked.

I shook my head. "You're very attractive, but you're just too young. I'm sorry."

I turned and walked toward the pool ladder. Sticking around here wouldn't do me any good right now. I'd never get rid of her. Besides, I had to go back to my room and shower before dinner.

Ruby would be at dinner. Maybe she'd be wearing more flattering clothes. Of course, why did I care what Ruby wore?

I didn't.

I was here to have fun, vacation, relax after such a busy and tiring wine season, and help my brothers celebrate their weddings.

And that was exactly what I planned to do.

★ ★ ★

Marjorie had made reservations at the Japanese hibachi steakhouse at the resort. There were eight of us, so we took up a table by ourselves. I had put on a pair of black dress slacks and a white shirt, no tie. I needn't have bothered with any of it, though. Everyone else was dressed in shorts and flip-flops. Casual seemed to be the way of it around here.

"Nice duds," Talon said to me.

"Yeah, I didn't get the memo on the dress code."

"It's all island wear here, even at dinner," he said. "Where were you, anyway? We would've told you what to wear."

"I walked over to the nude beach and took a quick swim in the pool."

Talon laughed. "Hey, guys," he said to the others. "Ry here already made a visit to the nude beach."

The razzing from my brothers began. Joe's friend Bryce joined in as well.

"Where are the ladies?" I asked.

"Jade was still getting ready when I left," Talon said. "She told me to go ahead."

"Ditto for Melanie," Jonah said. "I assume Marj and Ruby will be along with them any minute."

"Cool." I sat down and opened the menu. "I don't imagine they have any decent wines around this place."

"In your opinion?" Jonah said. "Probably not. But they should have some good wine."

I perused the list and was pleased to find a few I approved of. I ordered a couple bottles, while Talon ordered a bourbon, Jonah a martini, and Bryce a beer.

"So where's Henry this week?" I asked Bryce, referring to

his nearly one-year-old son.

"With my mother and my aunt."

"And how's your mom doing?" I regretted the words as they left my lips. Maybe he didn't want to talk about that. Then again, if Henry was staying with his mother, surely she was okay.

"She's better. It helps her to be around Henry. And she's with my Aunt Vickie too, so between the two of them, Henry's in good hands. Mom was suffering from a little bit of neurosis and some situational depression after she found out about my father. And then his suicide... To be honest, I think she's relieved that he's gone."

"Understandable."

"She's going to stay with Aunt Vickie for a while. They need each other right now. Now that Vickie knows for sure what happened to her son, and my father's part in it..." Bryce sighed. "Uncle Chase is there. They'll be all right." He smiled. "And I plan to call. A lot."

"Marj sure does adore Henry," I said. Marjorie had taken care of Bryce's son a few times. I had never imagined her as the motherly type. She hadn't been content to stay in the house like a good girl, much to my chauvinist father's chagrin. She worked right alongside us guys on the ranch. I never imagined her doing anything in the childcare department, but she had really taken to the little guy.

"Here come the women now," Talon said, smiling. His eyes were glued to Jade, his fiancée.

Jade was beautiful, her golden-brown hair tumbling down around her shoulders, and she wore a pink bikini top—yeah, she was my brother's woman, but she had an amazing rack—and a black-and-pink sarong tied around her waist.

Melanie, Jonah's fiancée, had wavy blond hair and was taller than Jade and not as curvy. She looked gorgeous in a casual black dress that showed off her great legs.

Our sister, Marjorie, was the tallest of the lot at around six feet. She was wearing a red sarong tied into a dress.

Coming up behind her was—

My eyes nearly popped out of my head. Who the hell was that?

Sleek dark hair with only slight waves hung well below her shoulders, resting on beautiful breasts. A light-blue V-neck tank showed lots of cleavage, and a denim miniskirt hugged her hips. Her legs were shapely, and so were her arms. This woman was athletic—athletic but still curvy and perfect in all the right places. Her full lips were painted scarlet, and her face...

Ruby Lee.

Still no makeup other than maybe some mascara and the red lipstick. Damn, she didn't need it.

She was beautiful. And God...that body.

Well, she was a cop. She was probably required to stay in shape.

Jonah and Talon smiled.

"You ladies all look beautiful," Talon said.

Ruby twisted her lips and looked down.

"Let's see," Marjorie was saying. "Where shall we all sit? Boy, girl, boy, girl, of course. Let's go Bryce, me, Talon, Melanie, Jonah, Jade, Ryan, Ruby. How does that sound?"

Sounded great to me. I wouldn't mind looking at Ruby Lee during dinner. Boy, she sure cleaned up nice.

CHAPTER FIVE

RUBY

My skin tightened around me. I felt like I was wrapped in cellophane. I knew I was turning twelve shades of red. Why did Marjorie seat me next to Ryan? Granted, we had shared a little conversation on the plane, but he was just being nice.

While the other guys were all wearing shorts and flashy print shirts, Ryan looked dashing in plain black dress pants and a white shirt with the top few buttons undone. A tiny bit of black chest hair peeked out, and again I looked down.

I had never been so attracted to a man.

I had never *let* myself be so attracted to a man. I had no intention of letting myself right now, but something about him made it difficult to resist. He wasn't just a beautiful creature. He was also a nice man. A generous one. I had no idea how much money he had shelled out for my first class seat on the plane, but I did know the Steels were loaded. Melanie had made that clear, and it was common knowledge, anyway.

Ryan would have no interest in me. He was simply a nice person.

My skin heated as he touched my forearm.

I turned toward him abruptly. "What?" I asked a little too loudly.

"You are miles away. I was asking if you want wine."

"Oh." I cleared my throat. "Yes. That would be nice. Thank you."

The waiter filled my glass.

"Did you order this wine?" I asked.

"Yeah. Their selection isn't great, but it's a little better than on the plane." He smiled.

Even his teeth were perfect. Not too big, not too small, and no doubt straightened by the best orthodontia Steel money could buy. Yet something told me he hadn't worn braces. No. Ryan Steel had been born perfect.

I looked over at his brothers. Steel brother number one, Jonah, the oldest, had hair a little longer and darker than Ryan's. It was graying at the temples and in his few days' worth of stubble. His eyes were dark, nearly black. We were sitting at the moment, but when standing he was tall. Around six-four.

Steel brother number two, Talon, the middle brother, stood about six-three. He had lived the most difficult life of the three. He looked a lot like number one and had the same coloring, though his hair was a little wavier with less gray. His jawline was a slightly different shape, and he had a barely noticeable crook in his nose. It had most likely been broken, probably when he was in captivity. I suppressed a shudder. What my father had put this man through...

I tried not to think about it as I concentrated on the man sitting next to me. The youngest Steel brother.

Ryan's eyes were slightly lighter than his brothers'—a chestnut brown rather than espresso. His hair was a little bit shorter and a little better groomed. Not in quite as much disarray as his brothers'. His eyebrows were dark brown and sculpted. Had he had them shaped? I had to stop myself from chuckling. No Steel man would have his brows threaded. They were perfect on their own.

I shook my head slightly. Was I really waxing poetic about Ryan's eyebrows when I'd just assessed his brothers as though they were suspects in a lineup?

The most amazing feature on Ryan Steel was his mouth. All the Steel brothers had gorgeous lips, but Ryan's were the pinkest and fullest.

Something in me surged at that moment. Something I hadn't let myself feel in over well over a decade. For a second I didn't recognize it.

Then it hit me.

Desire. Sexual desire.

I had come across attractive men in my lifetime. Even some close in looks to Ryan Steel. But I'd always held back, never let myself feel anything.

Now, looking at Ryan...

I couldn't. There was a reason I stayed away from men. There was a reason I dressed the way I normally did.

I didn't want the attention.

The clothes I was wearing weren't my own. I had only brought a few pairs of slacks and shorts, several button-up shirts, a one-piece bathing suit in an unflattering brown, a pair of flip-flops, and a couple pairs of sensible shoes. Melanie had told me not to worry about what to wear for the wedding, that she would take care of it. But I'd had no idea that her future sister-in-law would take over my wardrobe this evening.

Marjorie was about six inches taller than I, and I shuddered to think of what this miniskirt I was wearing looked like on her. It probably barely covered her ass.

But she had insisted, and Jade and Melanie had agreed, that I wear something a little more exciting to dinner. Jade and

I had the same size feet, so the strappy sandals I was wearing belonged to her.

They had oohed and aahed when I'd stripped down to my underwear to let them dress me like a Barbie doll. Yes, I was in shape. The only reason I didn't have six-pack abs was my own choice. I didn't particularly like six-packs on women.

★ ★ ★

"Wow," Marjorie said. "Why on earth do you cover this body up?"

"I don't know."

That was a goddamned lie.

"Well, that's over now. The three of us would love to look like that. How do you do it?"

All three of them were gorgeous in very different ways. I didn't know why they'd want to look like me.

"I work out," I said. "A lot."

"Do you diet?"

I shook my head. "Nope. I eat what I want. I have a huge appetite from all the exercise."

"Wow. What do you do for working out?" Jade asked.

"Weight training, interval training, kickboxing. When I get tired of that, I do a little yoga."

"Do you have to stay in shape?" Melanie asked. "To stay on the force?"

"No. The training was pretty vigorous when I was back in the academy, and we're encouraged to stay in shape, but a lot of the cops I know have grown beer bellies." I smiled.

"Wow," Jade said again. "Too bad we don't have a couple months before the wedding. You could get us all in tip-top shape."

I warmed. They were all very beautiful with great bodies. When I said as much, Melanie said, "Thank you. That's really sweet, Ruby. But you... There's no comparison."

Marjorie had taken it upon herself to pull my hair out of the bun. "And all this hair!" she exclaimed.

My hair fell nearly all the way down my back.

"Why do you keep it wound up so tight?"

"It's just the style I'm used to."

"I suppose it does suit you well when you're working," she said. "But this is not a week for work. We're going to relax, celebrate, have fun. You need fun hair." She began brushing my hair. "Amazing. Straight with just a little wave from being wound up. Not a bit of frizz on your whole head. You have a beautiful head of hair, Ruby."

"I... Thank you," I said.

After Marjorie finished combing out my hair and dressing me in her own tank top and skirt—"the color of this tank will go great with your eyes"—she painted my lips a dark red, which I wasn't sure I could deal with. Then she stroked on some blush and mascara.

"That's really all you need. Your skin is gorgeous. What products do you use?"

"Um...soap and water?"

"In Colorado? How do you keep your skin from drying out? You should be moisturizing."

Marjorie Steel certainly didn't mince words.

"Good genes, I guess." I nearly had to laugh at that one. They all knew where half my genes had come from, and they were not good. Although, even though my father was a complete psychopath, he was pretty damned good-looking. He had dark hair, nearly black, the same as mine, though his skin was olive

and his eyes brown. My skin was fair and my eyes blue, like my mother's.

Marjorie chattered on about getting me on a good skin care regimen. I gave up and stopped listening after a while. At one point, all three of them had their hands on me, doing something.

★ ★ ★

Ryan Steel was looking at me. I could tell. His eyes were burning two holes in my skin. I nervously picked up my wineglass and took a sip.

"What do you think?"

I set my wineglass down shakily, willing myself not to spill the red liquid. "What?"

"About the wine. What do you think?"

"Oh. It's good."

"I think it'll work well with the spicy Asian stuff we'll be having," Ryan said.

I nodded. Was I supposed to say something? I wasn't sure. The waiter came around and took our orders. I ordered teriyaki chicken, while Ryan ordered seared scallops and filet mignon. That sounded better than teriyaki chicken. I kept forgetting that this place was all-inclusive and I could order what I liked. But it was too late to change my order. Maybe Ryan would let me have a bite of his.

Of course for that to happen, I'd have to ask for a taste. No way would I have that much nerve.

I took another sip of my wine, this time letting it sit on my tongue for a moment to see what flavors I could identify. Mostly red fruit. Maybe a little earthiness.

"I want to propose a toast," Marjorie was saying. "To

Jade and Talon, to Jonah and Melanie, to all of us, and to this vacation that we all so richly deserve."

Laughter erupted from our group, and we all clinked glasses. Soon the chef came to prepare our food for us at our table. I was quiet. He gave me something to focus on. He kept us laughing with his antics, making an onion volcano and challenging us to catch little pieces of shrimp in our mouths.

When he got to me, I shook my head.

"Come on, Ruby," Marjorie urged. "It's part of the fun."

I didn't want to look like an idiot. Though neither Jonah nor Talon had been able to catch one.

I opened my mouth, and the chef effortlessly pitched a small piece of shrimp right onto my tongue. I couldn't help a smile before I closed my mouth and chewed and swallowed the seafood. The chef winked at me.

The guy was good. I smiled at him, silently thanking him for not making me look like a moron.

The teriyaki chicken was delicious, and of course I was too embarrassed to ask Ryan for a taste of his scallops and filet mignon. They looked amazing, though. The freshly made fried rice was the *pièce de résistance*, in my opinion. I gobbled up the stuff.

As I was pulling my napkin from my lap, hopefully daintily, a young blonde came bubbling up next to us.

"Hello there," she said to Ryan.

"Oh, hi, Juliet," Ryan said.

Juliet? She couldn't have been any more than eighteen. I might have a hard and tight body, but it was the result of a lot of work. At eighteen, no work was required. Well, maybe a little. At eighteen, I'd begun my quest for physical strength after I found out I couldn't get into the police academy until I was twenty-one. Up until then, I'd survived on leftovers at the diner where I worked as a waitress, thanks to a fake ID. I was never overweight, but I'd been a little soft. No longer.

Not that I didn't look feminine. I used my workouts to create long, lean muscles, not bulky ones. I had no desire to look like a body builder.

I looked up at Blondie and assessed her quickly. I had bigger boobs than she did, though hers weren't bad. I grabbed my wineglass, which the waiter had just refilled, thank God, and took quite a gulp. When was the last time I had compared my boobs to another woman's? And why did I suddenly care?

Blondie smiled. "I was walking by and I happened to see you in here, so I thought I'd come in and say hi."

"Hi back," Ryan said.

"Aren't you going to introduce me to your friends?"

"Well...sure." Ryan introduced all of us, ending with me.

"Hi, everyone. I'm Juliet."

A chorus of salutations echoed across the table.

I stayed silent. It hadn't taken Ryan Steel long to find a conquest for the evening.

A lump had lodged in my throat. I wasn't sure why. I certainly didn't have any designs on Ryan Steel. Did I? He was way out of my league anyway. And I wasn't looking for a man. Ever.

"Are you done with dinner?" Juliet asked Ryan. "It's a gorgeous night for a walk on the beach."

"It is," Ryan agreed. "But I've already got plans for a walk with Ruby." He took my hand. "Shall we?"

I arched one eyebrow. Was he using me to get rid of Blondie? Because I was nobody's tool.

"No, we don't," I said.

"Of course we do. You promised." He smiled.

No. Stop beating, heart. Don't let that gorgeous smile sway you. He's just trying to get out of walking with Blondie—although why is beyond me. I don't want him anyway. I could never handle him.

I wasn't playing this game. I stood. "Excuse me." I turned and walked toward the door of the restaurant.

CHAPTER SIX

RYAN

I followed Ruby with my gaze.

Juliet was tugging on my arm. "Doesn't seem like she's really interested," she gushed. "But *I* am."

I stood, shaking her off of me. "I'm sorry, but I'm not."

I left her standing by our table with a pout on her face. I'd no doubt hear from my brothers about this scene later, but right now I wanted to find Ruby. She had dashed out of the restaurant pretty quickly, but she couldn't have gotten far.

It was nearing midnight, but the resort was well lit. There she was...heading toward the beach. Surprising. I'd figured she'd go back to her room. I stayed quiet, just following her, until she came to the sand. She unstrapped her sandals and let her feet sink into the white plush.

I was wearing black loafers, no socks. I'd have to take my shoes off too. She was already walking toward the ocean when I got my shoes off and my pants rolled halfway up my calves.

"Hey!" I said to her.

She turned around, her eyes wide. "Who is it?"

"It's me. Ryan."

"Oh."

"Don't sound so excited to see me."

"Look, I don't appreciate you using me to get out of

walking with that blond bobblehead you picked up."

I walked up to her and touched her arm. Sparks instantly slid through my hand, but she nearly lost her footing and wrenched her arm away. *What...?*

"Did it ever occur to you that I didn't want to walk with her?"

"Did it ever occur to you to simply tell her that? Why drag me into it?"

Why had I? She looked gorgeous under the stars. Her dark hair glinted with indigo under the moonlight, her skin fair and opulent.

Her eyes were the clearest blue. Amazing I could see them in the dark, but they were mesmerizing.

Was this truly the mousy woman I'd sat next to on the plane? God, what would she look like when she was really dressed up for the wedding?

Wow. Just wow.

I grinned. Enter Ryan Steel ultra-flirt mode. "Maybe I wanted to walk with *you*."

She rolled her blue eyes. "Please," she said sardonically.

"Please walk with me?" I widened my grin. "Thanks. I'd love to." I touched her arm again.

Again, she pulled away. "Grabby, aren't you? And you know that's not what I meant."

Man, this wasn't going to be easy. Her lips were still dark, though the meal had probably taken care of most of her red lipstick. This was Ruby's natural lip color, darker than I remembered from the plane, and God, it was a turn-on.

I hadn't dared to think it before, but this woman was beautiful.

Stunning.

"We're both here, and it's an amazing night." I looked up at the night sky aglow with the moon and stars. "What would a walk hurt?" Though I longed to, I didn't touch her again. She obviously didn't appreciate it, though I wasn't sure why. I hadn't done anything to her that I wouldn't do to anyone else. Just touched her forearm pretty innocently. Man, she was jumpy.

She let out a sigh. "Fine."

I held out my arm, thinking it would be no big deal for her to slide hers through it. She shook her head and started walking.

This one was certainly going to be a challenge, but I hadn't yet met a woman I couldn't lure into my bed. The thought surprised me. When had I decided that I wanted Ruby Lee in my bed? But there was no doubt about it.

I did.

She was about Jade's size, probably around five feet seven inches. Although her boobs weren't quite as big as Jade's, they were close. Bigger than Melanie's, and even bigger than Juliet's. Perky too. Little hard nipples protruded through her blue cotton tank. She was clearly going braless, and if I had it my way, she wouldn't wear a bra this whole trip.

How to approach her—that was the question. Normally, I'd try taking her hand, especially for a midnight walk on the beach. But Ruby clearly didn't want to be touched. I didn't know why, though it could definitely have to do with her father. He had, after all, raped my brother and his own niece.

And then my jaw clenched.

Oh my God. Had that beast raped his own daughter?

That wasn't something I could ask her, obviously. Maybe Ruby was a woman to stay away from. Maybe I should leave her alone. After all, she hadn't asked for my advances, though I'd hardly even made an advance yet.

I should definitely stay away from her.

"It is a gorgeous night," she said, interrupting my thoughts.

And it was. I looked again at the myriad stars sprinkled across the night sky, at the nearly full moon reflecting light upon the water before us.

And I looked at her.

She was the most beautiful thing in the night.

The thought entered my mind from seemingly nowhere. Had I ever thought that of any woman? More beautiful than a starry night?

No. I hadn't.

The words sat at the edge of my lips. *Not as gorgeous as you are.* I ached to say them, but I feared Ruby wasn't ready to hear them.

So I swallowed them down, letting them lodge near my heart. Ruby Lee might be the most beautiful creature I'd ever laid eyes on, but I had to leave her alone. God knew what her father had done to her. No wonder she had jumped away every time I tried to touch her.

Suddenly I was aware of her silence, yet it didn't seem strange. I never really worried about conversation. I was a pretty talkative guy, and so were most women I was with, though whether they were just talking or trying to impress me, I didn't know. But for some reason, with Ruby, the silence didn't seem unnatural. In fact, it was kind of peaceful.

"Have you been to the ocean before?" I asked her.

"Honestly, no. This is actually..."

"What?"

"This is kind of embarrassing, but this is the first time I've been out of Colorado."

"And you weren't afraid to fly?"

"No. I've flown between Denver and Grand Junction before, for work. I knew if I could handle those little puddle jumpers, a big jet wouldn't be an issue."

"Luckily, it was a pretty easy flight," I said.

"It was...nice." She turned and looked straight into my eyes, stopping. "I'm not sure I've thanked you enough for the first class upgrade."

"Of course you have. You hardly stopped mentioning it during the whole flight."

"I wish I could repay you somehow."

"A gift doesn't require repayment."

She sighed. "That's what I don't get. No one's ever given me anything before."

I had to stop my jaw from dropping onto the sand. "Never?"

"Well, maybe not never. I get a holiday bonus at work."

"That doesn't count," I said. "I'm sure you earn every penny of it."

That got a laugh out of her. "No lie. I work my butt off for the department. But I do enjoy it. Most of the time."

"You've never had a friend give you a gift? A coworker?"

She shook her head. "Nope. I try to avoid getting close to people."

"Why?"

"This is getting a little too personal..."

"You can trust me," I said. I meant it. My word was as good as gold. The word of any Steel was.

"I'm sure Melanie has told you about my life," Ruby said.

"No, she hasn't. Other than who your father is. We can

deduce that you didn't have a great childhood."

"Melanie is a true friend," Ruby said. "Honestly, I think she's the best friend I've ever had. I don't know why I assumed she would tell you anything. I asked her to keep it in confidence."

"She's a good therapist," I said.

"I'm sure she is. But to me she was being a friend."

Ruby's hand dangled at her side, devoid of rings, bracelets, or any kind of ornamentation. Her fingernails weren't painted, nor were her toenails.

Her hand was small compared to mine, and I wanted to grab it, hold it in my own and protect her.

"You want to talk about...anything?"

"Not particularly."

Curiosity drummed through me. As much as I already hated Theodore Mathias for what he'd done to Talon, my hate ramped up a notch as I thought about what he could have done to the young woman walking next to me.

"How old are you?" I asked.

That actually got a smile out of her. "You're lucky I'm not one of those women who won't answer that question. I'm thirty-two."

"Hey, me too. I would take you for a bit younger, maybe mid-twenties."

"Thanks. I try to keep myself in shape."

I couldn't help myself. I looked over her body lasciviously. "Yes, you sure do."

I couldn't see in the darkness, but I was sure her cheeks were pinking.

"So are you happy your brothers are getting married?"

Nice change of subject. "Yes, of course. My brothers

deserve happiness. Talon has suffered so much, and so has Jonah, in his own way."

"Yes, unfortunately, there are many ways to suffer."

Horrible images entered my head of what she had gone through. I wanted to respect her privacy, but she had opened the door.

"Are you...okay?"

"Of course. I'm fine."

"I mean... Your father..."

"Is criminally insane. A psychopath. A murderer. A rapist. A certified nutcase. You can say it. I've no love for my father."

"Tell me about your mother, then."

"She was a good woman. She tried to be a good mother."

"What was your childhood like?"

"Probably a hundred and eighty degrees away from what yours was," she said with sarcasm, and then clamped her hand over her mouth. "I'm so sorry. What your brother went through. And the rest of you. I didn't mean..."

"It's okay. I get it. I mean, we went through a lot of shit, but at least we had money, right?" I was trying to be understanding, but a tiny red streak of anger niggled at my neck. "Let me tell you something, Ruby. All the money in the world couldn't buy healing for Talon. And let me tell you something else. I still sometimes have nightmares about the day he was taken. But for him, they'd have taken both of us."

Ruby stopped walking and plunked down onto the sand. "I don't know why I said that. I am so very sorry."

She sounded sincere. I sat down next to her. Her hand glistened in the light, and again I longed to grab it and hold it. But I didn't.

"It's all right." I sighed. "At least we were never hungry.

Were you?"

"Sometimes. Most of the time we did okay." She sighed. "It's hard for a cop to admit, but a few times I stole to eat."

"You were a kid. You were hungry. There's no need to be ashamed."

"I knew stealing was wrong. Even then."

"You don't steal now, do you?"

"Of course not."

"There's no shame in doing what you have to do to survive. You didn't hurt anyone."

"I kept people from making a bigger profit."

I let out a chuckle. "Yes, you did. I won't tell you that you didn't. But my guess is, since then, you've done everything you could to make it right."

She laughed. "Actually, I did. Once I started making money, I went around to all the stores that I used to steal from and I discreetly left twenty-dollar bills lying around. I don't know if the money got to the right person, but it made me feel a little better."

I stared at her. I was an honest person. So were my brothers and sister. But Ruby Lee was unbelievable in her honesty. In her sense of ethics. In her sense of right and wrong. How could she have been born to a psychopath like Theodore Mathias?

"You're pretty amazing, you know that?"

She looked at me, staring into my eyes with her own blue ones. "No one has ever called me amazing before."

"So that's another first, then. No one had given you anything before, and I gave you an upgrade to first class. No one had told you that you were amazing before, and I just did." Without thinking, I leaned toward her and brushed my lips across hers. "Has anyone ever done that to you before?"

CHAPTER SEVEN

RUBY

My heart nearly stopped beating. Tiny prickles raced across my skin, and warmth crashed through me, culminating between my legs.

What would Ryan Steel think if I answered his question honestly? If I said no, no one had ever done that to me before, because I had never let it happen? What would he think of a thirty-two-year-old woman who had never been kissed? He'd run as far as he could in the opposite direction. Which, as attracted as I was to him, was probably the best thing for both of us. So I decided to be honest.

"As a matter of fact, no."

He touched my cheek gently. Everything in me screamed at me to flinch, to go running, but something deeper told me to stay. Something deep within the core of me. Something I'd never felt before.

You're safe here. Safe with Ryan Steel.

Should I trust this soulful voice that spoke to me without words?

"Your skin is so soft," he said, lightly thumbing my cheek.

No reaction to the fact that I told him I'd never been kissed?

"You're beautiful," he said. "Very, very beautiful."

Beautiful. Another first tonight. No one had ever told me I was beautiful.

No one I cared to remember, that was.

I closed my eyes and inhaled. If only I could bottle this feeling, save it for eternity, stay on this beach forever and remember the feeling of being kissed, of being told I was beautiful.

But this was real life, not fantasy. And this was Ryan Steel, someone completely out of my league.

How I wanted to believe him. How I wanted to sink into his arms and find an escape.

But I wasn't beautiful.

Ryan was wrong. He was reacting to what his sister and the others had created. This wasn't the real Ruby. This was a mirage.

I picked up Jade's sandals and stood.

"Hey," he said. "Sit back down. Please."

"I can't do this," I said.

"Do what? We're not doing anything. Don't be afraid."

But I *was* afraid. I was afraid of the feelings he stirred within me. Feelings I had suppressed for far too long. Feelings so long buried that I'd foolishly believed they'd never surface again. I had learned to keep myself under the radar, to keep myself from being attractive to men by my clothing, hair, and makeup choices. Yes, some men had come on to me in the past despite my precautions. Up until now, I had never met a man I wasn't strong enough to resist. But Ryan Steel?

No woman had that much willpower.

"I'm sorry." I turned and walked briskly away.

When I heard him follow me, I began to run. He'd never keep up with me running in sand. Not in those black dress pants. And I doubted he was as used to running as I was. I did sprints for fun. No, he'd never catch me.

But he did.

I screamed when he grabbed my arm.

"Shh." He turned me around to face him. "It's okay. You don't have to run from me. I won't hurt you."

"You already have," I said.

He touched my cheek again, and again heat coursed through my veins. His touch felt good. It felt...right.

"I'm sorry. It's just... You look so beautiful in the moonlight. Your lips are so soft, glistening." He grinned. "So I'm sorry. Not for kissing you. But for frightening you."

"You must think I'm naïve."

"Maybe in a way. But I think in other ways you're far from innocent."

He had that right.

He continued, "I think you've seen things that no one should have to see, Ruby. And I'm sorry about that."

"I've been through nothing compared to what your brother has." My words were true. I had escaped my father. Barely, but I had. I'd worn a few bruises and scratches, but I had escaped his molestation.

I hadn't let a man touch me since.

I hadn't thought I'd ever want to.

But as I looked into Ryan Steel's brown eyes, his dark hair a mess, the tail of his shirt flapping lightly in the soft midnight breeze, his muscled chest and abdomen apparent underneath the soft cotton...

I wanted to be touched.

And that scared the hell out of me.

I pulled away from him. "I can't do this."

"You're not doing anything. We're just standing here."

"You...kissed me."

"I did. And were you serious when you said no one had ever kissed you before?"

Thank God for the darkness. My cheeks were burning so hot that I knew they were bright red.

"That isn't any of your business."

"Fair enough." He let go of my arm. "Walk with me?"

"I'm heading back to my room."

"It just so happens I have a room in the same house you do. Since we're going to the same place, maybe we can walk together."

"I suppose." The truth was I didn't want to leave him. I desperately yearned for his touch, his kiss, his...things I hadn't allowed myself to think about.

"Good."

He didn't try to take my hand, but he did take Jade's sandals. "I'll carry these for you."

Suddenly I felt like a juvenile, with the cutest boy in school offering to carry my books.

That had never happened, and it wasn't happening now. Ryan Steel was so far above anyone who could be considered the cutest boy in school. Ryan Steel was a fucking god.

"Would you like to meet for breakfast tomorrow?" he asked.

"I was going to get up early and go work out before breakfast."

"Great. How would you like a workout partner?"

I couldn't help myself. A laugh escaped my throat. Ryan Steel had no idea how hard I worked out.

But I looked him over. Clearly he was in great shape.

Maybe he could keep up with me. I guess we would see.

"Sure. I'm attending the six a.m. yoga class, and then I'm heading to the fitness center for some lifting. Then breakfast after that. Sound good?" No way would he be getting up at six a.m.

"Sounds great." Then he laughed. "You look surprised."

"I didn't think you were the type of guy who would be up at six a.m."

"Have you forgotten that I help run a ranch? My normal rising time on work days is five a.m., Detective."

I couldn't stop the smile creeping up on my lips. "All right, cowboy. Six a.m. it is."

We didn't talk much for the rest of the walk, and in about fifteen minutes we had reached the bungalow that housed our party. It was a six-bedroom house. My room was on the second floor, but Ryan's was on the first. Like a gentleman, he escorted me up the stairs.

"It's been a pleasure, Ruby." He leaned in toward me and gave me a chaste kiss on the cheek.

All my instincts told me to grab him, drag him into my room, and take him into my bed. Never mind the fact that I wouldn't know what to do with him once I got him there.

I doubted an instruction manual was needed though. I knew everything, but I was all theory and no practice. What I didn't know, I was sure he did.

Maybe I should've had a little more wine...

"I'll knock on your door tomorrow at a quarter to six. Be ready."

He smiled. God, he was gorgeous. "I will be."

He turned, and I watched his well-formed ass amble down the hallway to the staircase.

It was late, nearly one in the morning, but I was still on Colorado time. So I fired up my laptop. Time to see if I could locate dear old Dad.

CHAPTER EIGHT

RYAN

When I went downstairs, I was surprised to see my two brothers and Bryce just getting in.

In a low voice, so as not to wake up anyone who might be sleeping, I said, "Where are the ladies?"

"They'll be along. Marjorie dared them to go skinny dipping in the nude pool, and since it was dark, Melanie and Jade agreed to go."

I laughed. "What are you guys up to?"

"I should ask you the same," Joe said. "You took off after Ruby and we didn't see you again. Is she okay?"

"She's fine. She's up in her room."

"Anything we should know about?" Bryce asked.

"What do you mean?"

"You went after her pretty fast, and you were gone for a while..."

"No, nothing like that."

"She looked great tonight," Bryce said.

I eyed my brother's best friend. He, like me, was single. The fact that he'd made a comment about Ruby's looks didn't sit well with me.

"And that body..." Bryce whistled.

I took a step forward but then backed off. My hands were

clenched into fists. I was not going to haul off and punch my brother's best friend. But damn, I wanted to.

"What's going on between you two?" Talon asked.

"Nothing," I said. "I'm down here, and she's up there."

"But...are you interested?"

"Of course not." A lie.

"Too bad," Talon laughed. "You could have one of those couple names, like Ry-bee. Or Roo-an."

"Ruin? Ha. Doesn't sound too promising."

"Definitely Ry-bee, then." Bryce laughed as he grabbed some highball glasses out of the stocked kitchen. "Who wants to join me in a nightcap?"

"You don't have to ask me twice," Talon said.

"I'm going to pass," I said. "I have an early morning."

"An early morning?" Bryce said. "We're on island time here, man."

"I'm working out with Ruby." I yawned. "So I think I'll say good night." I headed toward my closed door, but Jonah stopped me.

"Ry."

"Yeah?" I turned.

"I need to talk to you."

"Sure." I opened the door to my room. "Come on in."

He shut the door behind him.

"What's up?"

"It's Ruby."

"What about her?"

"Melanie says she's been through a lot."

"I know that. I mean, I assume that, considering who her father is."

"So tread lightly there, okay? This wedding means

everything to Melanie and Jade. I wouldn't want anything to..."

"Fuck it up? What do you take me for, bro? You really think I'd screw up your wedding?"

"I know how you get when you want—" He patted me on the back. "Sorry. Of course not. I'm sorry, Ry. Really."

"Okay..." Something wasn't jelling here. Jonah wasn't a bad guy, but he had a temper, and he didn't normally back off so quickly when he got his mind on something.

"Sure you don't want to join us for a drink?"

"No. I'm good. Thanks."

Jonah smiled and left my room, shutting the door behind him.

Something was definitely off.

Maybe pre-wedding jitters.

No.

Even I didn't buy that.

★ ★ ★

Music blasted into my ears. Five thirty a.m. Really three thirty a.m. Colorado time. I hadn't drunk a lot last night, but damn, morning had come early. I rolled out of bed and headed toward my shower. Each room in this house had a private bath. Pretty cool. Marjorie had spared no expense.

Nothing was too good for my brothers and their brides. They deserved all the happiness in the world.

I thought again about my brief conversation with Joe last night.

He'd told me not to start something with Ruby, that she'd been through a lot, and not to screw up the wedding. Big brother crap. Classic Joe. What *wasn't* classic Joe was how he'd backed off suddenly, as if he'd thought of something else.

I'd have to talk to him about that later.

For now, I had a date for yoga and a workout.

I toweled myself dry and put on some athletic shorts and a muscle shirt. I figured it wasn't naked yoga, but on this resort, who knew? I'd strip if I had to. I wouldn't mind a look under Ruby's clothes. I ran my fingers through my wet hair. It would do.

I turned when someone knocked on my door.

I opened it, and there stood Ruby. Her hair was pulled back in that funky schoolmarm style, but it probably worked well for yoga. Her pretty face wasn't made up, but she didn't need it. Her lips were a dark pink. And that body... Workout clothes showed every curve, every muscle, every magnificent part of her shape.

Last night, I'd barely touched her, barely kissed her, but my groin had responded as if we'd been involved in some damned heavy petting.

And right now, it was tightening already, just from me looking at her.

Crazy shit.

I wanted to grab her and kiss her and then lead her to my bed and make gentle love to her.

Scratch that. I wanted to fuck her senseless, but I couldn't do that. She'd need a gentle touch first, as an introduction. Because if she hadn't ever been kissed—

Fuck.

That didn't mean shit. Her psycho father could very well have raped her without kissing her.

Not exactly a question I could ask.

She'd need an *ultra*-gentle touch if that was the case.

Did I have that in me?

Any other time, I'd have walked away in a heartbeat. Too much baggage. God knew my family had enough to deal with.

But something about her...

"You look great," I said.

"I look ready to work out."

Couldn't take a compliment, this one. How far was I willing to go? Did I like her that much? Want her that much?

Fuck, yeah. I did.

She carried a small cooler.

"What's that?" I asked.

"Our protein shakes for after yoga. We'll need some energy to burn for weights."

"Sure. Of course. Did you get up early to make them?"

"Yeah. Didn't you hear the blender?"

"I was in the shower."

"Oh. Let's go, then."

We walked around the bungalows and hotel to a grassy area. The instructor was just setting up. She was a pretty Jamaican woman, her dark skin a nice contrast to the white yoga pants and tank she was wearing.

"Good morning." She smiled. "I'm Herlinda. We don't get a lot at this early morning class. It might just be you two."

But a couple others showed up.

I had no idea how to do yoga, and some of the positions were a little out of my league, but Ruby executed them all beautifully, her muscles flexing.

Damn.

After class, Herlinda warned that we might be sore if we weren't used to yoga and to use one of the hot tubs at the resort.

Hell, I worked on a ranch. A little yoga wouldn't take me

out.

Ruby opened her cooler, pulled out two thermoses, and handed one to me. I opened it and looked at the thick shake inside.

"Uh...Ruby?"

"Yeah?"

"This is green."

She laughed. "Yes, it is."

"What the hell is in it?"

"Whey powder, almond milk, bananas, pineapple..."

"And?"

"Kale, chia seed, and wheat grass. Try it. It's really good."

I shook my head. "If you say so. Bottoms up." I took a drink. It wasn't very sweet, but it didn't taste like shit. Thank God.

"What do you think?" she asked.

"It's okay."

She laughed again. "You get used to it. Drink up. You'll need it."

It took some doing, but I managed to get the whole shake down.

"Now drink again." She handed me a bottle of water. "It's important to stay hydrated. Especially back home in Colorado."

I knew that. I took a few sips of the water.

"Off to the fitness center," she said. "Should we run?"

After I'd just drunk that shake? Doubtful. "I'll walk, I think."

"Good plan." She packed up the cooler. "Follow me."

"You know where you're going already?"

"Of course. I worked out yesterday before dinner. I hate

to miss a day."

"You like working out?"

"It's part of who I am. If I don't do it, I get pretty antsy. I make sure I work out at least four times a week. Preferably six. You don't work out?"

"Baby, my whole life is a workout. I'm a rancher, remember?"

"Yeah, but I thought you were the winemaker."

"I am."

"Do you actually stomp the grapes yourself?" She smiled a little.

"Of course not. No one makes wine like that anymore. This isn't Italy in the fifties."

"Then how exactly do you work out?"

It was a fair question. "I check the vineyards from spring until harvest. I go out during harvest and help if I'm needed. I'm always moving. Riding to one part of the ranch or the other."

"Riding?"

"Yeah. On horseback. It's how Talon and I like to get around the ranch. Joe not so much."

"So let me get this straight. If you're riding the horse, isn't the horse doing all the work?"

"Baby"—*why did I keep calling her baby?*—"clearly you've never been on horseback. It's work. Trust me."

"Whatever you say." She chuckled.

"You think it's not work? When we get back, I'll take you riding. How's that sound?"

"I didn't mean to—"

"I know you didn't. But if you think riding is easy, you have another think coming."

"Fine. Fine. Here's the fitness center. I'm going to do some reps with the free weights. What do you want to do?"

I had no idea. I hadn't been in a weight room in ages. "I'll just do what you do. How's that?"

"You can probably handle more weight than I can." She smiled. "I'm going to start with the dumbbells. I use the fifteens because I don't like to get bulky." She looked me over. "You should probably start with the twenties or thirties."

Twenties? Did she think I was that much of a wimp? I grabbed a fifty pounder in each hand and started doing some bicep curls. I'd show her.

My arms were strong, so I didn't have much problem doing the first ten reps. I rested a minute and then did another ten. She had moved onto tricep curls by the time I started my last set of reps.

The weights got heavier.

Damn. But I finished. No way was she going to show me up.

I moved on to tricep curls. As before, the first set was easy, but then...

God, what had I gotten myself into? I was strong, true, but the muscles I worked around the ranch were different from the ones I was working now, apparently.

"Don't overdo it," she warned.

"Don't you worry about me. I know my way around a gym."

"Whatever you say." She put down her dumbbells and picked up a yoga mat. "I'm going to do some crunches and push-ups. Go ahead and finish with the weights."

While she was occupied, I took the time to rest my arms. Then I decided to do some squats. I knew my thighs could hold up. I couldn't find anyone to spot me, so I decided to use the leg press machine instead. After a few sets on that, I looked over at Ruby. She was finishing up.

She walked toward me, wiping her face with a towel. Every part of her body that wasn't covered sparkled with shiny perspiration. She looked good enough to eat.

"Ready for breakfast?"

Was I ever. I grabbed a towel and wiped my face. "Sure am."

We each took a quick shower in the respective locker rooms and then walked over to the restaurant where the breakfast buffet was being served. Ruby piled a plate high with bacon, scrambled eggs, and pancakes. Then she added some fresh fruit.

"You're going to eat all that?" I said.

"You bet. I'm famished after a workout."

I went through the omelet line and then took a serving of ackee and saltfish, which I'd heard was a traditional Jamaican dish. The ackee looked a lot like the scrambled eggs on Ruby's plate.

Ruby had already taken a seat at a table outside, so I went to join her. I noticed she had also taken some ackee and saltfish.

"How's the ackee?" I asked.

"Good. Different." She munched on a slice of bacon. "I like trying new things."

I smiled. Good. Because I had a lot of new things in mind that I wanted to try with her.

CHAPTER NINE

RUBY

Never had a man looked at me the way Ryan Steel was looking at me now. Like he wanted to eat me alive. I couldn't decide whether it disturbed me, frightened me, or excited me.

Honestly, all three.

I wanted to get back to my room and continue the research I'd begun last night. My father was nowhere to be found, of course, but a lot was coming out in the wake of Tom Simpson's death.

But not now. Not this week. Not until we got home.

I couldn't burden any of them with this during our vacation. I needed the vacation as much as the rest of them did. So why was it that all I could think about was getting back to my research?

I let out a chuckle.

Because of the man sitting next to me. I needed an escape. An escape from him and the feelings he evoked in my mind and my body.

Needed an escape.

Not wanted an escape.

Oh, God.

"What's so funny?" Ryan asked.

"Nothing."

"I distinctly heard you laugh."

"It's just nervousness."

"Why are you nervous?"

Because the most magnificent man I've ever laid eyes on is watching me eat? "I don't know."

"You just had a killer workout. You should be floating in endorphins right now. I know I am."

He was. I could see it. He was as relaxed as anything. He was endorphins on steroids. Did anything ever get to him?

"How do you do it?" I asked.

"Do what?" He took a mouthful of omelet.

"Stay so calm. After all you and your family have been through."

His countenance became serious. "I owe my brother everything. I never forget that."

"I know that. I didn't mean to presume that you didn't. But you're always in a good mood. Always smiling. How do you manage?"

"I try to focus on the present. Tal is getting married. He's healing. Two of the monsters have been caught."

Monsters. One of those monsters, the one still out there, was my father. That fact always hovered around me, always colored my life.

"I'm lucky, I guess," he continued. "I've never been prone to the darkness that Joe and Talon are. That my mother was. I guess I take after my dad more than my mom."

"Your dad was always happy?"

He laughed. "I wouldn't say that. He could pack a mean punch. Figuratively, I mean. He didn't hit us. But he demanded our respect and didn't put up with any shit. So he wasn't always happy. But he wasn't prone to darkness either."

"But your brothers were?"

"Yeah. Joe always was. Talon was after he was taken. Understandable."

"Definitely."

"I was only seven when he got taken, but I have lots of memories before that time. Tal was usually happy. I think, anyway. I was just a kid."

"I can't even imagine how you all got through it."

"I can't imagine how you got through living with your father." He narrowed his eyes. "I'm sorry."

"Don't be. I didn't live with him for very long." Of course my esteemed father hadn't needed much time to inflict damage. "I can't help who my father is. I just hope I don't take after him in any of the bad ways."

He smiled. "You don't. You'd know by now."

I returned his smile, though tentatively. He was right, of course. Still, I worried. I didn't have to worry about passing any undesirable traits to children since I planned never to marry and never to have kids. I was fine on my own. The worry that niggled at me was for myself. I had to catch my father and stop him before he decided to come after me again.

So far, he'd kept his distance, though he'd reached out to me a few months ago when he was in town with his new girlfriend, Brooke Bailey, who just happened to be Jade's mother. Brooke was now convalescing at Talon and Jade's home after a nearly fatal automobile accident. Courtesy of my father, or so the Steels thought. They had no proof though.

I'd find that proof.

My father was a smart man. A cunning man. He'd never left a trail in his life.

But now I had an eyewitness. Talon Steel.

I already had enough proof to arrest him for what he did to Talon. And Talon, unlike my cousin Gina, was not afraid to press charges. He'd already pressed them against his half uncle, Larry Wade.

And there were others out there. Other victims of my father. I knew they were out there. Sometimes, in my dreams, I heard them calling to me for help.

I would help them.

Somehow.

"Earth to Ruby."

I jolted back to reality. "Yeah?"

"You seemed on another planet there for a minute."

No, just thinking about my father and bringing him to justice. "Sorry. A lot on my mind."

He eyed my plate. "Are you done?"

I'd eaten most of it. The ackee and saltfish had been... interesting. Not bad, but not something I'd be eating a lot of. I was glad I'd tried it though. I was more interested in sampling authentic Jamaican jerk chicken and curried goat. "Yeah."

"Good. Want to go for a swim?"

"What about waiting an hour after eating?"

"That's an old wives' tale. You don't really believe that, do you?"

I smiled. "No. But I'd rather wait until later. Right now I think I'll take a walk."

He nodded. "Great. I'll tag along."

I hadn't actually wanted company. My brain was churning now, mostly about my father. Besides, having Ryan Steel near me wasn't good for me.

It made me want things I had no business wanting.

"I..."

"You going to run away from me again?"

"No, it's—"

He stopped me by placing his hand on my forearm. My skin burned where he touched me.

"Look. You have nothing to fear from me. I just want to get to know you. We're both here for the week. We're both free as birds. I'm not asking for anything other than friendship."

"Friends don't usually kiss their friends on the mouth," I said. God, my skin was on fire.

"That won't happen again. Not if you don't want it to."

"I don't want it to," I lied.

He smiled. "I can't say I'm not disappointed, and I can't promise I won't try to make you change your mind."

My heart thumped. I needed some cool water on my forearm. If I didn't know better, I'd expect a red handprint to be there.

I cleared my throat. "I won't change my mind."

He finally let go of me and stood. "Okay, then. Where do you want to walk?"

"I figured the beach. Walking in sand is incredibly good exercise."

"Great." He smirked. "I'm a little more dressed for the occasion today." He held out his arm. "Shall we?"

I looked at him, raising an eyebrow, and he put his arm down.

Then we walked side by side out of the restaurant and into the gorgeous air that was Jamaica.

A concrete walkway led to the beach. When we hit the sand, I stopped to take off my flip-flops. He did the same and then took mine from me to carry them. Again I felt like a blushing schoolgirl. So un-Ruby-like. I crushed my toes into the soft sand. Wonderful.

"Feels good, huh?"

"Yeah," I agreed.

We walked toward the water. It was early yet, for island-timers, so there weren't too many people on the beach—a few dotted here and there, either sunning themselves or swimming. I looked around for jellyfish. I didn't see any.

We didn't talk much, just chatted about inane stuff, but when we'd been walking for about twenty minutes, I noticed something different.

More bodies appeared on this side of the beach. Naked bodies.

"Uh...Ryan?"

"Yeah?"

"I think we need to turn around."

He laughed. "Why?"

"I'm a little uncomfortable."

"You're a resort guest. You have every right to be here."

"Isn't this the nude beach?"

"Very observant, Ruby." He laughed again. "Does nudity bother you?"

"No. But honestly, I've never been around it like this."

"Neither have I. Except for last night when I visited the nude pool before dinner."

"That must be where you met Blondie."

"Juliet. Yes." He laughed. "Although Blondie suits her better."

"I don't mean to be rude or anything. I don't have anything against blondes."

For the third time, he laughed. "Ruby. It's okay. You're funny. I like your sense of humor. I don't think you have anything against anyone. Except criminals, of course. I mean, you're a cop."

"Doesn't everyone have something against criminals?"

"I do. My brothers do, obviously. Probably not everyone." He smiled. "Not the criminals themselves."

That got a smile out of me.

"How'd you decide to become a cop?"

That was a long story that I didn't want to get into right now. "Are you trying to distract me so I don't feel weird around all these naked people?"

"Guilty. But you know how you could feel a little less conspicuous?"

"How?"

He grinned. A real shit-eating grin. "Get undressed."

Yeah. When hell froze over. "You're kidding, right?"

"Hell, no. This is a nude beach. Look around you. There are all shapes and sizes of bodies here. No one will think anything of yours. If that overweight couple"—he glanced at a man and woman sitting nearby—"isn't embarrassed, why should you be? You have a great body."

It was too early in the trip to be sunburned, but my body felt like an inferno. God only knew what my face was doing. I didn't want to know. "I...can't."

"You *can*."

I looked around. He was right. No one was ogling anyone. People were talking, sunning themselves, swimming. Some were at the bar. Why not?

Wait. Was I truly considering this?

Yes, I was. And for only one reason. If I took off my clothes, Ryan would have to take his off too. And oh my God, I wanted to see him naked.

Not that I'd do anything with him naked. But to see him... To see, just once, what a perfect man looked like in all his glory. Something I never thought I'd see. Something I was curious about and wanted to see, but I had kept those feelings at bay.

I looked around again. No one on this beach could hold a candle to Ryan Steel. A few men looked good. A few women too. Most were average. Normal people who liked to get naked at the beach, I guessed.

I laughed. "Why not?" I gathered all my courage and lifted my sports tank, which doubled as a bra, over my head. My full breasts fell gently against my chest.

And Ryan Steel stared.

Shit. This had been a mistake.

Sure, no one else on the beach was ogling anyone. But I hadn't thought about what Ryan would do to me.

My nipples hardened instantly under his gaze.

I crossed my arms over my chest.

"That kind of defeats the purpose," Ryan said.

"You were staring."

"I was looking. I can't help it. You're beautiful. Your breasts are beautiful."

I hugged myself harder, clenching my tank in my fist. How could I get it back on without Ryan seeing my boobs again?

"Would it help if I took my clothes off?" he asked. "All of them?"

CHAPTER TEN

RYAN

Her eyes were circles. She didn't answer, so I walked over to a vacant lounge chair, put both our pairs of shoes down, and then pulled my muscle shirt over my head. I looked up at the sun. I hadn't brought any sunscreen with me, so we wouldn't be able to stay naked too long. But if I could get Ruby naked, get her out of her shell a little...

And then what? Seduce a virgin? This was new territory for me. But God, I wanted her.

I turned around and looked at her. She was still standing there, covering her chest. I met her gaze as I slid my shorts and boxer briefs over my hips.

My cock was at half-mast. I couldn't help it, being around her. At least I didn't have a raging hard-on. Though when I'd seen her nipples harden in front of my eyes, I'd had to will it down.

Her eyebrows rose slightly. Only slightly, as if she were trying to keep them down.

But I noticed.

It put another grin on my face.

"See?" I said, putting my clothes on the chair next to our shoes. "Not so hard, is it?"

And she burst out laughing.

"What?"

"I'm sorry. It's... You said 'not so hard.' And I thought..."

I couldn't help a laugh myself. "I know what you thought." I looked down at my half-erect cock. "You, Ruby Lee, have a dirty mind."

She covered her mouth. "I'm sorry."

"Don't be sorry. Just get naked. If I can do it, you can do it."

"There's a world of difference between you and me, Ryan."

"I think that's the first time you've called me by my name." And I liked the sound of my name from her red lips.

I liked it a lot.

"Is it?"

"Yeah." I tapped my foot. "I'm waiting."

"Oh, no. Not going to happen."

"Come on. Rip it off like you did the tank top. Like a bandage. Best to get it over with."

"I can't."

"I can't believe you'd be ashamed of that body."

She huffed. "I'm not ashamed of anything!"

"Well, then..."

She licked her full lips. I willed my cock not to respond.

"All right." She unclenched her arms from around her chest and slowly peeled off her shorts and underpants.

I deliberately did not stare. I didn't want to have her go charging out of here.

But God... That body had been created in heaven.

Sure, I knew she worked out. I knew her perfect musculature was the result of a lot of strength training and cardio, but surely a deity had carved those breasts, those perfectly formed hard nipples. That dark bush that was not too hairy and not too sparse, but just right. Those hips that swelled the perfect amount. Those long, slender legs tapering down to perfect ankles and feet.

Theodore Mathias might be a criminally insane psycho, but he had helped create an angel.

She stood with her knees together.

"Come here," I said. "Put your clothes on the chair."

"What if someone takes them?"

"Look around. Everyone leaves their stuff. It's safe here. And if your clothes get stolen, I'll buy you new ones. How's that?"

"I wasn't asking—"

"Ruby, I know you weren't. It was a joke. Okay?"

She smiled timidly. "Okay."

"You want to continue our walk? Get a drink? Go into the water?"

She twisted her lips. "Maybe a drink. It's hot out here. Do you think they have water with a twist of lime?"

I smiled. "I'm betting they do." I held out my hand. "Come on."

She came forward, placed her clothes on the chair next to mine, and again I tried like hell not to stare at her.

If only her gorgeous hair were down, falling over those milky shoulders, down her back nearly to the crease of that perfect ass...

I itched to touch her. To feel that smooth skin beneath my fingertips.

But I'd promised her a drink. I held out my hand again to her, and to my surprise she took it. Most likely for reassurance, not because she wanted to hold hands, but I'd take what I could get. I led her to the bar near the center of the nude beach.

The bartender grinned. "What can I get for you and your beautiful lady, mon?"

Ruby blushed.

"Just two waters with a twist of lime."

"Comin' right up."

I handed Ruby her water in a plastic cup with a wedge of lime on the edge. "See?"

"Don't you want a real drink?"

"Not this early. Maybe later. Besides, we have the rehearsal this afternoon. Joe and Tal would never forgive me if I showed up with alcohol on my breath." Actually, they wouldn't care if I had a drink, but I didn't want one at the moment. I wanted to enjoy this time with Ruby without alcohol. She, on the other hand, could use a heavy dose of the social lubricant. But I wasn't going to push it.

Despite the heat, her nipples were still hard as rocks, her areolas wrinkled. They were brownish pink and beautiful. I knew they were hard because she was nervous, embarrassed, but I hoped maybe she was a little turned on as well.

She took a sip of her water and cleared her throat. "Now what?"

"Whatever you want. We can keep walking. Take a dip in the water. Go over to the pool." I gestured. The pool was behind the bar. The same pool where I had met Juliet last night. We walked away from the bar.

And speak of the fucking devil.

Juliet came bounding toward us, her tits bouncing. In the light of day, she wasn't nearly as pretty as she'd been last night. Still, she wasn't bad to look at, and I would've looked my fill if not for the much better eye candy standing next to me.

"Hi, Ryan!" She turned to Ruby. "And hi..."

"Ruby." Ruby held out her hand.

Juliet took Ruby's hand and let it drop quickly. "Did you all enjoy your walk last night?"

"We sure did," I said.

A couple girls walked toward us.

"These are my friends, Shayna and Lisa," Juliet said.

Oddly, the roommates looked nothing like Juliet, the ultimate California girl, but they both had the same sorority feel. Shayna was African-American with a tight body. Maybe a dancer? Lisa was red-haired and freckled with a few more curves. I hoped she was wearing sunscreen.

"We're looking for some fun," Juliet continued.

You won't find it here. But I didn't say that. "I'm sure you can find lots of fun around this place."

Three Jamaican men ambled up then, dressed in board shorts. "Couldn't help overhearing you lovelies. If you're looking for some fun, we can take you for a ride on our Jet Skis."

"That sounds great," Juliet bubbled. "How about it, guys?"

"I don't know, Jules," Shayna said.

"Oh, come on, Shay," Lisa urged. "It'll be fun."

The first man held out his hand. "I'm Mark, and this is Rashaun and J.J."

"I'm Juliet. This is Shayna and Lisa. And Ryan and Ruby."

"Now that we know each other, come on, then." Mark smiled, his stark white teeth contrasting with his dark brown face.

Ruby pulled at my arm.

I turned toward her. "What is it?"

"I have a bad feeling about this," she whispered. "Tell them not to go."

Ruby was a cop. If she had a bad feeling, I couldn't ignore it. "Hey, ladies," I said. "Can I get you all a drink?" I wasn't sure what else to say. Although I might be able to take Mark and maybe one of the others, I wouldn't be able to hold my own against the three of them. Of course, there were plenty of people around. It was unlikely they'd start anything.

"That's sweet," Juliet said. "But I'd love a ride on a Jet Ski." She turned to the guys. "Are you all staying at the resort?"

"We have day passes. It's our day off. We live here."

Did this resort offer day passes? I didn't know. Ruby looked at me again with urgency in her eyes.

"I'm up for it," Lisa said, taking hold of Mark's arm. "I've never ridden on a Jet Ski before."

"It's lots of fun." Mark smiled. "We'll just stay around here. We won't be out long. I promise."

"I'm in," Juliet said. "Shay, come on. Please?"

Shayna's forehead was wrinkled.

Ruby spoke up, her eyes fearful. "You don't have to go if you don't want to. If it doesn't feel right."

I looked out at the ocean. Jet Skis were everywhere. These guys were probably okay.

Juliet rolled her eyes at Ruby's comment. "It won't be the same without you, Shay."

Shayna sighed. "All right. We won't be gone long, right?"

Rashaun winked at her. "Just tell us when you want to come back, and we'll bring you back. But we're locals, and we can show you some sights. It'll be fun."

Ruby tugged on my hand.

"Ladies," I said. "Don't go."

"Why not?" Lisa asked.

What could I say? I looked to Ruby.

She got serious. "You don't know these guys. You're in a foreign country. It's not safe."

Juliet scoffed. "Who are you? A cop?"

"As a matter of fact, yes," Ruby said. "Go ask the bartender if he knows these guys before you take off. Ask if the resort gives day passes."

"I'm sure they do," Juliet said. "I think I read it somewhere."

Juliet didn't look like she did a lot of reading. I opened my mouth to say something—I wasn't sure what—but Mark beat me to it.

"Hey, look. No problem, mon," Mark said. "You don't want to go, we'll go ourselves. Or find some other nice girls. Nice meeting you." He turned.

"No!" Lisa grabbed his arm. "I'm going."

"Me too," Juliet said and looked longingly at Shayna.

"All right."

"See you all later!" Juliet waved us off as she and her girlfriends followed the three men down the beach to where the Jet Skis were docked.

Ruby let out a sigh.

"I'm sure they'll be fine," I said.

"Probably. I hope so. But that's a new kind of stupid, getting on a Jet Ski in a foreign country with someone you've never met."

"I agree. But they're young. They don't know any better."

"Are you serious? I never would have done that, even at their age. By the time I was their age, I'd been on my own for years."

"Look. We'll wait here until they come back, okay? Will that make you feel better?"

"I'd like to, but it's getting toward lunchtime. We need to

shower and change and then meet the others for the rehearsal."

I checked my watch. Ruby was right. Jade and Melanie—and my brothers, for that matter—would never forgive us if we missed their planned rehearsal luncheon. They'd reserved a private dining area farther up on the non-nude portion of the beach. Ruby would get to try jerk chicken and curried goat. Both were on the menu, according to Marj.

"They'll be fine, Ruby."

She smiled. "You're probably right." Then she looked down. "I can't believe I'm standing here naked."

"Ha! The whole thing with the guys and the Jet Skis made you forget it for a bit. That's good. See? It's nothing."

"It's not nothing. Let's go." She walked toward the lounge chair where our clothes were still sitting.

We dressed quickly and walked back to the house. As much as I wanted to invite Ruby to shower with me, I held off.

But before this week was over, I'd get further than first base.

CHAPTER ELEVEN

RUBY

The luncheon was delicious. Real Jamaican jerk chicken was spicier than I'd imagined, but oh so delicious. Something called a Scotch bonnet pepper was the secret, though the chef, who came out to talk to us, said jalapeños could be substituted. It likely wouldn't be quite as hot though. Something to try when I got home. I loved to cook, but I rarely did, being single and all.

After the rehearsal, I decided to relax by the pool—the bathing-clothes-required pool, that was. Ryan was dragged off by his brothers to do God knew what. Some kind of bachelor party thing. Tonight we had a bachelorette dinner planned for Melanie and Jade, but my late afternoon was free.

I couldn't help taking my laptop with me. Why not do some research poolside?

I found a lounge chair, applied sunscreen, and then fired up the computer. A server came by, and I ordered a sparkling water with lime. I still wasn't ready to drink. I'd no doubt be doing plenty of that tonight, though maybe not. Melanie was pregnant and couldn't drink.

I checked my e-mails, checked in with work, and then, as I was about to search for my father, my server came back to me. I shook my head at him and then turned to a couple talking loudly next to me.

"She just got back. She got picked up by some tourists on a motorboat."

"Wow. Unreal."

"There's talk about it at check-in. They're issuing refunds for anyone who wants to leave. They'll make a big resort-wide announcement soon."

I looked to them. "I'm sorry to interrupt," I said, "but I couldn't help overhearing. What are you talking about?"

The man turned to me. "No problem. Most people haven't heard yet. A young woman jumped off a Jet Ski earlier. She was near drowning by the time a motorboat found her and picked her up. Her two friends are missing."

"Oh my God. Do you know who it is?"

"I only know she's a black woman. She looks young. Twenty or so."

My blood ran cold. Shayna. She hadn't wanted to go... But I hadn't been able to talk her out of it in the end.

"Is she all right?"

"Yes. She's fine. Just scared. My wife and I saw her when she came back. Security took her in to talk to her, and they called in the local law. She's with them now, and she's getting medical treatment."

"I met her this morning. Her name is Shayna. I was there when she and her friends took off with the locals. I tried to stop them."

The wife shook her head. "Young women can be so foolish. Thank God one of them got away."

Don't panic, Ruby. The others might be back by now. Shayna might have just gotten scared and jumped off early.

But in my heart I knew that wasn't what had happened. I thanked God that Shayna was all right. But Juliet and Lisa?

They might never be seen again.

Human trafficking. Young women stolen and sold into slavery.

A lump lodged in my throat. Why hadn't I tried harder to stop them from going with those men? Something hadn't been right, and I knew, after being a cop for eleven years, to trust my intuition.

Though I longed to go talk to Shayna, the local law might not allow it. This was way out of my jurisdiction, and I needed to stay out of it.

But those girls would never leave my memory.

More in a long line of people I hadn't been able to save. Thank God Shayna had saved herself.

★ ★ ★

"What's wrong, Ruby?" Melanie asked. "You seem a little distant tonight."

Jade and Marj were on the dance floor, enjoying the bachelorette festivities despite the resort-wide news we'd all gotten about the missing women. The resort wasn't closing down, but they had offered refunds to anyone who wanted to leave.

Juliet and Lisa hadn't yet been found.

They likely wouldn't be. They were probably long gone by now, though no one at the resort wanted to believe that.

I, on the other hand, had no issue with the truth. The truth was hard, and hard truth was a part of my everyday life. Had been for seventeen years.

Our party had decided to stay through the wedding tomorrow and then leave early. Not great to have our vacation cut short, but right now none of us felt like sticking around. I hadn't had a chance to talk to Ryan alone about Juliet and Lisa, but during the rehearsal he'd been watching me, his eyes sunken. Most likely he was wishing he'd tried harder to stop them. God knew I was.

"I'm sorry. I don't want to bring your party down. I just can't get those young women out of my mind."

"You tried to stop them. Ryan told us. It's not your fault. And one of them got away."

"I know. And I know it's not my fault. But God...this should be a safe place."

"This *is* a safe place. Security is everywhere. It was a fluke that those guys got in, and the girls didn't have to go with them."

"Shayna didn't want to go."

"And Shayna obviously figured out there was danger and got away."

"She could have easily drowned."

"But she didn't."

"Damn! Why didn't they listen to me?"

Melanie touched my arm. "Because they're twenty-one. They can't see past tomorrow. They came here to have fun, and three handsome strangers offered to take them Jet Skiing. When you're young, you don't think about consequences."

"I did."

"You didn't have a normal growing up experience, Ruby."

I sighed. "I know. I just wish I could talk to Shayna. Find out what happened."

"The locals are on it," Melanie said.

"I'm sorry to be such a downer," I said. "This is the night before your wedding."

"It's okay. I understand. We're all pretty broken up. But we came here for a wedding, and we're going to have a wedding."

"Definitely," I said. "Jade and Marj don't seem as affected."

"They are. They deal with it a little differently. I talked to them both after we found out. They're pretty freaked. So are the guys. Especially Ryan."

"Did you see the blonde who came up to Ryan last night at dinner?"

Melanie nodded.

"That was Juliet, one of the girls who's missing. She had a thing for Ryan." I sighed. "If he'd gone with her, given her what she wanted, she might still be here today."

"Ruby, Ryan wasn't interested in Juliet. In fact, it's pretty clear that he's interested in you."

I shook my head. "That's ridiculous."

"Why would you say that?"

"Because he's Ryan Steel. The most gorgeous man on the planet."

Melanie laughed. "I might beg to differ. Let's say second-most gorgeous."

I couldn't help a smile. Melanie was so in love. It was sweet.

Something I'd never experience.

Wouldn't let myself experience.

She continued, "You're as gorgeous as he is, Ruby. No matter how much you try to cover it up."

I warmed.

"Don't let what happened to you color your whole life."

"I'm not one of your patients, Melanie."

"I'm saying that as a friend. You're scared of men. It's obvious."

"Tomorrow is your wedding day. You should be having

fun, not giving impromptu therapy to your maid of honor."

"We're all in this together," Melanie said.

"I know. But the Steels and you have been through enough. I'm sorry to be such a downer. Feel like getting out on the dance floor with Jade and Marjorie?"

She smiled. "No, not really. I'm a little nauseated. Morning sickness and all. Turns out it's evening sickness as well."

"Okay. I'm sorry you're not feeling good."

"I'm not. The reason is great." She smiled.

Jade and Marjorie walked toward our table, both perspiring from dancing.

"I'm heading to the bathroom. Too much rum punch," Jade said.

Melanie stood. "I'll go with you. Seems my bladder fills up more quickly than usual since I've become pregnant."

That left me at the table with Marjorie. We weren't exactly strangers. I was wearing her clothes, after all. Still, I wasn't sure what to say to her.

Luckily, she didn't have that problem.

"Wow. I'm beat." She gestured to a server. "Could I get some water, please?"

I shoved my glass toward her. "Here. Have some of mine while you wait."

"Thanks. You're a lifesaver." She picked up my glass and took a long drink before setting it back down. "I never thought I'd say this, but I'm sick to death of rum punch. How come you're not out there dancing? You look hot."

Hot? I doubted that adjective described me, except that it *was* a balmy night and I felt a little hot.

"Must be the clothes." I smiled.

"Are you kidding? I don't look as good as you do in them.

I'd kill for that body."

"You have a great body. I wish I were taller."

"Eh. It's nice sometimes, but try finding a pair of pants that doesn't turn into capris after one washing. What I'd really like is to tone up, look more like you."

"Honestly, I think you look great. And trust me, the body I have is a lot of work."

"I'm no stranger to hard work. Try the ranching life." She laughed. "I was bound and determined to keep up with my brothers, and I did. I have a gym membership, and I go regularly. Would you mind going with me sometime? Show me the things you do? I'll buy you lunch."

I smiled. "You don't have to buy me lunch. I'd be happy to show you my workouts." I laughed. "You might want to talk to Ryan, though. I'm betting he's going to be sore tomorrow."

Marjorie laughed again. "He's just being a wuss. I can take whatever you can dish out. I promise."

I took a sip of my water and smiled. "You know? I think you could. Sure. Let's do it. Give me a call when we get home, and we'll set something up." I'd never had a workout partner before. I preferred to go at my own pace. But Marjorie Steel would be able to keep up with me. I could tell just by her disposition. This woman made things happen. Nothing got in her way.

I liked her.

A blondish man approached us. "Would you ladies care to dance?"

"Not me," Marjorie said. "I'm all danced out." Then she arched her eyebrows at me.

The man was nice-looking. No Ryan Steel, but handsome by anyone's standards, with sandy hair and dark eyes. He wasn't as tall as the Steel brothers, but was easily six feet.

"I don't think so," I said. "But thanks."

"I gave it a shot." He smiled and walked away.

"Why didn't you dance with him?" Marjorie asked.

"Didn't feel like it, and I'm not much of a dancer."

"Look, this might be a little forward of me, but blame it on the rum. We all know who your father is. Your life has been hard. So dance. Live a little."

As much as I hated being reminded of my father, maybe Marjorie was right. This was a dance, not a marriage proposal. Why not? I nodded to Marjorie and then stood, walked toward the man, and touched his shoulder.

He turned.

I cleared my throat, thankful for the darkness hiding the blush on my cheeks. "Still want to dance?"

"Sure, gorgeous. Come on."

He took my hand, and I resisted the urge to pull it away. It didn't feel nearly as good as Ryan's had when his hand touched mine. Though the song wasn't overly slow, he pulled me into his body, crushing me against him.

Whoa. Panic attack coming...

Breathe, Ruby, breathe.

We were in a public place, on a dance floor. There was nothing to freak out about.

Still, he moved slowly. My breathing got back under control, but I was uncomfortable with how close he held me. Once the song was over I'd bow out politely.

But when the song ended and the next began, he didn't let go of me, and one of his hands slid down and cupped my ass.

Enough.

I pushed my hands against his chest. "Let me go."

"Hey, gorgeous, don't be like that. We're just having a little fun."

"I'm done having fun, thanks. Let me go."

He tightened his arms around me. "Not yet. I haven't had a taste of your gorgeous skin." He lowered his head and touched his lips to a tender spot on my neck.

Come here. Show Daddy how much you love him.

I tried again to pull away.

Again, his strength outmatched mine.

"Goddamnit," I said through clenched teeth. "Let me go!"

He laughed, and this time sank his teeth into my neck.

Visions of my father clouded my brain. *No!* Not going there. I was a cop, for God's sake. I was well-trained in self-defense, and now was the time to put that training to use. I thrust my forehead against his neck, effectively pushing him back, and then landed a punch to his solar plexus and a knee to his groin.

He doubled over, and then—

Suddenly he was flung away from me, landing on his ass and knocking other dancers askew.

The music still played.

My heart thumped wildly as Ryan Steel thundered past me, grabbed the man by his collar, and yanked him to his feet. He dragged the man off the dance floor and outside.

I didn't know what to do other than follow.

When I got outside, Ryan was still holding the guy by the collar.

"I saw the lady try to get away from you."

"Hey, man. I was having some fun. This is a nude resort, and look at her. That body. She wants it. You know it."

"You bastard." Ryan pulled back his arm.

He was going to hit this guy, and I couldn't allow that. We were on a resort in a foreign country. I had no idea what could happen, what the laws were here. I had been acting in self-defense, but Ryan was just pissed.

I ran forward and grabbed his arm. "Ryan. Please. Don't."

He turned to me, his brown eyes blazing. "Did he hurt you?"

I shook my head, my fingers at my neck. "No. I mean... No."

"What did you do to her?" He eyed the man.

"Nothing, man. Just a little kiss on the neck, grabbed her ass. Look at her, man."

"You fucking son of a bitch!" He raised his arm again.

"No! Ryan. Don't."

"He deserves it." Still holding the guy, with his other hand he brushed my hand away from my neck. "Damn it." He turned back to the guy. "You bit her? What kind of animal are you?"

"Look, I'm sorry. She seemed into it."

"Bullshit. I saw her trying to push you away from across the room. I ought to punch you into tomorrow."

"You can try it."

"You fucking bastard."

This time I ran between them. "Ryan, don't. I'm okay. It's not worth it. Trust me."

Ryan let the guy go, and he crumpled to the ground. "If I see you again, I'll fucking kill you."

I'll fucking kill you. They were simple fighting words, but Ryan's eyes were dark and glazed over.

He truly meant those words.

That Steel darkness might not be quite as evident in the youngest son, but it was there. Definitely there.

The other guy stood, adjusted his pockets, and then leered at me before turning and walking away.

A few security guards walked swiftly toward him. "We'll take care of this from here," one of them said.

Ryan nodded at them and then turned to me. "What the hell happened? Are you all right?"

"I'm fine. I can take care of myself." True statement, though the guy had unnerved me. I'd dealt with worse than him in my life, so why had he affected me? Scared me?

"Why were you dancing with him?"

"Because he asked me. Because I don't want..."

"Don't want what?"

Why not admit it? "Because I don't want to be...scared of getting close to a man."

"Do *I* scare you?"

I trembled. But I couldn't lie to him. "You scare me most of all."

CHAPTER TWELVE

RYAN

Her words nearly broke my heart. I'd only kissed her once, brushed my lips softly against hers, and I wanted her more than I'd wanted any woman. She stood, in her tight black miniskirt and silver sequined camisole, strappy black slides on her feet.

"You look beautiful."

She blushed under the resort lighting. "These are Marjorie's clothes again. Jade's shoes."

"I didn't say the clothes were beautiful. I said *you* are beautiful." I touched her cheek, and to my surprise, she didn't flinch. Her skin was like silk under my fingertips. "Did that bastard hurt you?"

She shook her head. "He just scared me, like I said. I told him no and tried to push him away, but he wouldn't take no for an answer. Luckily we were in a public place, and my cop instincts kicked in."

"You wouldn't have put yourself in that position in a private place. You're too smart for that."

She blushed more. "Thank you for saying that. I..." Her eyes misted with tears.

"What is it, baby?"

She widened her eyes slightly at the word "baby," but then she spoke. "It's Juliet and Lisa. I wish they had been smart enough not to put themselves in a dangerous position. I wish I could have stopped them."

"You did all you could." God, her cheek was soft. "Maybe I'm the one who should have done more."

She sniffled. "We both should have."

"You're right. I wish we had done more. But Juliet and Lisa—and even Shayna, because she went along—were being stupid. They're grown women, and they were looking for a good time. They weren't thinking about the consequences. What young woman hasn't dreamed of being swept off her feet by a foreigner?"

"I haven't."

"No. Not you. But Juliet and Lisa probably haven't been through what you have." And I still didn't know exactly what she'd been through. I wanted to ask, wanted her to know that anything she told me was safe with me, but I wasn't sure how to approach it.

"I daresay that by now, Juliet and Lisa have been through way worse than I have." She shook her head. "I just wish..."

I stroked her gorgeous hair. "I know, baby."

"I want to talk to Shayna."

"She may not even be on the resort anymore. She probably wanted to get the hell out of here."

"You're right. But still, I'm going to check in the morning. Maybe she'll be willing to talk to me."

"All right. I'll go with you if you want. But why? Why is this affecting you so deeply?"

"Because, Ryan, my father... God knows how many other girls and boys he has hurt in his lifetime. I feel for every single one of them. And even though my father probably has nothing to do with Juliet and Lisa, I feel for them too."

"You can't save them all, Ruby."

"God, how well I know that. But I want to talk to Shayna."

"There's nothing we can do about that until morning."

She looked around. "I suppose I should get back to Melanie and Jade's party. Why aren't you with the men?"

I laughed. "It broke up pretty early. Those two are so ridiculously in love that they weren't in the mood for heavy drinking and strippers."

Just then, Melanie, Jade, and Marj came out of the dance club.

"There you are. Ruby, are you okay?" Marjorie asked.

"I'm fine."

"I'm sorry I pressed you to dance with that guy."

"It's not your fault. You couldn't have known he was such a lech. It was my decision."

"We're pretty wiped out," Jade said. "Plus Mel and I have to look gorgeous tomorrow for the wedding. We're going to head back."

"Okay," Ruby said. "I'll come along."

I touched her forearm. "Would you stay out here a little while longer? With me?" God, I sounded like a lovesick schoolboy. Ridiculous.

"I don't know…"

"Stay out if you want. You'll look great tomorrow no matter what." Marj laughed. "When we get back, I want you to take me to your gym. Show me how to get that body of yours. I'm holding you to it."

"And I've told you. There's nothing wrong with your body," Ruby said, smiling.

Marj was my sister. Somehow, I never thought of her as *having* a body. Although I was getting more uncomfortable by the minute every time she and Bryce were in the same room together. He'd been giving my sister some very unbrotherly looks.

Ruby turned to me then, and I saw something in her blue eyes that I hadn't before. I couldn't put a name to what I was seeing, but I liked it. I liked it a lot.

"I think...I would like to stay."

Marjorie smiled then and arched her eyebrows. "Okay. See you guys in the morning."

"Bye," Melanie and Jade both said.

Ruby smiled shyly. "What do you want to do?"

I smiled. "Whatever you want."

"A walk on the beach?"

"Sounds great."

I wanted so badly to take her hand, but I didn't. Ruby was a special person, a person who had been through a lot of shit. Whatever we had together, it would go at a snail's pace. As much as I wanted her, I had to be okay with that. Did I like this woman enough to move at a slow pace?

The truth of the matter was yes, I did.

We didn't talk much, just walked on the beach, me carrying two pairs of shoes. I had dressed better tonight, in shorts and a printed rayon shirt. Tomorrow, for the wedding, we were all wearing white pants and white shirts. I didn't know what the women would be wearing.

All I knew was that Ruby would look beautiful.

I was content to simply walk beside her, letting the soft breeze ruffle my hair and shirt. Her hair was down tonight—soft, silky, and straight, flowing over her creamy shoulders and down her back.

Then we came to the nude beach again. Other couples

were walking, and some were under cabanas. This part of the beach had several cabanas containing beds. They were walled off, but open on top so the stars were visible.

I longed to be alone with Ruby, to take her into one of the vacant cabanas.

But I knew how she would react to that.

"You want to go for a swim?" I asked.

She sighed. "Now that's something I would normally say no to, but I think I might like to. It's a beautiful night, and I haven't been in the ocean yet. But what will we do with our clothes?"

Here was my shot. "Why don't we put them in one of the empty cabanas? We can set them on the bed so they won't get all sandy."

"All right."

I led her to one of the straw cabanas, and we went inside. We stripped off our clothing, and my cock was at half-mast again. She turned away from me as she undressed. I didn't think anything of it. At least she was undressing. She folded her clothes neatly, set them on the bed, and then turned toward me, her arms over her chest. She had trimmed her bush since this afternoon. And, oh my God, I could see the lips of her pussy. So beautiful. Pink and fleshy. Plus, her sumptuous tits. Nice and plump with pink-brown pencil eraser nipples.

Fuck.

My cock tightened and threatened to grow. The cold ocean water would take care of that in quick order. I took her hand in mine. I ran with her to the water, and we splashed in.

Ruby laughed—she actually laughed—as her hair got wet and plastered to her shoulders and back. "Stupid move on my part. I should've put my hair up. This will be a bitch to brush out."

"But you look so pretty. Like a mermaid."

And she did. She was up to her belly button in water, her beautiful black hair plastered all over her body, her breasts plump, her nipples dark and hard. Her blue eyes sparkling. It was easy to imagine a glittering aquamarine fishtail underneath.

Of course, what was underneath was much better than a glittering fishtail. Between her legs was heaven. Beautiful heaven.

Shit, this water wasn't doing much for my cock. *Easy, Ryan. You walk out of the water with a giant hard-on, and she'll run screaming in the other direction.*

I touched her cheek again. She had let me do that before. Her lips were dark and glistening in the moonlight. I ran my thumb across the lower one.

"Ruby," I said, my voice low and husky. "I'm dying to kiss you."

She slid her tongue out and touched it to the tip of my thumb.

My God. My dick was raging. Just because this woman had touched her tongue to my thumb. What would happen if I actually kissed her? *Really* kissed her? Not a silly brushing peck like last night, but the joining of our mouths, our tongues, our lips sliding and slipping?

Just a kiss. That's all I needed. Just to kiss those beautiful lips, slide my tongue between them...

She closed her eyes and lifted her face.

Was that an invitation?

Whether it was or not, I decided to go for it. She would stop me if she didn't want it.

As much as I wanted to crush my lips to hers and take her mouth, I went slowly.

I leaned down and pressed my lips across hers once, twice, three times.

She tensed a bit, but then relaxed.

I cupped both of her cheeks and kissed her lips again. And then once more. I kissed her cheek, tiny little kisses until I got to her ear and gave her lobe a tug with my teeth.

"Let me show you a real kiss, Ruby," I said into her ear. "Open for me. Let me in."

She sighed, and I trailed my lips back to her mouth, gliding my tongue over her lower lip and then her upper, sliding it between the seam.

When she opened slightly, I slipped into her mouth.

She tasted of raspberries. Sweet raspberries. When I touched the softness of her tongue, I nearly exploded right into the ocean. From a kiss. A fucking kiss. A gentle kiss at that.

I quickened my pace, swirling my tongue with hers, running it over her teeth, her gumline, and then tangling it with hers again.

I pulled her closer to me, our chests touching, her gorgeous boobs rubbing against me, her nipples poking my chest.

She broke away, panting. "Oh my God."

"You're wonderful," I said.

"Oh my God," she said again. "Please. Kiss me again."

This time I smashed our mouths together, taking her tongue with mine, swirling them together. Again, she was tense at first, but within a few minutes she was kissing me back.

We kissed for several more minutes, until she broke away, panting again. She looked down at my rigid cock bobbing on the surface of the water. Her eyes were wide.

"I won't hurt you. I promise."

"It's not like I've...never seen one before."

"None of that matters. All that matters is you and me, the two of us beneath the moon, in this beautiful water. I can't help the way my body responds to you, Ruby. I enjoy kissing you. I think that's pretty obvious." I smiled. "But like I told you last night, you have nothing to fear from me. I won't do anything you don't want me to do."

"I never thought I could want something like this."

I touched her cheek. "What *do* you want?"

"I don't know. I only know what I'm feeling at this moment."

"And what are you feeling?"

"I'm feeling..." She looked up to the sky. "I'm feeling something I never thought I would feel. I don't even know how to describe it."

"Let me tell you what *I'm* feeling, then," I said.

CHAPTER THIRTEEN

RUBY

That kiss. I knew about kissing. I'd seen lots of kissing. I knew how it was done. I'd just never done it before. By my own choice. I'd had chances, despite trying not to attract men. I'd just never wanted to. Never imagined I'd ever want to.

Ryan Steel's lips were soft as suede, and when he touched them to mine, something inside me threatened to implode. Every cell in my body went on high alert. My nipples tightened and tingled, wanting to be touched, sucked. Sparks shot between my legs.

Kissing.

Had I really thought I could live my whole life without it? No longer. Now that I'd had a taste of it, I could never go without it again. As much as I didn't want to acknowledge it, my life, as of this very moment, had changed.

Or maybe it hadn't changed.

Maybe it had just begun.

I felt more alive, standing in the ocean with Ryan Steel, than I'd ever felt in my life. More alive than when I caught a criminal and saw him on his way to justice. More alive than when I'd graduated at the top of my class in the police academy. More alive than anything.

"Let me tell you what I'm feeling," Ryan said again.

"All right," I said softly.

"I find you beautiful, Ruby. Not just on the outside, but on the inside. You're different from any woman I've ever met. You don't know how beautiful you are. Or maybe you do, and that's why you try to hide it. You cover that body in androgynous clothing, pull that amazing hair back into that schoolmarm style. But you can't hide, baby. You can disguise your body, strap down your breasts, but you can't hide your beauty, because it doesn't just come from your physical attributes. It exudes out of every inch of you. Your integrity. Your demand for justice. Your concern for everyone around you."

I opened my mouth, but he silenced me by placing two fingers over my lips. His touch scorched me.

"You're beautiful in every way, and I want to kiss you. I want to touch your body. I want to show you pleasure. I want you to see the beauty in what I can show you. Beauty I'm sorry you've never seen before, because you deserve everything good. I'm fall—"

I shushed him this time. "Please don't say that."

"All right. That can wait. For now, I find you fascinating. I love being with you. Even walking in silence thrills me because you're beside me. Your presence is soothing, relaxing. And with all that's been going on in the Steel family, I crave that. I crave that steadiness that you provide for me."

Steadiness? Me? I was far from steady myself.

"Your strength," he continued. "Your physical strength is humbling, but your mental strength... I've watched my brother regain his mental strength in the last several months. He's like a new man. But you... I don't know exactly what you went through with your father, and I'm not asking, unless you want to tell me sometime. But you're still so strong. So ready to help others."

"But I—"

"Let me finish, please. Yes, you're strong, but underneath I sense the vulnerability of a child, Ruby. And I understand. I understand better than most because of what my brother has been through. It's killing me that you fear me. I don't want you to fear me, baby. I don't want you to run from me. I want you to run *to* me. Because I want to run to you."

I stared at him, at his gorgeous face in the moonlight, at his dark hair wet and slicked back on his head.

"I never imagined wanting to run to any woman. Even my former girlfriend, and we were pretty serious. But you... You stir something in me. You draw me in. And God help me, I want to be drawn in. I want to cocoon myself in you. Your beauty. Your goodness. Your amazingness. I've never wanted a woman this much."

I trembled, even in the warmth of the night. "I don't know if I can give you everything you want."

"Don't misunderstand me. I'm not asking for sex. Though I won't lie to you. I'd love to make love to you right now. But what I feel is more than that. It goes beyond the physical, beyond the emotional, even. I'm not even sure I can put it into words."

His words made sense to me. Because, though I was afraid of the physical, I understood exactly what he meant by "beyond the physical." But how could we have anything if I was afraid of the very essence of a relationship between a man and a woman? And how could I explain that to him? Because I did want him. And yes, I wanted him physically. I wanted him as much as I feared the act.

Did my desire overwhelm my fear?

There was only one way to find out.

I took his hand. "Take me to the cabana."

"Baby, you don't have to do this."

"Take me now," I said. "Before I lose my nerve."

"All right." He led me out of the water and to the cabana where our clothes lay on the bed. We brushed the sand off our feet.

The bed looked massive, and it grew larger with every beat of my heart.

But I wasn't going to run away in fear. He wanted me to run to him. I would run to him.

And I hoped I'd find the part of me that had been missing for so long.

He touched my cheek, his fingers burning my skin. "I need you to tell me first. Tell me..." He cleared his throat. "Are you a virgin?"

I gulped and nodded.

"Then your father never...?"

"No." My voice shook. "He tried. And he would have. But I got away."

He heaved a sigh. "Oh, thank God. I mean, I know whatever you went through with him wasn't good, and I'm so sorry for that. But I couldn't bear the thought of him taking you, violating you in that way."

"Believe me, neither could I. I was lucky to get away."

"Maybe. Or maybe you were just strong enough to figure out how to get away. Don't discount yourself."

"Ryan, I was fifteen."

His eyes darkened. "That bastard."

I swallowed. "What he did to me was nothing compared to what he did to your brother. And to many others."

He shook his head. "My brother went through hell. I won't deny it. And what's more, he saved me from the same fate. My brother is amazing. A real-life hero. But so are you, baby. So are you."

"I don't feel very amazing a lot of the time. And I sure as hell don't feel like a hero."

"You are."

"I doubt Juliet and Lisa would think so."

"Oh, baby." He cupped my other cheek as well, holding my face. "You're not responsible for everything bad in the world."

"But my father—"

"Hey. You're not your father. Any more than I'm my father. We've been finding out some stuff about him, stuff that I know isn't going to lead to anything good. But he isn't me."

"I know. You're right. I know that objectively."

"It's not your responsibility to right all your father's wrongs. Don't let him color your life. Don't let what he did to you color your life."

Easy for him to say. His words weren't any I hadn't heard before. From friends—the few I'd had over the years— but mostly from myself.

If only I could make myself believe them.

He roved his gaze over my body. "You're so beautiful."

"Oh!" I'd nearly forgotten we were naked. Our conversation had taken a turn away from what we both wanted.

Well, what *he* wanted.

No, that was a lie.

I wanted it. I just didn't *want* to want it.

But here I was, naked in a cabana on a nude beach with the most magnificent man in the universe.

I laid my hands over his and then smoothed them up his

arms, over his shoulders, to his face. I cupped his cheeks as he was cupping mine, and I pulled him toward me.

His soft lips landed on mine, and I opened slightly. Kissing was everything and nothing like I'd imagined it would be. It was wet and sloppy, yes, but it was also emotional and perfect.

At least it was with this man.

As he swept into my mouth, I let go of my fears, my worries. For this one night, I would have perfection.

Just once. That was all I needed.

Then I'd go back to real life. Back to what I'd been put on earth to do. Make up for the sins of my father.

No. Not going there. Not tonight…

I surrendered to the kiss, opened to it. My body heated, my skin prickling with fire. As I leaned into Ryan, his hardness nudged into my stomach. I resisted the temptation to back away.

You're safe here. Trust him. You're safe here.

I moved my hands forward and tangled them in his damp hair. He groaned into my mouth.

Did my touch do that to him? Did I have that much of an effect on him?

He broke the kiss and trailed his lips over my cheek to my ear, nibbling on my lobe, licking around the outer shell, and then poking his tongue into my ear canal.

"Oh!" The sensation was intense, traveling into my body like a strike of lightning.

"You okay?" he whispered.

"Yes. More than okay," I said.

He moved his hands from my cheeks down my neck, my shoulders, down my arms, until he cupped one of my breasts.

I inhaled a swift breath, my nipple pebbling further. I

wanted him to touch my nipple so badly. Thank God his mouth was on mine again, or I might have screamed out a command for him to.

And then he was. Thumbing my nipple.

The jolt surged between my legs, and I throbbed. Not only there, but also throughout my whole body.

I quivered, quaked in his arms. Ready to give in to whatever he wanted. Damn the consequences. I wanted to feel pleasure. Real pleasure. And I wanted to feel it with Ryan Steel.

Slowly I felt myself stepping backward. He was leading me toward the bed, still thumbing my nipple. When the back of my legs hit the mattress, I sat, Ryan coming with me, gently laying me down onto my back.

He slid his lips from my mouth to my neck.

I went rigid.

"Baby?"

"That's where he—that guy..."

"I'm sorry, Ruby. Do you want to stop?"

"No. I want to go on. I want to forget that guy. I want to forget my father. Every other horrible thing in the world. Kiss my neck. Please."

"Are you sure?"

"Yes. Please."

He obeyed, and I willed my body to relax. Neck kissing was supposed to be nice. And it was. When Ryan Steel was doing the kissing.

He continued down my neck, over my shoulder, to the top of my breasts. My nipples strained forward, longing for something... When his lips found one, I nearly flew off the bed.

How could anything feel so wonderful? He kissed my nipple lightly, his eyes meeting mine. He was looking for approval, so I smiled timidly.

And then he sucked the nipple between his lips.

I skyrocketed upward, my whole body tingling, my core hot and throbbing between my legs. Sighs and moans escaped my throat, lingering in the air around us, above us, as if they'd come from somewhere else.

Fire. Sparks. Electricity.

It was all here. All now. All around our bodies.

I closed my eyes as he continued to tug on my nipple. His fingers found the other one, and he touched it lightly first and then squeezed it.

I squeezed my thighs together, trying to hold in the wondrous feeling, my blood boiling like liquid gold in my veins.

When his mouth left my nipple, I opened my eyes, whimpering at the loss.

"Everything okay?" he asked.

I nodded. "Yes."

"You sure?"

"It feels good, Ryan. It feels...more than good."

He smiled. "Good. You deserve more than good. You deserve the best."

I had it. Right here, naked beside me, was the best. Ryan Steel. He was the best.

He kissed my nipple and then went lower, gliding his lips over my abdomen, down to my vulva. He inhaled.

"You smell amazing, baby. Vanilla and musk."

My thighs were still squeezed together. He nudged them apart. "Open for me. Please. I won't hurt you."

I willed my body to relax once more, and I opened my legs. I was bared to him now, the moonlight shining upon my most secret place.

A place no man had been.

No man save this one.

"God, you're beautiful," he said. "Beautiful everywhere. Beautiful down here."

I sighed and then jerked when he slid his fingers through the folds of my pussy.

"And wet. God, you're so fucking wet."

I didn't doubt it. I'd never imagined anything could feel this good. This...right.

"Don't be frightened," he said. "I want to taste you."

I nodded.

When his tongue touched my clit, my whole body jolted. Was that an orgasm? I had no way of knowing. The sensation was intense, vibrant. Nearly sent me whirling. But when he slid his tongue through my folds and then clamped back onto my clit, I knew what I'd felt before had been nothing.

This was only getting better.

I closed my eyes, lifted my hips off the bed. His damp hair wet my thighs. Or was that my own juices?

God, I had no idea. Didn't care.

"Let me show you the world, baby," he said. "Let me make you come."

I hadn't already? Well, he would know. I had gone past the point of resistance. "No" wasn't a word my lips could form anymore.

"Yes, please," I whimpered.

He clamped his mouth onto me and sucked, and then something entered me. I gasped.

"Easy, baby. It's just my finger. Let it go. Let me make you feel good."

He slid it in, out, and then in again. I relaxed and let him take me along.

And when he swirled his tongue over my clit in tandem with the thrusts of his finger, I whirled into oblivion.

CHAPTER FOURTEEN

RYAN

Her pussy walls clenched around my finger, and her body stiffened.

She cried out, and I lapped up the juice of her orgasm. Honeyed vanilla. So good. I'd never tire of the taste of her. Sweeter than any other woman I'd had.

I always got a thrill from making a woman come, but this was more than a thrill.

This was heaven. Pure heaven. And I hadn't even released yet.

She continued to cry out as I milked the last drop of climax from her, tonguing her sweet folds and finger fucking her tight little pussy. When her body started to relax, I kissed her inner thighs, wet from her nectar and oh so sweet. Then I moved forward.

She opened her eyes. "Wow."

"Feel good, baby?"

"I can't believe it," she said. "I just can't. I always imagined it would be amazing, but oh my God."

As I suspected, that had been her first orgasm. I felt privileged—no, honored—to have given it to her.

My cock was harder than it had ever been, but I couldn't ask her to take care of me. This had to go slowly, and I didn't have a condom with me anyway.

I could resist. Not like I had a choice.

But then she looked down at my groin.

"Are you...okay?"

I laughed softly. "I'll be fine."

"Do you want me to...?"

"No, baby. Don't worry about me."

"But that hardly seems fair. I could...touch it for you."

I was too weak to turn down that offer. "God. Please." I took her hand and guided it to my granite-hard cock.

She fingered it timidly. "It's warm."

I closed my eyes and groaned. "Yes, it is."

"Show me what to do. I feel so stupid, Ryan."

"Just do what feels right, baby."

I opened my eyes, expecting to see her lubricate her hand with her mouth, but instead she reached between her legs and coated her fingers with her own juices.

And I almost spent my load right there. What a fucking sight.

She gripped my cock then, rubbing her nectar all over it. I groaned again.

"Good?"

"You have no idea."

She rubbed her hand all up and down my shaft, and then, with her other hand, added more pussy juice.

Oh. My. God.

Then she began pumping me, her hand like a vise around me.

"Ruby, damn," I said through clenched teeth. "So good."

She continued, increasing her speed and then decreasing it. For a novice, this woman was a natural tease. I wanted this to last forever, but I had no resistance at this point. My balls scrunched into my body, and my cock convulsed. I was going to shoot.

I had to warn her.

I opened my mouth, but instead of words, a long groan erupted as I came all over her hand.

The straw walls of the cabana spun around me as my body shook.

Fuck.

That was a big one.

When I finally came back to reality, she was looking at me, her hand covered in my cum.

"Wow," she said.

"Is that a good wow?"

She laughed a little. "I just didn't expect it to be so much."

"I'm a stud, baby."

She laughed again.

"Don't laugh at that. A man could get a complex."

"Believe me, there was never any question in my mind that you were a stud."

"Damn right."

She laughed again. I was growing accustomed to the sound. I wasn't sure she had laughed much in her life. I intended to change that.

I checked in the drawer of the nightstand by the bed. Sure enough, clean towels had been provided. I handed her one, and she wiped off her hands.

"I'm wondering..." she began.

"Yeah?"

"What does that feel like to you? To come?"

I smiled. "It's hard to describe, but probably pretty

much the same way it makes you feel. Just really good. Really euphoric. The perfect mixture of tension and relaxation with nirvana coating it all."

"That's a really good description."

I looked straight into her vivid blue eyes. "Was tonight truly your first orgasm?"

She nodded. "There were times, after a particularly vivid dream, when I thought I'd had one in my sleep, but those were nothing compared to tonight."

I couldn't help puffing out my chest a little. "You never masturbated?"

"No. I found men attractive, of course. But an orgasm, or sex, or a man, wasn't anything I thought I'd ever want. Until now."

"What made you change your mind?"

She picked up a pillow and smacked me with it. "You did! But you already know that."

I puffed my chest out even farther.

She sighed. "This has been a wonderful night, but I want you to know that I don't expect anything from you."

"Meaning...?"

"I'm not the kind of woman who thinks we have some kind of relationship now, just because we enjoy kissing each other and..."

"Giving each other orgasms?"

"Yeah," she said shyly. "That."

She was gorgeous in the moonlight. Still naked, she glowed, her pale skin luminous and opulent. Her countenance was relaxed, still showing her afterglow. Next time she came, I wanted to see her in the sunlight. I wanted to see how rosy pink her cheeks and body got when all that blood was flowing through her.

"Are you saying you don't *want* a relationship?"

"No. Not exactly. I never thought I wanted a relationship, and just because we've had a good time together doesn't make it a relationship. I know that. I don't expect anything from you."

"So you *do* want a relationship?"

"No. Not exactly."

I cupped her glowing cheeks. "Ruby, you're going to have to actually say what you mean here. You're talking out of both sides of your mouth."

She sighed. "I don't mean to. I just mean this. I don't expect anything from you. I'm not ready for it anyway."

"What if I am?"

She arched her eyebrows, her eyes wide.

Had I truly just said that? Anna and I had broken up two years ago, and I'd had a few dates and one-nighters, but I hadn't been looking for anything substantial. I hadn't found it either.

But here it was now, staring at me with wide blue eyes.

Ruby Lee.

Detective.

Virgin.

Full of integrity.

Beautiful.

And bombshell sexy, whether she knew it or not.

"We don't have to be looking for a relationship," I said. "I never thought you expected anything from me. You're not that kind of a woman. You know your own mind, and you've been taking care of yourself for nearly two decades. You're amazing." I stroked her cheek. "Why don't we just take it one day at a time?"

She nodded. "All right. I just don't want you to feel—"

I trailed my fingers over to her lips, shushing her. "I don't feel anything but the desire to get to know you better. To spend time with you. I promise you're not forcing me into anything."

She nodded, puckering her lips and giving my fingers the softest kiss.

My groin tightened.

I could go again. But no condom. Not that it mattered. She was a virgin, and I was clean. But it was too soon, and I couldn't ask her to suck me off. Her father hadn't raped her, but I didn't know what he *had* done. And now, basking in the afterglow of our mutual orgasms, was not the time to find out.

She yawned. "I'd better get back and get to bed. I want to hit the yoga class in the morning again, and then, instead of going to lift, I'm going to see if I can talk to Shayna. If she's still here."

"Sounds good. Yoga at six it is."

She laughed. "You want to go again?"

"Sure. Why not?"

She laughed again. "Let's see how you feel about it in the morning."

★ ★ ★

An elephant had stomped on me overnight.

I could barely move the next morning. My phone alarm had gone off at five thirty so I could shower before Ruby came to get me for yoga, but I was still lying in bed.

Fuck. Today was the wedding, too. I had to escort Ruby down the aisle.

I sat up in bed.

Ouch.

I moved my legs to the side.

Ouch.

I stood.

Fucking ouch.

I walked to the bathroom and reached out to turn on the shower.

Ouch.

I stepped inside.

Bliss.

The hot water pelted me, and I turned it even hotter and stood for a few moments, just letting it coat me. It was heaven on my sore muscles.

Yoga and a little weight lifting. This was the result?

I wasn't out of shape. I was in damned good shape. I was very active.

What a wuss.

I couldn't let Ruby see me like this.

Then I remembered her words from last night. *Let's see how you feel about it in the morning.*

The little vixen knew.

I forced my body to move as I washed up and then stepped out of the shower. Bringing my arms above my head to towel off my hair was excruciating. I had barely struggled into my boxer briefs when her knock came at my door.

I groaned as I walked toward it and opened it.

"Morning!" she said, looking gorgeous and chipper as ever.

"Morning," I said back through clenched teeth.

She held up the little cooler, presumably filled with protein shakes and water again. "Ready for yoga?"

"Sure." I'd show her. I'd get through that hour on the mat if

I had to wince through the whole thing. Which I'd definitely be doing. I quickly put on my shorts and muscle shirt.

Ouch.

"Great!" She grabbed my hand and pulled me out the door.

I had to stop myself from groaning in pain. When we opened the door to the bungalow, we were surprised to see two envelopes taped to the door. One was addressed to me, the other to Ruby.

"I wonder what this is about?" I said.

"I've actually been expecting something. I would imagine the resort security and the local police want to talk to us. Shayna probably told them that we saw the three guys."

"She didn't know our last names."

"It probably wasn't too hard to look up all the Ryans and Rubys at the resort. We were probably it, and we're staying in the same place."

I nodded. Made sense.

She glanced quickly at the paper inside the envelope. "Yes, that's what they want. They want us to come by at eight o'clock this morning."

"Come where?"

"To the resort security office. There's a map here."

I quickly opened my envelope and confirmed what Ruby said. "All right. Maybe we should skip the yoga then?" *God, please let her say yes.*

"Why? We don't have to be at the office for two hours. We can do yoga, grab a quick shower, and get something to eat."

"I thought you wanted to try to talk to Shayna this morning."

"If she's still here," she said. "And I can find out when we talk to the police this morning."

Shit. Looked like I was in for an hour of torture.

After a ten-minute walk to the greenbelt, my thighs were really whining.

Herlinda was stretching. "Good morning! Nice to see you again. Grab a mat, and I'll see if we get any more stragglers."

Ruby and I both grabbed mats and set them down. Ruby began stretching. My muscles balked, but I was determined.

I did a few wimpy stretches, and soon Herlinda was calling the class to order.

"Let's start with some deep breaths in the lotus position," she said.

The lotus position? I pulled my legs into my body with a smile plastered on my face. Inside I was grimacing with pain.

Just breathe, Ryan. You can get through this.

I got through the hour but didn't make it into all the positions. Ruby was concentrating, so I hoped she didn't see what I was doing. I was sure Herlinda noticed, but she was too nice to say anything.

Ruby rolled up her mat at the end of class. "Ready to hit the showers?"

"I... I was thinking more along the lines of a hot tub?"

She smiled at me. "Anything you want to tell me, Ryan?"

"Nope."

"Come on..." she teased.

Oh, what the hell. "My body feels like it's been run over by a Mack truck."

Ruby burst into laughter. As much as I want to be irritated with her, it was such a joyful sound I couldn't help smiling.

"I had a feeling you'd be sore today, but you're just too much of a man to admit it. I can't believe you got through the entire yoga class."

"Barely."

She laughed again. "You're a good sport. I like that. All right, the hot tub it is."

I grinned. "Since we didn't bring our suits, we'll have to go over to the nude pool and hot tub."

She dropped her mouth open.

I moved forward and pushed her chin up. "Careful. Lots of mosquitoes around here." Then I took her arm and led her toward the nude pool and hot tub.

Because it was so early, the hot tub was vacant. We stripped our clothing, and she seemed a lot less inhibited now as we stepped into the warm water.

Heaven.

Ruby opened the cooler. "We'll have to save the protein shakes for later. Right now, we need hydration in this hot water." She removed two bottles of water and handed me one.

I opened it and took a deep drink. Cool, fresh water. Nectar of the gods.

I closed my eyes for a few moments and inhaled the rising steam. Then I opened them. Ruby was sitting across from me, her lovely breasts floating near the surface of the water. I chuckled.

"What's so funny?" she asked.

"Here I am, in a hot tub on a nude beach, with the most beautiful woman in the world sitting across from me, and I'm too fucking sore to do anything about it."

"You'll be fine. We'll have lots of time to do something later."

Did that mean she was up for doing "something?" Hell, yeah. But would we truly have the time? We had decided to leave the resort early, tomorrow, after the wedding today.

I didn't want to leave yet. I wasn't ready to leave paradise.

But the arrangements had already been made. Still, we had today. Ten minutes in the hot tub and then a megadose of ibuprofen, and maybe I'd feel a little better. Hell, I had to take part in the wedding today. I'd better do something about the sore body.

We didn't speak much, just relaxed and inhaled the steam, until Ruby said it was time to get out.

"Oh, come on. It feels so good."

"Yes, but too much of a good thing is bad for you. Especially when it's 104-degree water. It's time to get out, get more hydration, go get breakfast, and then we have to go speak to the security and the police."

Right. I'd almost forgotten. The hot water sure was relaxing. I stood and exited the tub like a decrepit old man.

"Did that help at all?" Ruby asked.

I looked at her, her beautiful body dripping. Damn, if I didn't hurt so damned much right now... "It felt great while we were in there."

"It will help. I'm sorry you're hurting so badly."

"Oh, yeah? Why didn't you tell me this would be the result yesterday?" I smiled.

"You assured me you were in great shape."

"I am. Look at me."

She dropped her gaze to the floor. "I *have* looked at you."

I walked toward her—*ouch*—and lifted her chin up so our gazes met. "I want you to look at me. I want you to *see* me."

"All right."

"I hope you like what you see, Ruby. Because I sure as hell like what I see when I look at you."

Her cheeks reddened, and her gaze dropped again. My

fingers still on her chin, I lifted it again. "Please. Look at me. I want you to. Don't be afraid. Don't be shy. We've been... intimate, remember?"

Though I had toweled off, I was still wet from perspiration from the heat of the water. My cock was flaccid as she raked her gaze over me.

"You are beautiful, Ryan. There's no doubt about that."

No woman had ever called me beautiful before. The way she looked at me, almost reverently, I knew it was a compliment.

"So are you. But I've told you that many times before."

She smiled shyly. "We really should go get something to eat. Before we know it, we'll need to meet the security guys."

"Fair enough." I put my clothes on, struggling to get into my shorts. Damn, those aching muscles.

"We should see if you can get a massage later today. Maybe before the wedding," Ruby suggested.

"That's a great idea. But only if you join me."

"All right. After we talk to security, we can stop by the spa and see if they have any openings."

I had been hoping she would offer to give me a massage. Hell, I'd love to give her one. If I weren't in so much pain.

CHAPTER FIFTEEN

RUBY

"Ms. Thomas says the two of you saw the three men who took her and the other two ladies that day," a local police officer said.

"Yes, sir, we did," I said.

"Can you describe them?"

"They were three dark-skinned males, probably aged twenty-five to thirty," I said. "They identified themselves as Mark, Rashaun, and J.J."

"Last names?"

"They didn't tell us, and no one asked."

"Those are all very common first names here on the island. They are likely aliases. Anything else?"

"They had Jamaican accents. The individual named Mark did most of the talking. One of them, not Mark, was bald. All very good-looking, well muscled. Mark was about six-two, two hundred pounds. The bald one was a little shorter, maybe five-eleven or six feet, one hundred and eighty pounds. The third one was the same size as Mark."

The officer turned to Ryan. "Can you add to any of what Ms. Lee said?"

"I don't remember their names, but I'm sure Ruby is correct. She has a mind for facts."

"Can you describe them?"

"Not any more than she did. I agree with her description. The one named Mark seemed to do most of the talking. He wasn't the bald one."

The officer nodded, made some notes, and then addressed me again. "Can you tell me what they said?"

"They walked up to us just as the girls said they were looking for some fun. Mark invited them to get on their Jet Skis. They said they were locals and could show them some great sights." I frowned. "I told them not to go. I really tried to stop them."

"Yes, Ms. Thomas corroborates that. You have good intuition, Ms. Lee."

"I'm a police detective myself." I didn't have to tell them where my intuition really came from.

"Thank you for trying. Unfortunately, sometimes young women just don't sense the danger they might be in. This resort is usually quite safe."

"They said they had day passes," I said.

"The resort doesn't offer day passes," the officer said. "But there was no reason for you to know that."

My heart sank. I had suspected that. I should have called security. I should have, should have, should have... "I wish I had been more successful stopping them."

"So do we, ma'am, but don't blame yourself."

"Is Ms. Thomas still on the property?" I asked.

"Yes. She has a flight leaving today. A shuttle will be picking her up in an hour or so."

"Do you think I might be able to talk to her?"

"That's up to her, ma'am," the officer said. "She's really distraught right now."

I nodded. "I can imagine that she is. I won't do anything to disturb her further, I assure you."

"It's still up to her."

"Do you know where she is?"

"Probably in her room. We kept security stationed there since she was unable to leave the resort yesterday. I can't tell you what room she's in, but I can have the front desk operator connect you. Then it's her decision."

"That would be fine. I don't want to bother her. If she doesn't want to talk to me, I'll respect that. But I have to try."

The officer made a quick call to the front desk and then turned to me. "I've set it up. All you need to do is go to the front desk, show your ID, and the operator will connect you to her room. You can use one of the phones behind the desk. If she wants to come out to meet with you, she is certainly welcome to do that."

"Thank you so much. I appreciate it." I turned to Ryan. "I guess I'm headed to the front desk."

"You want me to come along?"

"That's up to you."

"Then I'd like to. Besides"—he smiled—"they might have some ibuprofen at the front desk."

★ ★ ★

"Thank you for agreeing to talk to us," I said to Shayna.

The three of us sat at a table outside her room in the hotel portion of the resort, a security guard nearby, watching.

"I'm not sure why this is of any interest to you," Shayna said.

"I'm a police detective in Colorado."

"But I live in LA."

"I know that. But this interests me."

She looked down. "You have no idea how much I wish I'd listened to you yesterday. Both of you."

I took her hand. "Hey. You got away. You're safe now."

She sniffled. "But Juliet and Lisa. The police don't have a trail. They have nothing."

"None of this is your fault," I said, hoping to soothe her but knowing I wasn't.

How well I knew the guilt that ate at her soul. The same guilt ate at mine. Gina, Talon, Colin Morse, Luke Walker, among many others—all victims of my father. I hadn't been able to stop him so far. But I would someday.

How I wished I'd been able to stop the three men who had taken Juliet and Lisa.

"The locals think they were taken as slaves," Shayna said, weeping. "I'm glad I got away, but my God, how can I be glad when my two best friends are missing?"

I had no words of wisdom for her, except to say, "I know exactly how you're feeling."

"How would you know?"

"It's a long story. When we both get back to the States, feel free to call me anytime." I took a card out of my bag and handed it to her.

"How long have you been a detective?" she asked.

"Only a few months. But I've been on the force for eleven years."

"You've seen a lot, then."

"More than you know." She was right. I'd seen a lot as an officer of the law. I'd seen *more* as Theodore Mathias's daughter.

"Can you talk about what happened?" I asked. "How you escaped? And why?"

She shook her head. "A lot of it is a blur. I wish I could be more help. I've already told the local police everything I know."

"I'm sure you have. I hate to make you relive it, but if you could tell me, maybe I could help."

"How? You're a detective in Colorado. You can't do anything here."

"Let's just say I have an interest in this case. I've seen these types of things before."

She swallowed. "All right." She sighed. "Let me think."

"Take your time."

"It was fun, at first. I'd never been on a Jet Ski before. I kept my eyes on the beach. As long as I could see a beach, with people, I felt we were okay. We rode along the coast for a while. Everything seemed fine."

They were getting the women comfortable. Classic. But I didn't say this.

She continued, "The guy I was with pointed out each beach. It was hard to hear him with the noise from the Jet Ski, but I made out some of it. It seemed like they were showing us sights, like they said they would."

"When did you start to feel uncomfortable?"

"We started moving away from the coastline. Away from the beaches. I asked where we were going. The guy—I think I was with J.J., but honestly I'm not sure—said something, but I couldn't make out his words."

"I see. And then?"

"We kept going, and when I couldn't see any land at all, I got really nervous."

"Is that when you jumped off the Jet Ski?"

"Not yet. I tried to get Juliet's and Lisa's attention. But they were laughing and having a great time. They didn't seem worried at all."

"But you were."

"Yes. My father taught me to trust my intuition. He was a cop too. He's dead now."

"I'm sorry."

"Thank you. It was two years ago. I still miss him. He was a great dad."

"Sounds like he really was. He gave you some good advice." I patted her forearm. "What happened next?"

"I can't be sure. But I thought I saw..."

"What?"

"We were still so far away, but I thought I saw a ship in the distance. We seemed to be going toward it."

"A ship? Or a boat?"

She shook her head. "I can't be sure. It was so far away, and maybe I was seeing things. At that point I was really freaked out. I didn't know what to do. I'm a good swimmer. I swam in high school and college, so I made a rash decision. Even though I couldn't see a coast, I jumped off the Jet Ski into the water and started swimming as fast as I could. I had no idea which direction to go since I couldn't see any land. All I knew was that I had to get away. I swam so fast because I feared J.J. would come after me."

"But he didn't?"

"No."

"Thank goodness."

"I can't be sure how long I was in the water. Once I realized he wasn't coming after me, I calmed down a little, but I still had no idea where I was, where the coast was. And the waves were strong. I treaded water for a while and then began to swim as best I could, but the waves got to be too much." She closed her eyes, inhaling. "I swallowed some water. Started to have trouble breathing." She choked on her words.

"It's okay. You're okay. You're safe now."

"I know." She broke into sobs. "I'm so sorry."

"Don't be sorry. You have every reason to cry. It's okay."

She nodded and gulped. "I thought for sure I would drown, actually became resigned to it, and then a motorboat arrived. They dragged me on board. For a second I thought it was the boat that J.J. was heading toward, and I figured I was dead anyway. But it wasn't. It was four locals, two men and two women. One of them gave me mouth-to-mouth until I coughed up a bunch of water. They calmed me down, told me they were friends. I wasn't sure if I could trust them at first, but what did I have to lose? They brought me back to the resort." She shook her head. "They are heroes. I'd be dead if it weren't for them."

"Did they tell you their names?"

"Yes. I have it all written down."

"Did they ask you what had happened?"

"They did, but I wasn't in any condition to speak at that point. I didn't get the whole story out until I was back here, talking to security and then the police."

The security guard walked toward us then. "I'm sorry to cut this short, but the shuttle is at the front of the resort to take Ms. Thomas to the airport."

I smiled. "I'm sure you're anxious to be on your way."

"I am. Very. I never want to come near this island again." She stood.

"I'll get your bags, ma'am." The guard walked into the room and came out with a suitcase and carry-on.

I moved toward Shayna and gave her a hug. "Thanks for talking to me. Please, call me anytime if you need to talk. I'm a great listener."

"Thank you," she said through sniffles.

She unclenched from me, and the guard escorted her away.

Ryan came toward me and took my hand.

"You were quiet during all of that," I said.

"You were doing fine without me."

I sighed. "I feel so bad for her."

"I know. But she'll be okay. She got away."

I shook my head. "You don't understand. She's going to feel guilt. I know what that feels like."

"And you think I don't? I was spared the wrath of your father and the others because *I* got away that day. Because Talon made sure I got away."

How could I have been so obtuse? Of course Ryan understood. "You're right. I don't know what I was thinking. Of course you of all people understand guilt. How do you cope?"

"I just try not to let the guilt eat me alive. I watched it eat Joe alive for the last twenty-five years. He's only now letting it go, thanks largely to Melanie. Believe me, it affects me. I just don't let it consume me. I can't."

"How do you escape it?"

"Work. Play. All three of us are workaholics, thanks to our father's indoctrination."

"Work didn't keep the guilt away from Jonah."

"No, it didn't. Joe has a different personality than I do."

"He's prone to depression, like your mother?"

"I think so, yes. Talon too, to a lesser extent."

"But not you."

"Not so much. Don't get me wrong. I feel the guilt. I feel it like an anvil on my chest sometimes. I've just learned to focus on other things. Like I said. Work. Play."

"You're amazing," I said. And I meant it. He was whole, and he had every reason in the world not to be.

"You know?" I said. "When I grow up, I want to be just like you."

CHAPTER SIXTEEN

RYAN

I smiled and cupped her cheek. "That's the best compliment I've ever gotten. But you're all grown up, baby, and I think you're perfect just the way you are."

She touched her hand to my cheek, and her caress scorched me. "I mean it. You're so together, Ryan, despite what you've been through. Your brothers know it. I know it. Everyone knows it. You're known as the most jovial Steel, after all. Nothing in the world could shatter you."

"Nothing except you." I stroked her silky cheek.

"I don't have that kind of power." She smiled. "Let's go check out the spa and see about that massage for you. Pretty soon it'll be time to meet the others for lunch, and then we need to get ready for the wedding."

Sounded good to me.

Ten minutes later we arrived at the spa, and sure enough, they had two openings. Ruby suggested a hot stone massage for my muscles, and I wasn't about to argue. She chose a traditional Swedish massage for herself.

"You're going to be feeling great soon," she promised.

★ ★ ★

The massage, along with the ibuprofen, helped, though I was

still sore. For now, though, I had to get dressed and wish my brothers well. The wedding would begin in about fifteen minutes.

Talon and Joe both wore white shirts and pants, as did Bryce and I, though they had white orchid boutonnieres while Bryce's and mine were bluish-white. I had no idea what the women would be wearing. All I knew was that Ruby would look gorgeous.

"Nervous, guys?" Bryce asked Joe and Talon.

Talon shook his head. "This is the best thing I've ever done."

"Ditto," Joe said.

"I'm just glad it isn't me," Bryce laughed.

"Thought you and Marj were hitting it off," Joe said.

"Are you kidding? Your kid sister? I'm not taking on the three Steel brothers."

"Not that I like thinking about you bopping my baby sister," Joe said, "but Marj couldn't do any better than you, man. Plus, she loves Henry."

Bryce scoffed. "Marj is gorgeous. I can't deny it. But we'll see. I'm not really in the market right now. Plus, I've got my hands full with a soon-to-be toddler. I miss him."

"How could you? You call him ten times a day." Joe laughed.

"Hey, guys," I said, checking my watch. "We need to get out there. The ladies are waiting."

Bryce and I followed Talon and Joe out to the makeshift altar on the beach. Brian Roberts, Jade's father, had flown in early this morning. Other than that, we had no guests except ourselves. Our parents were both dead, and Melanie was estranged from hers. Jade's mother, Brooke Bailey, wasn't recovered enough for travel, and they didn't have a great relationship anyway.

We took our places next to the officiant at the altar.

A string quartet started playing, and I looked up to see my sister walking down the makeshift aisle covered with a white runner. She looked beautiful in a light-blue sundress, carrying a bouquet of orchids that matched my boutonniere.

And then—

I nearly lost my footing.

Ruby. My Ruby.

Well, not *my* Ruby...

Not yet, anyway.

She was following my baby sister down the aisle. Her dress was the same color as Marj's but a slightly different style. Hell, I knew nothing about style, but it was spaghetti-strapped and silky, and her nipples poked through.

God... Didn't need a boner now.

She also carried a bouquet of orchids, but another small orchid had been entwined in her hair behind her ear. Her hair was pulled back from her face, and the glossy locks tumbled down her back.

So beautiful.

The blue in the dress and the orchid in her hair brought out the sparkling sapphire of her eyes. Her lips were dark, as usual, and a slight blush tinged her cheeks.

I couldn't take my eyes off of her. I hardly noticed as Melanie walked down next, solo, and then Jade, escorted by her father.

"Dearly beloved," the officiant began in his Jamaican accent. "We are gathered here on this joyous occasion to join Jonah Bradford Steel and Melanie Lynn Carmichael in marriage, and to join Talon John Steel and Jade Bailey Roberts in marriage. The couples have written their own vows for the occasion. We'll begin with Jonah and Melanie." He nodded to Joe.

Jonah took Melanie's hand and looked into her eyes. "Melanie, I've never known anyone like you. Your propensity for caring for others is beyond description, and your strength humbles me. You chased the darkness from my life and replaced it with love and acceptance. I can never begin to repay you for what you've done for me—the joy, peace, and love you've brought to my life—but I will spend every day of my life trying. I give you my life. I will love you always." He smiled. "And I cannot wait to meet our child." He touched her still-flat belly.

Melanie sniffled, and Joe wiped a tear from her eye.

"Jonah," she began, "you came to me for counseling and guidance, but it was you who ended up guiding me. You helped me see the beauty in my life, to see that I could be special to someone. You showed me love when I felt unlovable. And when my life was in peril, all I wanted was to get back to you to tell you how much I loved you. I vow to you today that a day will never go by that you don't feel that love, that appreciation and respect I have for you. You say I led you out of the darkness. The truth is, you led me out as well. Together we are stronger, and I know we'll make a wonderful home for our child." She blinked, and a tear fell down her cheek. "I give you my life, today and always."

"May we have the rings?" the officiant said.

Ruby stepped toward Melanie, and I stepped toward Joe, and we handed them the rings.

Jonah took Melanie's hand and placed the ring on

her finger. "Melanie, I give you this ring as a symbol of my commitment to you and our children, today and forever."

Melanie took Joe's hand and repeated the same vow.

"Jonah," the officiant said, "you may kiss your bride."

Joe grabbed Melanie and crushed his mouth to hers, in what was visibly a deep and openmouthed kiss. It went on and on, and I was afraid I'd have to pry them apart, until they finally let go of each other, their smiles palpable.

"And now, Talon and Jade."

Jonah and Melanie stepped aside, and Talon and Jade took their places in front of the officiant. The officiant nodded to Talon.

He took Jade's hand. "Jade, my love." He shook his head. "What can I ever say to tell you what you mean to me? Language is insufficient. Words aren't enough." He blinked, gulping. "You made me want to live, to grasp life and pull myself out of the hole I'd been buried in for too long. You never gave up on me, even when I pushed you away. For that I'm eternally grateful. You gave me your love, and you gave me your trust, even when I didn't deserve it. No matter how hard I fought, you fought harder. You fought for us, and you broke down my walls. You're everything to me, blue eyes, and I'll spend every last day I have on earth trying to be everything to you. I love you."

Jade wiped at her eyes and smiled, looking at my brother—my brother who was now whole, thanks to her. "Talon, you're the strongest person I've ever met. Looking back, I think I fell in love with you that first night you kissed me in the kitchen. I'd been humiliated, left at the altar, and I wasn't sure I wanted another relationship, but you called to me. Maybe not in words, but our souls cried out for each other. I know in my heart we are meant to be. You are my life, my love, my everything. I thank the universe for bringing us together, and I promise to love you with all my heart and soul, today and always."

Joe and Marj stepped up with the rings, and Talon and Jade were pronounced husband and wife. They, too, shared a clenching openmouthed kiss.

The string quartet began to play, and they finally unclenched and headed up the aisle. Joe and Melanie followed, and then Bryce with Marj on his arm. I looked at Ruby and held out my arm to her. She took it this time, and we followed Bryce and Marj.

Hugs and kisses all around for everyone. I finally took a look at the two brides, and they were, of course, radiant. My brothers both wore wide grins, and my heart soared. They both deserved this happiness. This joy and light.

I turned to Ruby. She looked serene and contemplative.

"Penny for your thoughts," I said.

She smiled. "Nothing. Just very happy for everyone."

"Everyone?"

"Well, everyone here."

"Hey, baby," I said. "I know you're worried about Shayna and the others. But let's not let that spoil the party. We're going to have a great reception, and then tomorrow we go home. We can face life then, okay?"

She nodded. "Sounds good."

I touched her cheek. "Have I told you how beautiful you look today?"

"Thanks to the salon," she said.

"Ha! Thanks to whoever created you." Then I cursed myself inwardly. She didn't want to be reminded of who created her. Half of her had been created by her father. Before she could think about it, I leaned down and brushed my lips across hers. "Come on. Let's go get a drink to toast the newlyweds."

Servers were pouring Dom Pérignon—sparkling cider for Melanie—and I grabbed two flutes for Ruby and me.

"Time for the toasts!" one of the servers shouted.

"I'll start, I'll start!" Marjorie laughed, taking front stage on the dance floor that had been set up on the beach. "To my best friend in the world, Jade Roberts. Oops, Jade Steel!" She laughed. "You've always been there for me, and now I know you'll always be there for my brother Talon. Tal, you couldn't do any better."

"Don't I know it," Talon said.

"And also to Joe and Melanie. The love I see between you two, and between Jade and Talon, makes me think anything is possible. And I'm really excited to be an aunt!" She held up her glass. "Cheers!"

Joe took the stage next, as Talon's best man. "Tal and Jade. Wow." He looked at Jade. "I've never seen my brother as happy as he's been since you came into his life. Thank you for that. And Tal, God, you amaze me. No one deserves happiness more than you, and I'm so glad you found it. I'm proud to call you my brother. To Talon and Jade!"

Again we all clinked our glasses and took a drink. I nodded to Ruby. "I think it's your turn."

"I don't know what to say."

"Just speak from your heart."

She smiled and raised her glass. "I'm the new person around here, and I'm so happy to have been accepted into this amazing family. Melanie, you and I are a lot alike, and even though we haven't known each other very long, I know I can count on you and you can count on me. I'm honored to be standing with you today, and I wish you and Jonah a long and happy marriage. To Jonah and Melanie!"

More clinking of glasses. I touched Ruby's arm. "That was great."

She blushed.

Then I went forward. "Technically, I'm Joe's best man, but right now I want to talk to both of my brothers. Joe, you're my oldest brother, the one I always looked up to, the one who taught me things, bossed me around." I paused while everyone laughed. "I've watched you since I was a kid, looking to you for guidance, and you've never failed me. I'm so glad you've found happiness with Melanie. And I promise I'll be the best uncle your kid has!" He held up his glass, and we all clapped. "And Talon... There's so much I could say to you, but I'll keep it brief. You're my hero. We all know why, so I won't go into detail. I wouldn't be who I am today if it weren't for you. You're not just a hero to me but to so many others too. Live your life, bro. Enjoy it with your lovely lady. You deserve every minute of it." I held up my glass again.

Finally, Bryce stood. "I've known most of you for what seems like forever. Joe, you're the best friend a guy could ask for. Thank you for sticking with me, even when I tried to push you away because of things I didn't want to see. Melanie, you couldn't ask for a better guy, and I'm really happy that Henry will have a playmate soon. Jade and Talon, Marjorie, Ryan, Ruby, thank you for letting me share this special day with you. So to all of you, I wish you happiness and love!"

The string quartet began, and the two couples enjoyed their first dances as husband and wife. After a few minutes, Bryce took Marj onto the dance floor, so I turned to Ruby, offering my arm.

She took it, neither of us saying a word, and I led her onto the dance floor.

She felt so perfect in my arms. I inhaled her earthy scent laced with berries and vanilla. I leaned down to whisper in her ear. "You're so lovely. I want to eat you up."

She tensed for a moment but then relaxed. "I think we have wedding cake and then a big dinner tonight."

"I'll still be hungry for you after all of that."

She didn't respond. Was I going too far? She was still so innocent, even after our time last night. Perhaps she wasn't comfortable with such dirty talk. Which really wasn't even that dirty.

When the dance ended, the servers brought out the wedding cake. It was too sweet, but I ate a piece anyway. Ruby had a smudge of white frosting on her lower lip. How I longed to lick it off. But I held myself in check and just removed it with my thumb.

She smiled. "What?"

"Just a little icing," I said.

She smiled again.

And I knew I had to have her.

Completely.

Tonight.

CHAPTER SEVENTEEN

RUBY

After our celebratory dinner, Ryan, who seemed to be feeling much better thanks to the massage and ibuprofen—or maybe the champagne—asked me to go for one last walk on the beach before we left tomorrow.

I agreed. Not so much because I wanted a repeat of what had occurred last night, but because I wanted one last night of peacefulness, listening to the waves, looking at the stars.

I had to force myself not to think that the beach was where I'd last seen Juliet and Lisa. I was thankful that Shayna was safely home by now. She'd have a lot to deal with, but she seemed very strong to me. Anyone who could jump off a Jet Ski into the ocean with no land in sight had a lot of courage. I had enough on my plate with my job and trying to bring my father to justice, but still, I was going to keep in touch with Shayna and follow Juliet and Lisa's case. I had to.

But tonight I was determined to enjoy the peace of the beach. With Ryan.

He wanted a lot from me. I wasn't deluding myself otherwise. I also wasn't deluding myself that I meant anything more to him than any other woman he'd been with.

So, as we walked for the last time along the beach, our toes sinking into the soft wet sand, I made a decision.

I'd give Ryan what he wanted.

I'd give him me.

Thirty-two was way too old to be a virgin, and he'd already allayed a lot of my fears. I trusted him to be gentle, to lead me through it. And I certainly couldn't ask for a more appealing man. Ryan Steel was magnificent.

So I'd give him my virginity, let him show me what I'd been missing.

After that, I'd let him go.

We walked along in the moonlight, as we had the previous two nights. I let him take my hand, reveling in the warmth that coursed through me at his touch. When icy tingles of apprehension threatened me, I held his hand tighter. This was going to happen tonight.

I needed it.

Maybe he did too. He'd just watched both his brothers say I do. Was he feeling alone?

I didn't know.

When we hit the nude beach and the cabanas came into view, my nerves prickled again. Could I do this?

Yes, I could. No second thoughts. It was high time for me to experience sex. Way past time, actually.

I slowed down, my heart beginning to thunder wildly. Ryan turned and looked at me, his dark eyes afire.

"Have I told you that you look beautiful tonight?"

I smiled. "You tell me that all the time."

"Today, when I saw you walking down the aisle, that orchid in your hair... I'd never seen anything so beautiful, Ruby."

My cheeks heated. Ryan had no doubt been with a lot of women, many more beautiful than I. But I let his words sink into me, warm me, erase all the doubts in my mind.

I had never thought of myself as beautiful.

I had never *let* myself think of myself as beautiful.

"I know you think I'm talking about your outer appearance," he said. "And I won't deny that you have a smoking-hot body, a gorgeous face, and the most luxurious head of hair I've ever seen. That's not where your true beauty lies. Your true beauty lies in your heart. You care."

"Yes. I do care."

"I know you do. I've seen it. Just in the short time we've known each other."

His words warmed me, and I did something I had never done before. I took the initiative and reached forward, pulling him to me and opening my lips to him for a kiss.

It was a gentle kiss at first, but it became more frantic, our tongues dueling, our lips sliding against each other's. Our mouths seemed fused together, and my nipples tightened, poking into his chest. Tingles raced through me, making me feel both warm and cold at the same time, and every bit of energy pulsing through my body coursed with concentrated aim between my legs.

I would be wet for him tonight. I was wet for him already. My nipples were aching for his tongue, the folds of my pussy aching for his fingers. And, dare I say it?

His cock.

We kissed and we kissed and we kissed, ravishing each other's mouths, our groans vibrating into each other like the low hum of a bass beat.

A few moments later, he broke the kiss, panting. "I need you. I want you so much, Ruby."

"I want you too."

I didn't regret the words that tumbled out of my mouth. In

fact, I rejoiced in them. I hadn't lost my nerve.

"I mean," he said, "I *want* you. I want to...make love to you."

"I want that too."

He arched his eyebrows. "Are you sure? If we do this, we can't take it back."

I cupped his cheeks, the dark stubble rough beneath my fingers. "I don't want to take it back. There was a time in my life that I didn't think I'd ever want to do this with anyone. I do now, with you. I'm not asking for anything past tonight, and I promise I won't have any regrets. Please, Ryan. Make love to me."

"Oh, God," he groaned. "Do you want to go back to the house?"

"No, I want to make love here. Under the stars. In the same cabana where you showed me an orgasm last night. I want to treasure this moment, remember it always."

"That sounds amazing, baby." He grabbed my hand and led me to the cabana where we had been last night. Luckily, it was vacant. "You tell me what you need," he said. "We'll go as slow as you need to go."

"Don't be so focused on me. This is for both of us." I meant that, with all my heart. This would be a first for me, but in my soul of souls I hoped that some part of it would be a first for him as well. I yearned to give him something he would remember forever.

"I want to undress you, baby. I want to unwrap you, like a beautiful gift to be savored."

I was still wearing the dress I had worn to the wedding. He caressed my shoulder, gently pushing the strap over my skin. He repeated the action on the other side, and the dress fell to my waist, baring my breasts. My nipples stuck out, hard and dark, ready to be kissed, sucked—whatever he wanted to do to them.

He thumbed them gently. "So beautiful, baby."

Though apprehension filled me, shakily I reached forward and unbuttoned his white shirt. With each inch of tan skin exposed, my heart beat faster.

Ryan Steel was so beautiful, so perfect and magnificent. Never in my wildest dreams had I imagined someone like him would want me.

I touched my fingers to his chest, so warm, and then brushed the shirt over his shoulders so it fell into a white heap on the floor. His erection tented his white pants.

His cock. I had seen it before, had touched it, had made him come.

He was large. This might hurt. I had thought about that. But the first time would no doubt hurt anyway, and if I was going to do this, I wanted it to be with Ryan.

I bit back my fear and apprehension and surged forward. Gathering my courage, I trailed my hand downward and grasped the bulge in his pants.

"God," he groaned.

He slid his hands down my waist to my hips, where he pushed the silk of my dress over them. It landed in a tousled blue circle around my feet.

I stood, bared to him except for my blue lace panties.

"Wow," he said. "You and lace? Definitely nice."

I scrunched my toes into the straw mat covering the sand inside the cabana, determined not to let my nerves scare me. He'd seen me naked several times before, but this time we were definitely heading somewhere.

I throbbed between my legs. I was wet. I could already feel it.

I inhaled a deep breath and moved forward. I unbuttoned his pants, unzipped them, and then brushed them over his hips until he was now standing in a puddle of white. His cock sprang out at me.

"Commando?" I said. "You went to a wedding commando?"

"I didn't have any white underwear." He laughed. "I tried some lighter ones, but they all showed through."

I laughed along with him. My gaze was drawn to his cock. It rose from a bush of black curly hair. I wanted to touch it, explore it, search underneath and look at his balls, his inner thighs. I wanted to lace my fingers in his pubic hair. I wanted to turn him around and look at his ass. Run my palms over it.

This was all new to me, and I wanted to savor every moment, explore his perfect body with my hands, my mouth—every part of me.

I looked down at my panties. I could already smell the arousal in the air between us. He was right. It smelled like vanilla and musk. I inhaled deeply.

"Looks like I'm a little more naked than you are," he said, and he slid his thumb under the lace waistband of my panties. "You're amazing. So amazing. Your body. Wow."

I was thankful he couldn't see the blush on my cheeks in the darkness. Only the moonlight shone upon us, and he looked like a god. A god about to deflower a virgin.

Slowly he slid the panties over the cheeks of my ass, baring me to his view. "Your pussy is already swollen. You're so hot."

I didn't doubt it. I was throbbing down there, aching for something. Now I knew what I was aching for. Ryan Steel.

Ryan Steel's cock to fill that emptiness. The emptiness I had always known existed but never quite knew how to fill. I had been waiting for this man.

"What do you want to do, baby?" he asked.

I swallowed my fears again, determined to be honest with him this one night. "I want to touch you. I want to get to know every inch of your body."

"Sounds great." He pulled me close to him. He kissed my lips, taking my tongue with his. After a few moments, he pulled away. "I could kiss you forever. Your mouth is so soft, and you taste of fresh raspberries." He stroked my jawline with his finger. "So lovely."

I took advantage of our position and raised my own hand to stroke his jawline, letting his stubble prickle my fingers. I'd meant what I said. I wanted to touch and explore every part of him, and I would begin with his gorgeous face. I trailed my fingers over the contours of his cheeks, over the outer shell of his ear down to his ear lobe, which was soft under my fingertips. I moved my hands over his scalp, threading my fingers through his beautiful hair. Then I came back to his cheeks, and I moved upward, combing through his eyebrows, rubbing his forehead, and then touching my thumbs to his temples. Then down to his neck, massaging a little as I went.

Next, his shoulders. Those broad, masculine shoulders. His skin was a light bronze, darker than my own fair skin, and the contrast between my hand and his shoulder mesmerized me. His skin was soft, softer than I had expected.

"I love your touch, baby," he said.

His words warmed me, giving me courage. I glided my fingers over his chest, his glorious pectorals, his coppery nipples that hardened under my touch. Low moans left his throat. He was so firm, so warm. I slid over the black hairs covering his pecs and nipples. So gorgeous. Downward to his tight abs. He had a classic six-pack, the perfect amount of hair that thickened slightly as it led to his crotch. I moved outward, to his hips, their slight indentation so erotic and masculine. And then I did it. What I'd dreamed of. I slid my hands around his hips to the globes of his perfect ass.

So smooth. So warm. I trailed my fingers through the crease, and he jolted slightly when I touched his asshole.

I hadn't meant to. I was enjoying touching him so much that I'd let myself go, did what was feeling right, not thinking about where I was going.

"I'm so sorry," I said, bringing my hands back to my sides.

"It's okay. I was just a little surprised. You can touch me wherever you want, baby."

"I'm so embarrassed."

He smiled. "Don't be." He took my hand and led it back to his chest. "Touch me. Please. I want you to."

His skin heated my fingertips, and I trailed to his nipple once again. I flicked it, and it hardened. "Does that feel good to you?"

He closed his eyes. "Mmm. Yes, it does."

I flicked it again and then moved to the other one. It hardened instantly. Then, gathering my courage, I moved toward him and swiped my tongue over one.

He tasted of salt and musk. I licked it again and then kissed it, wrapped my lips around the nub and sucked. If I liked this, why wouldn't he?

"Ahh," he groaned.

I pulled back. "I didn't know men liked that."

"I can't speak for all men, but I love it."

I clamped my lips to his nipple again and tugged. His cock, already erect, nudged against me, bobbing as though looking for attention.

I trailed my lips down his chest, his smooth abdomen, to the black curls between his legs. With my hands, I fingered them, their roughness, and inhaled. Male musk. So tempting.

"God, Ruby. You're killing me."

His cock was mere inches from my lips. I knew what he wanted, and I wanted to touch every part of him. I lowered my head slightly and slid my tongue along the top of his cock.

He groaned.

I moved toward the head and licked at it. A drop of liquid coated my tongue. It was salty.

He groaned again, and his cock pulsed.

I couldn't help a smile. I had power over him right now. He was at my mercy. Instead of taking him between my lips as I knew he craved, I knelt down farther and licked the underside of his cock, all the way to his balls. They were coated with fine black hair and scrunched up close to his body. I touched my lips to them and kissed them. They smelled musky and masculine, like the rest of him. I inhaled the earthy scent. Mmm.

"Jesus," he said.

"Move your legs apart," I said.

He obeyed, and I kissed the softness of his inner thighs while I trailed my hands over his quads. So firm and warm, while the inner part was so soft.

Ryan Steel was the perfect combination of hard and soft. Of strength and compassion.

I laid my cheek against his hard thigh and sighed.

And then I found myself lying on the bed. He'd lifted me so quickly and with such minimal effort I'd hardly noticed.

"Baby, you're driving me slowly insane." He hovered over me, perspiration rivering over his face.

"I just wanted to touch every part of you."

"I get that. I hope I didn't disappoint."

"Of course not. Except that I didn't get past your thighs."

"Later," he said. "Time for me to give you a little of the torture you gave me."

CHAPTER EIGHTEEN

RYAN

I was pulled tighter than a drum skin. I'd been clenching my teeth, tensing my muscles, trying not to spew my load just from her fingers and tongue on my flesh. She had no idea what her touch did to me, but she was about to find out.

I began slowly, as she had, sitting next to her supine body, softly fingering her cheeks, her ears, her brows. I stroked her jawline and slid my fingers over her neck to her shoulders. Goose bumps erupted on her skin, and I smiled to myself. I had as much effect on her as she had on me.

Her breasts were rosy and swollen, her pink-brown nipples hard and protruding. I longed to take one between my lips, to thumb them. But not yet. I would tease her as she had teased me.

I moved my hands over her chest, fingering the soft skin of the upper parts of her breasts. I ached to touch those tight nipples with my fingers, but I circled around her areolas, avoiding the pink-brown skin.

She closed her eyes, moaning, and I knew what she wanted. Just one touch to the turgid nipples. It would feel so good to her. But no. I moved over the beautiful globes of her breasts and then down her flat belly to her navel, a perfect little wink in her smooth skin. I glided my fingers down her sides, over the swells of her hips, and then I spread her legs ever so slightly. I fingered her vulva and entwined the hair of her short bush through my fingers. And then I dipped below. Smoothed my fingers through her wet folds.

She tensed up, moaning.

But I moved to her inner thighs, stroking them as she had stroked mine. Her skin was so soft, so silky, and just touching her made my dick grow even firmer. How I longed to place myself between her legs and shove it into her deeply.

But even if things were different and I wasn't teasing her, I couldn't do that.

She's a virgin, Ryan.
Don't forget that.

So though her cunt was right in front of my view, her dark-pink lips glistening with her juices, I avoided it, instead nibbling on her inner thighs, licking the musk that had dripped there.

I kissed my way over her thighs, to her knees, massaging her as I went. I kissed down her calves to her lovely feet. I kissed her toes and massaged her insteps.

She sighed. I looked up at her. Her eyes were closed, her lips slightly parted and glistening. So beautiful.

I moved up the bed toward her and turned her over gently. She squirmed.

"Relax, baby. You'll have your turn again."

I kissed the tops of her shoulders, between her shoulder blades, and down her smooth, glossy back to the crease of her ass. Such a gorgeous ass, so perfect and muscular. I smoothed my hands over the round globes, and she turned red. So adorable. I brought my lips down upon her sweet cheeks.

I nibbled at the plumpness of her ass, and goose bumps

erupted again. I smiled to myself, moving toward the crease of her ass. How it beckoned me. Though she had touched my asshole, I knew she wasn't ready for me to touch hers. But oh, how I longed to. How I longed to slide my tongue through the crease, find that puckered hole, show her the pleasure it could bring.

Maybe someday...

Instead, I moved down her ass to where her cheeks joined her thighs, and I licked and nibbled across that little crease. I kissed down her thighs to the back of her knees, downward until I got to her feet again. I gave each of them another quick massage.

At the head of the bed she was murmuring unintelligible things.

"What is it, baby?"

"I want... I need..."

"All right." I smiled. "You've been a good sport. Now get on your hands and knees. I want to lick you. I want to lick that pussy. That sweet cunt."

The C word made her tense. Just for a moment, but I noticed. Still, she obeyed, coming up on her hands and knees, laying her cheek on the pillow.

And her paradise was bared to my view. Deep pink, engorged. Glistening with nectar. As much as I wanted to kiss, suck, bury my tongue between her sweet folds, I took a moment to just look at her. The beauty of her female form. That pussy that was made to attract men.

So fucking beautiful.

Her hips wiggled.

"Baby?"

"You said..."

"Yes?"

"Damn it, Ryan. You said you were going to lick me."

I couldn't help a small chuckle. "Yes, I did say that."

"Then why in hell aren't you?"

She was adorable. Time to put both of us out of our misery. I dived into her.

Her flavor. That intense female flavor. Her fragrance rose above us, scenting the air around us. Every time I inhaled, my cock grew harder.

Slowly I slid my tongue between her labia. I savored her, resisted the urge to shove my tongue up into her cunt. I wanted to go slowly. I wanted this night to have so many memories for both of us.

She wiggled her hips again, pushing her pussy into my face. God, she turned me on. My cock was throbbing between my legs. But I had to get her ready. Couldn't rush her. This was new to her. I had to remember that. So I slurped at her pussy, nibbled at her clit, took a deep breath, and then slid upward, over her asshole.

She tensed up.

So I went back down, concentrating on her pussy. I sucked at it, bit it, ate at her like an animal devouring its prey, lapped at her like a cat lapping at cream. Sweet cream—for that's what she was. Rich and decadent.

"You taste so good," I said before diving back into her. "Does it feel good to you, baby? You like it?"

"God," she sighed.

"Answer me, Ruby. Tell me if you like it when I suck your pussy."

She wiggled her hips again. "Yes. Yes, I like it."

"Are your nipples hard right now?"

"God, yes."

"Your pussy is wet. So fucking wet."

Again I shoved my tongue into her heat, but this time I concentrated on her clit. It was time to let her have an orgasm. If she truly wanted me to put my cock inside her tonight, I needed her relaxed.

I buried my nose in her, finding her clit and nibbling, sucking. When she tensed and her pussy clamped down, I inserted two fingers into her heat.

She pulsed around me, and I licked her further, ate her, lapped at her, couldn't get enough of her sweet silky pussy.

She cried out, not in words.

"Yeah, baby," I said against her quivering folds. "Come for me. Show me how much you love me sucking your pussy. I need you. I need to put my cock in you soon, Ruby."

When her clamping subsided, I took one last lick of her. She was so swollen, so coated in juice. I almost didn't want to stop. But perhaps it was time.

I moved toward her head and brushed my lips across hers. "Did you like that, baby?"

"God, yes."

"Do you still want to make love?"

Her eyes shot open, and for a moment, I feared she'd changed her mind.

But then, "Yes, Ryan. I want to feel what it's like to have you inside me."

"I can't wait to be inside you, baby. My cock is so ready for you."

I gently turned her over so she was lying on her back.

"I'm going to ask you this one more time because I want to know that you're sure. Do you want me to make love to you?"

Her blue eyes sparkled as she stared into mine. "Yes, please. I've waited too long for this."

"Oh, thank God." I got off the bed, found my pants on the floor, and retrieved my wallet. This time I had remembered a condom.

I sat down next to her and held out the condom. "I don't know if you're on birth control," I said. "But if you are, I want you to know that I'm clean. You're safe from diseases with me."

I feared she might not be on birth control. If she wasn't sexually active, why would she be?

"I'm on the pill," she said. "It just always seemed the... responsible thing to do."

"That's wonderful, baby. But I want you to be comfortable, so we can still use the condom if you want to."

She shook her head. "Ryan, I want to experience this. I don't want any barriers. I want to feel what it's like to have a man inside me."

I let out a groan without meaning to. Thank God.

I smoothed my fingers through her pussy lips. "You're nice and wet. Lots of natural lubricant. It might still hurt, but you're definitely ready."

I climbed atop her, hovering over her, my cock dangling, touching the hair on her vulva. I slid the head down over the wetness of her pussy lips. And I groaned. God, it felt so good. What would it feel like to breach the pussy of a virgin?

I was about to find out.

"I've never made love to a virgin before," I said. "I can go slowly or I can go quickly. It's up to you, although quickly might be less painful."

"Quickly," she said. "Come inside me. Please, Ryan."

CHAPTER NINETEEN

RUBY

He kissed my lips softly, touching his tongue to mine.

"Relax, baby," he said.

And then he thrust into me.

I cried out against his lips. The pain felt like a knife slicing me in half.

"Shh," he said. "I'm all the way in. Just get used to it. Get used to the fullness. I won't move until you tell me to."

My jaw was clenched and my eyes squeezed shut.

"Relax," he said again.

"I feel so full," I said.

"You *are* full. Full of me. I promise it will be good. We just have to get through this rough part. People all over the world wouldn't be doing it if it weren't good."

I smiled at that, and then I forced myself to relax. I had wanted to ease the emptiness, and I couldn't deny that he had done that.

The sharp pain subsided fairly quickly, and then it was just fullness. Then the walls of my pussy began to tickle. I had liked how his fingers felt sliding in and out of me, and now, would I like the feeling of his dick sliding in and out of me? There was only one way to find out.

I opened my eyes and looked into his dark orbs. "I'm

ready."

"Are you sure?"

I nodded. "Yes. I want to experience this. I want to experience it with you."

He pulled out and groaned as he thrust back into me.

Again the fullness, but no pain this time. Just a welcome feeling within my walls.

"Again," I said.

He plunged back into me, and this time the force of it aroused the tip of my clit.

A moan escaped my throat.

"Good, baby?"

Good? This was so much more than good. This was filling an emptiness that had been within me for far too long. He wasn't just filling my pussy. He was filling my heart, my soul. My very being.

How had I gone so long in life without this? Without the joy of this joining?

Sex didn't have to be a violent thing. It didn't have to be a horrifying thing. It could be a lovely thing. A very loving thing between two people.

Ryan Steel wasn't in love with me. I wasn't in love with him, either. But my God, I felt something for him. Something I'd never had the urge to feel before.

He slid in and out of me again and again, and my muscles tensed, my blood began to boil, my nerve endings began to tingle. Another orgasm was coming.

"Oh my God, Ryan. Oh my God."

"Enjoy it, baby. This is what life is about." He grunted. "Just this."

His words, though not romantic, not even that sexy,

somehow spoke to something deep and primal within me.

And I crashed around him.

He continued pumping into me as my climax took me higher and higher, my skin tingling, my pussy throbbing. Faster and faster, his hips pistoning, until finally—

"Ah!" He plunged deeply into me and stayed there.

As the last waves of my orgasm left me, my pussy walls were so sensitive that I felt the contractions of his cock as he emptied into me.

And I knew my life, as of this moment, had been changed forever.

★ ★ ★

"I'd like to see you again," Ryan said to me. "When we get home."

"I told you. I don't expect anything from you."

"Baby, I understand that. I don't expect anything from you either. And I know you don't have any frame of reference, but that was some of the best sex I've ever had."

I smiled. He was right. I had no frame of reference. But I had a hard time imagining that sex with anyone else could ever be this good.

Still, was I ready to have sex with only one man? Was that fair to me? Was it fair to Ryan?

"Let's just see how things go," I said. "I'm so involved in my work right now. I'm not sure I have the time to devote to anything else."

He frowned a little.

Shit. Had I really hurt his feelings? Offended him? Ryan Steel? The most gorgeous man in the universe? Surely I didn't have that kind of power. Not mousy, inexperienced Ruby Lee.

But I was no longer mousy...and no longer inexperienced.

I'd slid under the radar for so long that I'd become comfortable with being "invisible." Now? Thanks to Marjorie, suddenly I'd become noticed. And as uncomfortable as it had made me at first, I found now...

I could hardly even imagine the words.

I found now...that I *liked* it. I liked feeling attractive. I liked the attention I got from Ryan Steel.

Yes, *Ryan Steel*.

I couldn't believe some beautiful supermodel type hadn't snagged him before now. So I turned to him.

"Have you ever had a serious relationship?"

"I've been around the block," he said, "but I've really only had one serious relationship."

"Can you tell me about it? I don't mean to pry, but as you've said, I have no frame of reference. I'm not saying I'm looking for a serious relationship, whatever that may mean. I'm truly just interested."

He turned on his side and propped his head in his hand, looking down at me with those dark, deep eyes. The Steel brothers all resembled each other, but there was no question that Ryan was the best looking in a model-handsome kind of way. His features were a little bit finer, his jawline slightly more sculpted, his eyelashes just a bit longer, and his irises ever so slightly lighter. Right now, glowing in the moonlight, they were a dark amber, his lashes an onyx curtain.

Women would kill for lashes like that.

"Okay. What would you like to know?"

"Everything."

He laughed. "That narrows it down."

"Again, I have no frame of reference. So start at the beginning."

"All right. Her name was Anna. Anna Shane. Her family owned a small ranch adjacent to ours."

"How did you meet?"

"Ranch business. She acted as bookkeeper for her family's business, and when they were slow, we hired their ranch hands so they could have full-time work."

"So her ranch wasn't as big as yours?"

"No ranch is as big as ours, baby."

I couldn't help a smile. "Sounds like a personal problem to me."

"Ha! I actually meant it literally. We own the biggest ranch in Colorado."

"I know that. What I wanted to know was how big hers was in comparison."

"Not big at all. The Shanes had a small-time operation."

"So you met her...and...?"

"We hit it off, went out a few times. Had a good time. It blossomed from there."

"How long were you together?"

"About two years."

"And when did it end?"

"A couple years ago."

"What happened?"

"She brought it up, actually. Said she loved me but didn't feel like it was forever love."

"Were you upset?"

"No one likes to hear those words, but I actually agreed with her. I loved her too. She was a great woman. Very pretty, very smart. But I didn't hear bells, if that makes any sense."

Made perfect sense. And what scared me most of all is that I heard the fucking Bells of St. Mary's when I was in Ryan's presence. Could he possibly hear them too?

"Now that I look back," Ryan continued, "it came on pretty suddenly. We were happy. We never discussed marriage—I guess because neither of us heard bells, as she put it—but I definitely didn't see a breakup coming."

"Were you hurt?"

"Yeah. Of course. I cared about her. I loved her. But when push came to shove, I had to agree that I didn't see it as anything permanent."

"I wonder what made her bring it up."

"She didn't mention it at the time, but about a week later, her family sold the ranch and they all moved to Hawaii."

"Hawaii? That's a strange place to move. They must have gotten a great price for the ranch."

"I have no idea what kind of price they got, but they must have had a lot of money set aside."

"Doesn't Hawaii seem strange to you?"

"Not overly. It's a great place to retire."

"Never been there." I'd never been anywhere other than Colorado and Jamaica, but that was neither here nor there.

"You'd love it," he said. "Maybe we can go someday."

Big doubts there. But heck, we were in Jamaica together. Why not Hawaii? Maybe we *could* have a relationship...

"Do you keep in touch with her?"

"I tried to contact her through social media a few times, just to check in, but I never got a reply. So I gave up. She has her own life now in Hawaii with her family. Maybe she met someone. I only wish her the best."

"Hawaii..." Why was I having such a hard time wrapping

my head around this?

"Yup."

"It just seems so unreal. How long had her family owned the ranch in Colorado?"

"Several generations, same as us."

"And they just up and leave? Something doesn't make sense there."

"Never thought about it."

"And she doesn't reply to you on social media? Why wouldn't she? She's the one who ended the relationship."

"Again, never thought about it. Which I guess tells you that we were right to end it."

"Was there any time during the relationship that you thought maybe she felt more than you did?"

"No, not really."

I swatted his arm. "You're no help at all."

"I don't mean to sound unfeeling. It just wasn't a relationship that meant that much to me."

"But you loved her."

"Yes. I thought I did. But looking back, I think it was more of a comfortable thing. I did care for her deeply, but I think the love I felt for her was more like that of a big brother or a good friend. It wasn't her fault at all. She was great."

"You can't help what you feel. Something just doesn't sit right with me."

"About my relationship with her?"

"No, not that. About why they left so abruptly, to Hawaii of all places."

"I can't think of a lot of reasons *not* to go to Hawaii."

"I guess it's the detective in me. Something just doesn't add up."

"I think we all have enough mysteries to keep us busy without adding one more."

I couldn't fault his observation.

Still, I had a feeling the mystery of the Shanes would come up again.

CHAPTER TWENTY

RYAN

A few days later I was back at my office, thinking naughty thoughts about Ruby Lee. We'd sat together on the flight home—I'd talked her into allowing me to upgrade her to first class again—and talked a lot about wine. I'd promised her a tour of our winemaking facility and the vineyards if it was warm enough.

"Warm enough? You're a rancher," she'd said. "Any temperature you can take, I can take."

I didn't doubt it. She'd been on her own since her teens. She'd probably learned to exist being cold.

I hated thinking of her living like that, but I couldn't help but admire her fortitude. She was something special, this one. Scared shitless of a relationship with me, but still special. Frankly, I was a little scared myself. I was feeling things that were foreign to me. I truly had loved Anna, but while talking to Ruby the last night at the resort, being put on the spot and having to describe those feelings, I realized I was feeling something for Ruby that was new.

Completely new.

I wasn't scared so much of the feelings as I was that she might not return them.

What the hell? I had her number. I was going to call her.

I picked up my phone to call her, when it buzzed in my hand.

Hmm... I didn't recognize the number.

"Ryan Steel."

"Ryan?"

"Yes."

"Is it really you?"

"Uh...yeah. Who is this, please?"

"Oh, darling. It's your mother again."

My heart slammed against my sternum. Was that the same voice of the woman who'd called me before? It could have been. I hadn't paid much attention the first time.

Who was this nutcase?

No, wait. I'd blocked the number the previous time this had happened. This had to be a different number. I looked at my phone and quickly scratched the number on a sticky note. Then I hung up.

Why would anyone do this to me?

My mother was dead. Had been for over two decades. I was only nine when she died, and I didn't have many memories of her. I wasn't sure why. Talon and Joe had lots of memories, but they were older. Still, nine wasn't exactly young. Why were my memories of her so few? I had lots of memories of my father and brothers during that time. Honestly, I hadn't thought much about her in a while. Not until Jade had uncovered my mother's true birth certificate and we found out she was the half sister to Larry Wade.

Then, all of a sudden, Daphne Steel had invaded my thoughts, and it had hit me like a cement block. I didn't remember much about my own mother.

Very strange.

Maybe I'd talk to Melanie about it. She'd helped both my

brothers deal with the demons of their pasts. Maybe she could help me. Not that my mother was a demon. She had been a loving woman.

I thought, anyway.

How much was my own memory, and how much was me just remembering what my brothers had told me?

At any rate, the loon who'd called me was *not* my mother. My mother was dead and buried. At least I remembered a little about her. Poor Marjorie had no memories at all.

I had to call my brothers and let them know that this had happened twice now. Once could have been a fluke. Twice? That merited looking into.

I called Joe on speed dial.

"Hey, Ry. What's up?"

"How's married life, bro? How's Melanie?"

"Great." He laughed. "And she's good. A little nausea, but she's handling it like a pro."

"Glad to hear it."

"I doubt you called to ask about my wedded bliss."

"Yeah, well, there is something else. I got a weird phone call this morning. In fact, I got another one before we left for Jamaica. Both different numbers though." I explained the situation.

"That *is* weird." Joe's voice had a slight edge to it. "Did the woman give you a name?"

"A name? Why would she give me a name? I only have one mother, and she's dead."

"Right. Of course."

What was up with my brother? "I saved the second number. I'm going to give Trevor Mills a call and have him look into it."

"No, don't." My brother's voice was stern.

"Why the hell not?"

"Because this is just some prank. Mills and Johnson are on Mathias. That's where they need to be concentrating."

"Joe, what gives? You know as well as I do that tracing a phone number will take Mills all of three seconds."

"Yeah, you're right. I'm sorry. It's just..."

"Just what?"

"Shit. Nothing. Go ahead and give them a call. Let me know what you find out. Do you want me to call Talon?"

"Go ahead if you want. I'm going to get Mills on this first."

"Sure, I'll call him. And Ry?"

"Yeah?"

"Love you, bro. No matter what."

What? When was the last time either of my brothers had said they loved me? Probably the fifth of never. Not that I doubted their love. We just weren't a touchy-feely bunch.

"Love you too," I said and ended the call.

That was weird. Very weird.

After a quick call to Mills to look into the number—I left him a voice mail—I called Ruby.

"Detective Lee."

"Hey there, baby."

"Oh, hi, Ryan."

"Don't sound so excited to hear from me." I smiled into the phone.

"No. I'm happy you called. I'm just in work mode."

"What are you working on?"

"What am I *not* working on? I have a huge caseload, plus all my spare time is spent tracking my father. I'm also looking into the situation with Juliet and Lisa."

"Any leads?"

"On my father? No, I'm sorry to say. On Juliet and Lisa? Still no, but I'm investigating kidnapping rings in the Caribbean. There are more than a few. Several women have gone missing from resorts in the area. Not just Jamaica, but the Virgin Islands, the DR, even a few from the Bahamas. These guys don't discriminate, that's for sure."

"Is there any way to find Juliet and Lisa?"

"Not without money I don't have. They were essentially naked when they disappeared. They had no ID, nothing."

My nerves rattled. "Ruby, what happens to these women?"

She sighed across the phone line. "It's not pretty, Ryan."

"I've seen a lot of 'not pretty' in my life. You can tell me."

"They're usually drugged, deprived of food and water, and beaten and raped to learn submission. Once they submit, they're fed to gain weight. They need to be attractive for buyers."

"What if they don't submit?" A lump was lodged in my throat.

"Then they don't survive. They are eventually starved and beaten to death."

God. I didn't know those two women, but the thought of this... "Thank God Shayna got away."

"I say that every day," she said.

"I didn't mean to start this conversation on a downer."

"Most of what I do is a downer. Detectives don't usually investigate good people."

I chuckled. "Touché. How do you deal with it? All day and every day?"

"I guess you could say I'm driven."

"What drives you?"

"My father. The guilt I feel for not being able to bring him to justice. So I bring a lot of others to justice instead. It helps."

Her answer didn't surprise me. "You'll bring your father to justice, Ruby. We're all here to help."

"I know. But believe me, he's cunning. He doesn't slip up."

"He will. We've taken out his two partners. He'll screw up eventually, and when he does, you'll swoop in and get him. I promise you."

"I hope you're right."

"Of course I am. Hey, it's Friday. Do you want to come to my place for dinner? Maybe spend the weekend? You could use a break."

She laughed. "I just got back from vacation."

"Yeah, and you're back at your job and everyone else's already."

"I was going to do some research this weekend."

"Funny thing about my place. I have Internet."

"Okay, okay. Sure. Can I bring anything?"

"Like a bottle of wine?"

She laughed. "No. Like...I don't know. Dinner? Do you cook?"

"I happen to be a great cook," I said. "I'll make you seared scallops a la Ryan."

"Seafood? On a beef ranch?"

"Man cannot live on bovine alone."

She laughed once more. It was a musical sound. I was glad I had that effect on her.

"All right. What time?"

"Be here around six if you can."

"How about six thirty? I get off at five thirty. I'll have to... pack a bag."

"Six thirty it is. Come hungry."

"I will." She ended the call.

No sooner had I put my phone down when it buzzed again. The same number that had called before...

CHAPTER TWENTY-ONE

RUBY

A weekend with Ryan Steel.

Things could definitely be worse.

Before I let myself freak out about it, my phone buzzed again.

"Detective Lee."

"Hi, Ruby. It's Marjorie Steel."

Marjorie? Why was she calling? Right, to get together for exercise and lunch. "Hey. How are you?"

"Good. You?"

"Can't complain. What's up?"

She sighed across the phone line. A heavy sigh. "Are you seeing Ryan again?"

"Tonight, actually."

"Wow. That's quick."

"He called me. I told him I didn't expect anything from him." Shit. Was that the kind of thing I should say to his sister? Of course, she didn't know we'd had sex. I wasn't one to kiss and tell. Especially since this was the first time I'd ever been kissed.

"No, that's not what I mean. I'm thrilled for both of you. We all are. It's just..."

"What?"

"I've talked to my brothers and their girlfriends—I mean, wives." She laughed shakily. "Anyway, we agree there's something you need to know. About Ryan."

My heart began to thump wildly. I didn't have a good feeling about whatever was coming.

"What?"

"Has he told you about any mysterious phone calls he's gotten?"

"No..."

"Someone has been calling him, claiming to be his mother."

"I'm sorry. Isn't your mother...?"

"Dead? Yeah. At least that's what we're all hoping."

Say what? "What are you getting at, Marjorie?"

"Call me Marj. Everyone does." She sighed. "This is still so surreal... There's a chance that Ryan has a different mother than Talon, Joe, and I do."

I went numb. I had no idea where this could be leading, and a feeling of dread overwhelmed me. "Oh my God. Who?"

"Wendy Madigan."

I knew the name well. She was a member of my father's infamous future lawmakers club in high school, and Melanie and I had talked in detail about her. She was currently in psych lockup here in the city.

"It's a long story, but she told Jonah and Talon that she was Ryan's biological mother, and that she gave him to our father in exchange for five million dollars."

"She's obviously lying."

"That's what we all thought at first too, but it makes an eerie sort of sense. The psych ward assured Jonah that she didn't have access to a phone. But how hard can it be to hijack a cell?"

Not hard at all. As a police officer, I knew that security in psych detention centers wasn't the best. "Why are you telling me this?"

"Because Jonah and Talon have a lock of her hair. We need a lock of Ryan's to get a DNA test done. We need you to get one for us."

I about fell off my office chair. "Excuse me?"

"I know it's a little unorthodox—"

"Unorthodox? That's a pretty tame word for what you're talking about here. It's a total violation of his trust. I can't have any part in this."

Marjorie sighed across the phone line. "Melanie and Jade agree with you. But Jonah, Talon, and I are determined to keep this from him for his own good. Even thinking there's a possibility that he might not be our full brother will cause him tremendous trauma. We want to avoid that. If we find out he's not Wendy's son, he never has to know there was an issue."

"You're his sister. How can you possibly condone this?"

She sighed again. "I don't like it, not at all. Neither do the guys. It's the lesser of two evils, though. We want to protect our brother as much as we can."

"Wouldn't it make more sense to let him know there might be an issue than to spring this on him all of a sudden if the DNA proves he's Wendy's son? That way he can at least prepare for it."

"You think just like Melanie. That's what she said. And Ruby, we have considered it. But our family has been through so much already. Why create more havoc if there's no need?"

Poor Ryan. What if this turned out to be true? He'd be devastated. I was just starting to know him. Maybe even starting to fall in love with him. If he found out I had a part in this deception, what would he do?

I couldn't take that risk.

"I'm sorry, Marj, but I can't help you. It just feels wrong to me in so many ways."

"I understand. I really do. We'll figure out another way to get a strand of his hair."

"Why not just grab his comb or brush? Certainly there are hairs there. Or get another type of DNA sample?"

"We'd need his blood or his saliva or a piece of his skin. Those are impossible to get without his cooperation. As for taking hair from a brush or comb, there's no way to make sure that it's actually his. Plus the root needs to be intact."

I shook my head, even though she couldn't see me. This was rattling me. Really rattling me. I had a lot of respect for all the Steels, but what they were planning to do was wrong on so many levels. "How do you know the hair sample from Wendy is usable?"

"Jonah pulled it right out of her head. The roots are intact."

"So you just need Ryan's hair to compare?"

"Right."

"You really want me to pull a strand of his hair off his head?"

She sighed once more. "It's impossible, isn't it? Please forgive me. I'm sorry I asked. I truly am. We'll figure out another way. He's just dealing with so much right now, with someone calling him, claiming to be his mother. Wendy isn't supposed to have access to a phone."

"Security is pretty lax in those psych units."

"Not surprising. The phone calls have alerted him to

something. I don't blame you for wanting no part of it."

"I get that you want to protect your brother."

"We Steels take care of our own. I'm glad to be one of them."

One of them.

Could I ever be one of them? Did I want to be?

The answer frightened me.

Yes.

I wanted to be a Steel.

I hardly knew Ryan Steel, but I was drawn to him like I'd never been drawn to anyone. Of course, I'd never let myself be drawn to anyone...

"You are all pretty amazing," I said, though that didn't convey at all what I wanted to say. Amazing wasn't strong enough. *Strong* wasn't strong enough. They'd fought battles that made mine look like mere schoolyard quarrels. But while I understood their need to protect their brother, I couldn't go along. From what little I knew about Ryan so far, he would want to know what was going on.

"Who will tell Ryan?" I asked. "I mean, someone will have to tell him eventually...if you get a sample and the test is positive."

"I imagine Talon and Jonah. They're the closest to him. I'll keep you posted."

"Thank you. I appreciate that."

★ ★ ★

Ryan Steel had a dog—a gorgeous golden retriever named Ricky. I fell instantly in love. I loved dogs but had never had one of my own. I kept my life simple, and a dog didn't fit into simple.

"Joe has one of his siblings. Her name is Lucy."

"Ricky and Lucy." I laughed. "Cute. He's just gorgeous."

"The whole litter was. There's some champion blood running through his veins. A few of their littermates actually do shows. Ricky and Lucy weren't considered show quality."

"Really? I know nothing about showing dogs, but he's beautiful. The most beautiful golden I've ever seen. How old is he?"

"Four."

I sank my fingers into his soft yellow coat. "I love him already."

"Looks like he loves you too. Lucy's a little darker than he is. More golden. He's more blond."

"I hope I can meet her."

"Anytime. I'm sure Joe and Melanie would be happy to introduce you."

The mention of Joe and Melanie made me think of my earlier phone call with Marjorie. I regarded Ryan, handsome as always in perfect-fitting jeans and a black button-down shirt. He wore cowboy boots. Yes, cowboy boots. I hadn't seen him looking cowboyish while we were in Jamaica, but wow, he was made for western wear.

He looked happy. So happy.

I hoped to God his happiness wasn't about to be destroyed.

"I opened a bottle of my Rhône blend," Ryan said. "Would you like a glass?"

"Sure, sounds great."

I followed him into his kitchen where he poured two glasses and handed one to me.

I swirled it in the glass. "Gorgeous color," I said.

"This is a younger wine, hence the deep ruby hue."

I chuckled. "Hence?"

"Would you prefer thus?"

"Neither are words I hear used in everyday conversation. At least not around a bunch of balding cops. Hence my surprise."

"Do I look like a balding cop to you?"

And I laughed once more. "Definitely not."

He joined in my mirth and swirled his own glass. "Give it a taste. I want to know what you think. This is Jade's favorite of my wines."

I inhaled its fruity fragrance and took a sip. "Mmm. It's good. Really..." I searched for words. "I don't know how to say this."

"What's the word that came to mind?"

I smiled. "Meaty. But not meaning meat, like beef."

He smiled back. "Like meaty fresh fruit. A meaty plum, right?"

"Yeah, that's exactly it. By gum, you are a genius!"

"I'll take the compliment, but 'by gum?'"

"Haven't you seen the original Willy Wonka film, where Violet blows up into a blueberry?"

"About a million years ago."

"That's what she says. 'By gum, it's gum.'"

He smiled. "You're pretty adorable."

"Not quite as adorable as when you said 'hence,' but I'll take it." I took another sip. "This really is great wine. Which grapes do you use?"

"This is a blend of grenache, syrah, and mourvèdre. Three classic Rhône blend grapes."

"Mmm. It's excellent."

"Glad you approve."

I was beginning to feel a little self-conscious. He hadn't tried to kiss me. Had barely touched me. Maybe this was just an overnighter between friends. I could deal with that. Not that I had a choice. Besides, I did have a ton of work to do over the weekend. I'd brought my laptop and some files.

But then he walked toward me, took my wineglass from me and set it on the kitchen table, and cupped my cheek.

CHAPTER TWENTY-TWO

RYAN

I couldn't go one more microsecond without touching her. Her cheek felt the same—smooth as silk, warm. Her lips as dark and luscious as ever. She was wearing her signature Dockers and button-down white shirt—probably her work clothes, or maybe all she had in her wardrobe—but she'd pulled her hair back into a sexy high ponytail instead of into that tight schoolmarm bun. It flowed down her back in a sleek, dark waterfall.

"Let me taste that meaty fruit," I said, and I brushed my lips across hers.

She parted them, and I slid my tongue inside. She was more assertive in her kisses now, meeting me with her own tongue, opening her lips more freely. Still, I could tell she was holding back. We both were, truth be told.

We were testing the waters. Deciding if the chemistry we'd had on the island was still there. Had it just been an island romance between two single people whose friends were all paired up?

I deepened the kiss, groaning into her mouth.

No. The chemistry was definitely still there.

As much as I wanted to lift her in my arms and take her into my bedroom, I knew that would be a mistake. She had only just lost her virginity. I couldn't move too fast. I didn't want to scare her away.

I broke the kiss and smiled at her. "Hungry?" I asked.

She nodded. "Definitely."

Did she mean hungry for food...or something else? After that kiss, any other woman might mean something else. But Ruby Lee? I knew her well enough to know she meant food.

"Then step aside while I sear some scallops. It doesn't take long."

"Can I do anything to help? I'm pretty good in the kitchen."

"I already made a salad, and green beans are steaming. I'm serving the scallops over a fresh corn relish, which I already made as well. You can get that out of the fridge if you'd like."

"Sure. Can I set the table or anything?"

Set the table? I was used to eating alone. I never set the table. I just grabbed a plate out of the cupboard, utensils out of the drawer, and served myself from the stove. I should have thought of that. I hadn't had a woman here in quite a while.

"Yeah, that'd be great." I gestured to a cupboard. "Plates are in there. Silverware in the drawer below."

She fiddled around setting the table while I seared the scallops. I seasoned them only with salt and pepper. The succulent flesh of sea scallops needed nothing else. I quickly put them on a serving platter. This was all so new. All I could think about was that I'd have three times the dishes to clean up, but hey, this was a dinner date, after all.

Once all the food was on the table, I filled two glasses of water and refreshed both of our wineglasses. "Dinner is served," I said.

She smiled and sat down.

I took her plate. "This is a dish I invented. The corn relish is made with fresh corn, a mild vinaigrette, and salt and pepper.

Top it with the seared scallops. I hope you like it."

"It looks wonderful," she said, as I set her filled plate in front of her.

"Shit. I forgot the salad." I got up and got it out of the fridge, tossed it in some balsamic vinaigrette, and served her some on her already filled plate.

"You gave me enough to feed an army," she said.

"From what I recall, you're not shy when it comes to food."

"True enough." She took a bite of scallops and corn. "Mmm. This is fantastic."

Watching her eat was a joy. She relished her food. She wasn't worried about eating too much in front of a guy or getting fat. As much as she worked out, she didn't need to worry about that. Plus, the stress of her job probably kept her metabolism moving at a rapid pace.

She cleaned her plate in short order and had seconds of green beans.

"Save any room for dessert?" I asked her.

"Oh, no. I couldn't possibly eat another bite," she said, licking her lips.

"Good," I said. "Because that's not the kind of dessert I was talking about."

She fidgeted nervously. "I see."

"Look, we don't have to." Though the thought of the case of blue balls I'd be nursing was nearly unbearable.

"I... I think I'd like to. I just wasn't expecting anything, you know?"

"What do you normally expect when a man asks you over for the weekend?" I regretted the words as soon as they left my mouth. She'd never spent a weekend with a man before. She'd never dated before, never had sex before...until recently. "I'm sorry. I didn't mean that the way it sounded."

"It's okay. Most women my age have spent the weekend with a man before. It was an honest mistake."

"Not really. I know you now. I shouldn't have been so thoughtless."

"It's okay." Her lips trembled a bit.

I stood and helped her out of her chair. I looked into those soulful blue eyes. "Ruby, I want to go to bed with you. I want to go to bed with you a lot. We give each other something. You may not realize that since you don't have any experience, but I can truly say that what we have together is special. I've told you that before, haven't I?"

She nodded. "You have. And I...enjoyed our time together very much. Too much, really."

"What do you mean?"

"You have to understand. This isn't anything I ever wanted. I mean...ever *thought* I'd want."

"So you don't want it?"

"No, I want it. I just don't *want* to want it." She shook her head. "No, even that's not true. I want it. Plain and simple."

"I'm very happy to hear that. Because I want it too. I want *you*."

She fell against me, and I crushed my mouth to hers. She opened instantly, not tentative as she usually was. She was giving in. Giving in to the heat between us, the desire thick in the air.

I kissed her thoroughly, deeply, letting our tongues tangle, our lips slide together. I grabbed her ponytail, and with my other hand, began unbuttoning her perfectly pressed Oxford shirt.

She tensed under my fingers at first, but then relaxed.

Her breasts were still encased in her bra—I'd never seen her in a bra before—and I cupped one, full and firm in my hand.

We kissed and we kissed. I ached for her to unbutton my shirt as I had hers, but she didn't. Perhaps she was feeling too timid. So I broke the kiss.

"Undress me, baby," I said breathlessly. "Please."

She looked around. "Shouldn't we..."

"What? Go to the bedroom?"

She nodded.

"What's wrong with here? I'm going to set you on the table and slide my cock inside you. God, I'm hard just thinking about it."

"Lord," she moaned. "All right." She shakily started on the buttons of my shirt. "You look great in black," she said shyly.

"You look great in everything. But you look the best in nothing."

She let out a nervous chuckle and continued. Soon she parted the two sides of my shirt and ran her hands over my chest. My nipples hardened for her instantly. My cock was already granite solid.

"You look the best in nothing too," she said, out of breath.

I closed my eyes, reveling in her touch. "Yes, touch me all over. My chest. My abs. Your touch drives me crazy."

She smoothed the shirt over my shoulders, and I opened my eyes. For the first time, I regarded her bra. Basic white, no lace or adornments of any kind. So very Ruby. I couldn't help but smile.

"What?" she asked.

"Nothing, baby. Let's get that bra off you." I brushed her shirt over her shoulders and then unclasped her bra, throwing both garments to the floor.

Ricky clambered around us, looking for attention. I let him outside.

"You didn't have to do that," she said. "I don't mind him."

"I do. I want you all to myself." I set her on the table and removed her loafers and socks. Then I unbuckled her belt, undid her Dockers, and slowly pulled them over her hips and onto the floor. Her underpants were basic white cotton. How I missed the blue lace she'd been wearing the last night in Jamaica.

I inhaled. She was ripe for me already. Sweet vanilla musk. I resisted the urge to rip the panties from her. I didn't want to scare her. So I dragged them over her hips, leaving them on the floor with her pants. Then I spread her legs.

And saw paradise.

I had bright track lighting in my kitchen. Every other time I'd seen Ruby with her legs spread, we'd been outside in the dark under the stars. The moonlight had done her justice, but right now, I could see her dark pinkness, her wetness, every part of her delicious pussy.

I fingered her folds, relishing the soft sigh from her lips. "You're beautiful, baby. Absolutely beautiful."

"I'm feeling...embarrassed."

"Why?"

"Because you're looking...down there."

I laughed. "I've seen you 'down there' before, you know."

"I know. But it was dark. And we were in a foreign country."

"What's a foreign country have to do with it?"

"I could... I could pretend. I could pretend I was someone I wasn't. That I was beautiful. That I was the kind of person who wasn't afraid of..."

"Afraid of what? You don't strike me as a person who's

afraid of anything, Ruby. You're a cop."

"Cops are still afraid," she said. "But that's not what I'm talking about."

"What, then?"

"Afraid of men, damn it. Afraid of men."

I looked into her searing blue eyes, removing my fingers from her pussy. "You know you have nothing to fear from me."

"Of course I know that. I wouldn't have come if I were afraid. It's just..." She heaved a sigh. "Now is now. Now is reality. We're no longer on a tropical island."

"No, we're not."

She shook her head. "Of course, even that beautiful island had a dose of reality."

I cupped her cheek. Those perfect lips were in a frown, but God, she was still beautiful. "Do you really want to go there right now?"

"No. Absolutely not. I'm sorry."

"Ruby," I said, "we're no longer in Jamaica, but that doesn't mean we can't be the people we were then. We're the same people no matter what, baby."

"Of course. I know that. I wish I could make you understand what I mean."

I thumbed her soft cheek. "I do understand. I do. We were in paradise, under the stars, the waves rolling in the distance. But I promise we can recreate paradise right here." I laughed. "I'll even turn on the television. I'll bet we can find ocean sounds on one of the music channels."

That got a laugh out of her. "You just made me see how ridiculous I'm being. But please understand, this is still all very new to me."

"I do. I get that. We don't have to do anything if you don't want to. Even though you're sitting on my kitchen table naked."

"And it's cold on my butt, by the way."

"I can take care of that." I lifted her in my arms and carried her out of the kitchen, through the hallway, to my bedroom. I set her down on my comforter. "Better?"

"I suppose."

"You suppose?"

She nibbled on her lower lip. "I knew what would probably happen when I agreed to come here. I'm not naïve."

"Never thought you were."

"I don't really know how to explain what I'm feeling. It's not apprehension. I want you. I do. It's not fear. I'm not sure what it is."

My balls were aching, but I'd go at her pace. Not like I had a choice. "Tell you what. Do you want to go sit in the hot tub and relax for a while? We'll see how things go. However they go, you are welcome here. I have plenty of spare bedrooms."

She smiled. "You have a hot tub?"

"Right outside. By the pool."

"You have a pool? I thought you said this is Talon's guest house?"

"It is."

"Wow."

Now wasn't the time to impress her with Steel money, so I divested myself of my boots and jeans, wrapped a towel around my waist, handed her a large towel from the bathroom, and then scooped her up. "Ready?"

CHAPTER TWENTY-THREE

RUBY

I felt like such a teenager! What the hell was wrong with me? I was in my thirties, and I'd *already had sex with him*. Why was I freaking out? I wanted him. I hoped I'd made that clear. But that crazy imp in my mind just wouldn't let go.

I stepped into his hot tub. The evening was cool and crisp, and steam rose from the water. The warm water bubbled around my foot, and then my leg, and then the rest of my body as I sank into the warmth, and I let go of my inhibitions.

Well, tried to, anyway.

Part of me was still mousy Ruby Lee. The girl who intentionally flew under the radar to avoid situations like... well, like the one I was in now.

"Ahh," Ryan said as he sank into the water beside me.

We were naked, our arms and sides touching. He felt so good against me. So...right.

How could this be happening?

Looking up at the night sky—not nearly as clear as it had been in Jamaica—I breathed in.

The darkness soothed me, and I realized what had caused my discomfort. The harsh lighting in his kitchen. I'd been in the kitchen with my father when he'd first tried...

I shook my head to clear it. Now was not the time to go

there. But at least I knew why I'd been uncomfortable.

I timidly moved my hand onto his thigh. It was soft and smooth in the warm water. And it felt good. So good beneath my fingers.

He didn't reach to touch me, and after a few minutes it became clear that I'd be setting the pace tonight. As freaked out as I'd been, I'd probably freaked him out just as much.

I smoothed my hand up and down his thigh, enjoying the feel of his slick skin.

And then, I went all in.

As I smoothed my hand from his knee upward, I grabbed hold of his cock.

He groaned.

And his hardness grew thicker in my hand.

I did this to him.

I did this to Ryan Steel.

I still couldn't quite wrap my mind around that truth.

Slowly, with the warm water a gentle lubricant, I pumped him with my fist.

He lay back, closing his eyes. "Good, baby."

My nipples tightened up as my breasts bobbed on the surface of the water.

I was turning him on.

And that was turning *me* on.

I threw out all my inhibitions and let them float upward on the rising steam. I let go of his cock and climbed atop him, positioning my pussy entrance right at the large head.

"Baby..."

"Shh," I said and slid down upon his erection.

It was tight. So tight, but I felt only the stretching and no pain this time.

"God," he gritted out, as I seated him to the hilt within me. So full, so very full.

"Show me," I said. "Show me what to do."

He cupped my cheeks and stared into my eyes—his own dark as night. "Do what feels good, baby."

An urge swept through me. To pull myself off him and then plunge back down.

So I did that, and my clit rubbed against his rough pubic hair.

And skyrockets erupted.

So quickly. How could I be climaxing so quickly?

"Yeah, baby," he said. "Let it go. Let it feel good."

"This is impossible." My nerves skittered, my body shuddered as the orgasm whirled through me.

He pulled me up off him and thrust me back down, groaning. I soared with the steam rising from the hot water.

Again, he pulled me up and then down.

"Ah!" he ground out.

This time he held me down, and I felt him pulsing within me. His orgasm. Nearly as quick as my own.

Wow.

I brought my head down onto his shoulder, breathing in his salty, masculine scent.

"That was amazing," he whispered into my ear.

I couldn't respond. I was still recovering.

How had I climaxed so quickly?

He simply held me, didn't try to move me, let me stay sunken against him, breathing rapidly. He rubbed my back, whispered soothing words to me.

"Breathe, baby. Relax. It's okay..."

When my breathing finally steadied, I moved backward

and looked into his dark eyes.

"You're amazing," he said.

"I can't believe that just happened. It was so quick."

"For me too," he said.

"Is that...normal?"

He laughed.

"Hey, don't laugh at me."

"It's not *at* you. But yes, it's perfectly normal...when two people want each other the way we do."

Embarrassment swept through me, but I couldn't deny the truth of his words.

"I just never thought I could want a man like I want you," I said, thankful for the darkness that covered what I was sure was a crimson blush in my cheeks.

"Believe it or not, I never thought I could want a woman the way I want you."

"You? After all your women? After your relationship with Anna? You've never wanted anyone the way you want me?"

He cupped my cheeks. "Look at me, baby. Look into my eyes. See the truth in there."

His eyes were dark, dark and beautiful, as they always were. But truth did shine within them. A truth I'd never seen before.

I looked for truth all the time as a cop. I knew when I saw truth in someone's eyes...and when I saw lies.

But this was a truth I'd never seen. A truth of emotion, a truth of...

No.

Not ready to go there.

I touched his cheek, rubbed my fingers against his stubble.

"Can you see it?" he asked. "Can you see the truth in my

eyes?"

"Yes," I said, and then I swallowed all my apprehension. "What do you see in mine?"

He smiled. "I see a lot of things that you're probably not ready to face yet, and that's okay. We have all the time in the world."

And it hit me like a wheelbarrow full of river rock.

Love.

That's what he was seeing.

That's what I wasn't ready to face.

I was in love with Ryan Steel.

I, who had no idea what love even was…so how could I know?

But I did.

★ ★ ★

"See you later," I said to my father, who was sitting at the kitchen table with a cup of coffee. I'd left him a plate of dinner that was currently heating in the microwave.

"Where are you off to?" The harsh fluorescent lighting in the kitchen illuminated his features—was he angry, or simply mistrustful?—in an eerie way.

"Just meeting a friend for a milkshake. I'll be home before dark."

I'd had dinner alone. My father was rarely home for dinner, and I had learned to fend for myself while living with my mother. She had worked three jobs to keep us afloat, and I'd been doing my own cooking since I was eight years old. Real cooking, because the processed meals were more expensive than buying actual meat and vegetables. I'd been shopping and cooking for what seemed like most of my life.

Since I was only fifteen, it had been most of my life.

I walked toward the door, but his footsteps followed and he overtook me. He stood against the door. "You're not going anywhere tonight."

I'd only lived with my father for a couple of months. So far, he'd given me an allowance. More money than I'd ever seen. He'd been good to me. He'd helped me get acclimated to my new home, the community, and had helped me make friends in the neighborhood. I was planning to meet one of those friends tonight for a shake.

"Dad." The word fell from my lips in slow motion. It still didn't feel right. The man was still a virtual stranger to me. But he'd been trying. At least up until now. "Dana's expecting me. I won't be late." I reached for the doorknob.

"Not tonight, Ruby." He brushed my hand from the knob.

I looked up at him. His eyes were so dark, almost black. He was a handsome man, olive complexion and dark hair, but something sinister lurked in his gaze tonight.

Something I hadn't seen before.

Maybe I hadn't been looking.

A knife of fear lanced into me.

I was in danger.

I turned to run back into the kitchen and toward the back door, but he grabbed me by the arm and yanked me against his chest. Hard.

"What do you want?" I asked breathlessly. "Why can't I go meet Dana?"

"Because I need you here tonight."

My heart thumped wildly. "Okay. What do you need?"

He yanked me over to the couch in the living room. "Take

off your clothes."

I jolted backward. "What?"

"You heard me. Take off your clothes. You're beautiful. Let me see that body of yours."

I crossed my arms over my chest. "No. I won't."

I scrambled away, but he caught me again and then dragged me into his bedroom. I wrenched away, but he grabbed me and turned me around to face him.

"Come here. Show Daddy how much you love him." His grasp was firm. "Now take off those clothes."

"I won't!"

"Don't make this harder than it has to be."

"Are you crazy? I'm your daughter!"

"Makes no difference. Let me see that body."

I gathered every ounce of strength and ran toward the door, but again he caught me.

"You asked for it now." He punched me in the cheek, and a dull thud echoed in the room.

For a second, nothing happened, and then the pain hit. I cried out.

"Scream. Go ahead and scream. It's better that way," he said, an evil gleam in his eye.

I made a deal with myself at that moment. I would not scream again, no matter what he did to me.

"You're a slut, just like your slut mother. She wasn't good for anything but a fuck. A one-nighter that went wrong, and now I'm saddled with you."

My heart thrummed wildly and ice filled my veins as fear overtook me. "You don't have to be. I'll leave. I'll never bother you again." And I meant those words, for now I knew who and what my father truly was.

"Not yet. Not until I see what you have to offer. You're a pretty thing, with your mother's fair skin. My dark hair. And you don't mind showing off that tight little body in those belly tops and tight jeans you wear. What do you expect?"

"I don't expect my own father to rape me!"

He grabbed me and tossed me onto the bed. "Well, little daughter, rarely in this life do we get what we expect."

He fell down on me, and something hard nudged my belly.

God. Him. His penis. He was hard for me.

Acid bubbled in my stomach and meandered up my throat. I turned my head and retched, but nothing came up.

He punched me again.

"You throw up, and I'll make this worse."

As if in answer, I heaved again and vomited onto his bed.

"Bitch!" He punched me again and then shook me. Then he ripped my shirt off me. "Pretty nice tits," he said, eyeing me.

I closed my eyes. Maybe I could escape into my mind. Think of something else.

But instead, without looking, I raised both my legs and pushed outward, kicking.

He flew across the room.

I opened my eyes in time to see him land with an oof.

I got up and ran for the door, but again he caught me, turning me.

Scrunching my eyes shut again, I kneed him between his legs, hoping I had the strength I needed to incapacitate him.

"Auugh!" This time he yelled and crumpled to the floor. "Bitch. You fucking little slut!"

Thank God my purse was where I'd left it in the living room. I grabbed it and headed out the door in my bra and jeans, my own vomit coating one side of my body.

I ran as hard as I could with no idea where I was going.
Only that I was never going back to my father, no matter what I had to do.

★ ★ ★

I woke up, perspiration sliding over me.

Next to me, Ryan slept soundly.

My breathing was rapid, couldn't get enough air.

I was hyperventilating. It had happened before, though not for quite a while.

Why now? Why tonight?

I rubbed my shivering arms, trying desperately to calm my body and my mind.

Ryan stirred and opened his eyes. "Ruby? Is everything okay?"

No, everything was *not* okay, but I couldn't saddle him with this. He'd go hightailing it away from me if I told him I'd just had a nightmare of my father attempting to rape me.

"Fine," I said quickly.

"You're not fine." He leaned over to his nightstand and turned on his lamp. "You're shivering. What's going on?"

I opened my mouth to say "I'm fine," but the words never made it to my lips.

Instead, I burst into tears.

CHAPTER TWENTY-FOUR

RYAN

All I could do was hold her and let her cry into my shoulder.

She shook as she sobbed, her nose running. Every time I tried to reach the nightstand to grab a tissue for her nose and eyes, she held onto me for dear life, and I couldn't move.

So I let her cry.

And I hoped, when she finally stopped, I would be able to soothe her.

She was so strong, and this burst of crying didn't sway my opinion of that. Something had gotten to her, and I prayed it hadn't been me.

No, it hadn't.

We'd come in from the hot tub, dried off, taken a quick shower, and then snuggled in bed, kissing.

Yes, we'd made out, and I'd felt like a teenager again in the back of my car. That's how thrilling making out with Ruby had been.

We hadn't made love again, although I'd been more than ready to. I'd promised her I'd go slowly, and I meant it. But right now I wanted to move heaven and earth to help her, to kill with my bare hands whoever had done this to her, had made her feel this way, so sad and upset.

"Baby, baby, it's okay." I said the soothing words over and

over to her, until the sobbing became weeping, and then soft whimpering.

Finally, she pulled away from me. Her eyes were red and swollen. Her nose was pink. And my God, she'd never looked more beautiful to me.

I was in deep. So deep. I hoped I could deal with the baggage she was so clearly carrying.

"What can I do for you?" I asked. "Anything? A cup of tea?" I handed her the box of tissues. "Glass of wine?"

She shook her head, sniffling and taking a tissue. She blew her nose loudly and then grabbed another and wiped her eyes. "I must be a complete mess."

"You look beautiful."

That got a smile out of her. "Now I know you're lying to me."

"Never." I touched her hair.

"I'm so sorry. I never cry. I'm serious. I don't know what came over me."

"It's okay to be emotional, baby. I sometimes have that effect on women."

That actually got a chuckle out of her. I was on a roll.

"But seriously. Is there anything I can do to help?"

She shook her head. "I'm good. I just had a dream. Well, it was more of a nightmare."

"Do you want to talk about it?"

"No. Absolutely not."

"Are you sure? I'm a good listener." I smiled.

She swallowed audibly. "I'm not ready to talk about it."

"Oh." I held back a sigh. "All right." I couldn't force her to tell me anything, of course, but for some reason, I wanted to know what had upset her. And then go eliminate it from the universe. Anything that made Ruby Lee cry had to go. Simple as that.

"Could you excuse me for a minute?" she said.

"Sure. Of course."

She got up and went into the bathroom, closing the door. I heard the water running in the sink for a few moments, and then it shut off. I figured she'd come back out momentarily, but instead the whoosh of the shower made its way to my ears.

A shower? In the middle of the night?

Should I join her?

I waited a few minutes. Maybe she was just going to rinse off. I'd give her some space. After ten minutes, though, I started to worry.

I got up and went into the bathroom. "Baby?"

Then I heard her quiet sobs. She was in the shower scrubbing her skin with a shower pouf. I opened the glass door.

"Ruby? Please, let me help."

"Have to get him off me," she wept quietly. "All of his filth. All of his grime. I'm contaminated. Contaminated with his disgusting filth."

"Baby, you're clean. You can't wash anything else from you."

"I have to. He's inside me. He's...part of me." She continued scrubbing herself.

"Who, baby?"

"My father. Theodore Mathias." She stopped scrubbing and looked up at me. "Who else?"

I took the opportunity to gently take the shower pouf from her clasped hands. "Let go. It's okay."

She reluctantly let me take the soapy pouf from her. I rinsed it off under the pelting water and then set it aside.

She was still quietly weeping. I didn't know what to do, so I just held her, the water still pummeling us. I couldn't think of anything to say, so I said nothing.

After a few minutes, she pulled away. "I'm sorry."

"For what?"

"For having this silly meltdown. You'd think I was some drama queen teenager. This isn't me."

"I know it's not you. Not the normal you. We all break down sometimes."

"You don't."

"Are you kidding? After what my brother went through to save me? I've done my share of overthinking it, believe me."

"There's a big difference between overthinking and having a meltdown in the shower," she said.

"Not so much." I moved toward the faucet. "Okay if I turn this off now?"

"Yeah. I suppose I'm as clean as I'm going to get." She gave me a half smile.

I opened the shower door and grabbed two big bath towels. I wrapped her in one, dried her off as best I could, and then wrapped one around my own waist.

"You want to come back to bed?" I asked when we were both dry.

"Maybe I should just go home."

"Look, if you don't want to sleep in the same bed with me, that's fine. You know that. I'll set you up in a different room. But I'm not letting you drive home when you're obviously so distraught."

"No," she said.

"What do you mean, 'no?' You can't drive right now. It's the middle of the night. You're a cop, for God's sake."

She let out a tiny laugh. "I mean no, I don't want to sleep in a different room."

Warmth spread through me. I hadn't realized, until she said it, how much I wanted to share my bed with her for the rest of the night. I wanted to protect her from whatever was bothering her.

"You want to talk about this now? About what brought this on?"

She shook her head. "I'd rather forget about it."

"Okay. For now." She would have to talk to me—or someone—about this at some point. She was an intelligent woman. She probably already knew she couldn't keep it inside forever.

I walked her over to the bed. She lay down, and I got in beside her. I opened my arms to her, and she snuggled into my shoulder.

"You smell so good," she said.

"Well, I'm squeaky clean now," I said.

She let out another soft chuckle. "Why are you being so nice to me?"

"I'm a nice guy."

"But I'm such a mess."

"Baby, I've been around messed-up people my whole life. You're not even close." I pulled her closer to me.

We lay there for a few moments, and I listened to her breathe softly. My cock was growing hard, just having her so near to me, but I knew she didn't need sex.

So I nearly jumped out of my skin when I felt tiny kisses on my shoulder.

My cock hardened further, and I was ready for action.

I pushed her away from me slightly. "Are you sure you

want to do this? Because I won't be able to stop if we go much further."

"Yes," was all she said.

I pulled her to me and kissed her gently. I worried she wasn't ready for more, but I didn't need to be, because she deepened the kiss, exploring my mouth with her tongue, all around my teeth and gum line, the inside of my cheeks.

She was kissing me more fervently than she ever had before.

It would have been so easy to let her continue, to fall into her beautiful body and make love to her.

But damn, I wasn't going to be anyone's escape. I cared too much for her for that.

So I stopped again. "Ruby, I don't feel right about this."

"Oh? I'm...sorry. I thought..."

"Don't get me wrong. I want you big time. I'm hard as a fucking rock. But right now, you're trying to escape something. This isn't the way to do it."

"No, I'm not—"

I silenced her with two fingers to her lips. "Come on, baby. You were just in the shower not half an hour ago trying to scrub the filth out of your pores."

She sighed. "Yes, but that doesn't mean I don't want you now."

"Oh, I believe you want me. I just don't think it's for the right reasons."

She let out a laugh. "So what? So what if it's for the wrong reason? What if I am trying to run from something, and running into your gorgeous body with one of the toe-curling orgasms you give me feels right? What's wrong with that?"

She was offering me a free fuck with her tight little body,

her succulent lips on mine.

Shit. That was the problem. I didn't want to be just a fuck to her.

"You're new to this. I don't want you to do something you'll regret."

"Look, I may be inexperienced, but I'm thirty-two years old. I'm educated, I'm street smart, and I've seen things that most people would never want to see in their lives. I'm not naïve, nor am I ignorant."

"I wasn't suggesting that you were."

"Then why won't you be with me? Why won't you give me the comfort I crave?"

"I will always give you comfort. Let's just lie here for a while, and if something happens, it happens. I just want you to think about it first."

Frankly, my own willpower was shot. All I could think about was getting balls deep inside that hot little pussy. But damn it, I cared about this woman. I desperately wanted her to talk to me about what had brought on the meltdown.

She sighed and lay back down in the crook of my arm. "All right. Let's just lie here together."

My cock was tenting the sheets. No doubt she had noticed.

A few moments later, her breathing became shallow. She had fallen asleep.

★ ★ ★

Ruby had her red lips around me. Her little pink tongue slithered around my cock, wetting me, poking into my tiny slit. Then she wrapped her lips around my glans and sucked, short little tugs, and I imagined shooting my semen into her throat.

God, so good.

I shot my eyes open.

The comforter had been thrown to the bottom of the bed, and Ruby was down between my legs, her pretty, dark lips around my cock.

I'd thought I was dreaming.

Reality was so much better.

She sucked and she slurped. She was new to this. I knew that. But my God, I felt like a teenager getting his first blow job.

Her naïvety was a plus. She wasn't sure how to please me, so she just did everything. And consequently I was about ready to spurt down her throat.

"Easy, baby."

She took her lips from my cock—I whimpered at the loss—and looked at me. "I know men like to come in a woman's mouth. I want you to know... It's okay to do that."

God, what a fantasy—to come down her hot little throat, watch her swallow all of me.

But I wasn't quite sure she was ready for that, no matter what she said, and I wanted to come in her sweet cunt anyway.

"Baby," I said. "Come sit on my cock. Ride me."

I had no idea what time it was, so I glanced at the clock radio on my nightstand. Five o'clock in the morning. My normal wake-up time, but not on Saturdays.

She crawled on top of me, her beautiful tits bouncing, and positioned herself on top of my cock. Slowly she sank onto me, soft sighs coming from her throat.

I clenched my fists and grimaced, holding back. I could shoot so easily right now. But I needed to see her move on top of me. It was still dark outside, but moonlight streamed in through my window, illuminating her.

Her dark hair, dark lips. She was a goddess, and oh my God, I wanted her.

"Now move on me, baby. Make it feel good."

She began gyrating her hips, first in circles and then up and down. Then a combination of the two.

She looked so sexy. She gripped me so tightly, hugged me so sweetly. And then she did something I didn't expect. She grabbed my hands that were at my side, brought them up to her tits, and cupped them in my palms.

"What do you want, baby?"

"Play with them," she said shyly.

"While you fuck me?"

She nodded. "Yes."

"Say it, baby. Say the words. Tell me what you want me to do to you while you fuck me."

She closed her eyes. "Play with them. With my...breasts. While I...fuck you."

I almost squirted into her channel right there. I cupped her beautiful peach breasts, thumbing her nipples ever so slightly. She gasped, moving on top of me harder and faster.

And all I wanted, in that moment, was to love her until the sun came up.

The sun wouldn't be up for almost an hour, but that was okay. I wouldn't last much longer, but after that I could make her come. And come. And come.

CHAPTER TWENTY-FIVE

RUBY

It happened in a flash. Ryan was cupping my breasts, lightly touching my nipples. Everything I had asked him to do, and when I sat down on his cock, I came.

Just like that. No stimulation to my clit. I just came. Stars danced before my eyes. It was so sudden, so unexpected, and so powerful.

From the inside out, I exploded, and then imploded back inside myself, everything culminating in the core of me, my innermost depths. The orgasm rocked through me, and I cried out. "Ryan, oh my God!"

"Yes, baby. I can feel you coming. I can feel you clenching my cock in your pussy."

"You can really feel it? When I come?"

"Ruby, I have felt you come every time. Every time is amazing."

Just those words made the orgasm skyrocket back. He could feel this. He could feel my body responding. How fucking empowering.

Before I knew what was happening, he had flipped me over onto my back, and then he was pounding into me. He seared me with his dark eyes melting into my own. He didn't speak, but sweat beaded on his brow and dropped on my face.

His teeth were clenched, and he was grunting, groaning as he pushed into me again and again.

Every drop of perspiration that fell on my face left a trail of fire in its wake. He pushed into me so far, nearly touching my heart, it seemed. I closed my eyes, and the tiny convulsions began once more.

"Goddamnit, I'm coming again."

He continued to grunt and plunge. His hairline was wet with perspiration.

And then—

He groaned and plunged so deeply inside me, I almost felt that we were inside each other's skin. Truly one body.

He stayed there for a moment, lying on top of me, breathing rapidly, still groaning.

And though he was way too heavy for me, having him there, sweating, having just climaxed, still one with my body... It was unlike anything I'd ever known.

I made a decision right then and there. I would talk to Melanie about finally getting through what happened to me, what happened to Gina, what happened to all those other innocent people my father had preyed upon. I would make myself whole.

I needed to be whole. Not for Ryan Steel, but for me.

Because I needed to be worthy of him.

★ ★ ★

I woke up a few hours later. Ryan was still sleeping soundly beside me. Ricky had nudged the door open and was panting in my side of the bed. I reached over and gave him a pat on his soft head and then got up to use the bathroom. When I had finished, I grabbed the shirt Ryan had been wearing yesterday and put it on. It covered me midway to my thighs.

I reveled in the soft cotton. Wearing his clothes felt very right.

"Come on," I said to Ricky. I took him down the hallway to the kitchen and let him out the back door.

Then I went back into Ryan's bedroom. He was still sleeping, and I glanced at the clock. It was nearly eight. It was Saturday, so I didn't wake him. He knew when he had to be up.

I went back to the bathroom to comb the tangles out of my hair. I picked up Ryan's brush and then noticed a short dark hair sticking to my neck.

We'd been so sweaty last night. I probably had Ryan's hair plastered to my body and vice versa.

I pulled the hair off my neck and examined it.

Damn. The bulb of keratin on the end was intact.

This was a fresh hair. Ideal for DNA testing.

Without thinking much more on the matter, I held the hair between my fingers and sneaked back into the kitchen. I searched through the cupboards until I found a box of zippered plastic bags. I grabbed one, stuffed the hair inside, and zipped it. Then I went back to the bedroom and hid it in my purse.

My heart beat wildly.

I didn't have to do anything with that hair. I was only taking it because...

Because why?

Was I going to betray Ryan's trust and give that hair to his brothers to have it tested?

Take it out of your purse, Ruby. Take it out and flush it down the toilet.

But something held me back.

Just having that hair was not a betrayal.

I hadn't done anything yet.

It would be safe. Safe in my purse.

I let Ricky in and gave him some fresh water. I rooted around for dog food, and when I found a can I opened it and fed him.

My skin chilled.

Why had I taken that hair?

No. Wasn't going to think about that right now. It was safe in my purse. I searched the kitchen again and found some eggs and veggies. I thought I'd surprise Ryan with an omelet for breakfast.

A few peppers, tomatoes, and mushrooms later, I'd made two omelets and brewed a pot of coffee. Ryan still hadn't come out to the kitchen, so I figured I'd go wake him up before the eggs got cold.

I walked to the bedroom and made a quick decision.

I would get rid of that hair in my purse.

I grabbed my clutch and opened it, ready to take out the hair and throw it away, when I noticed I had a new text message.

Stay the fuck away from my son, bitch.

CHAPTER TWENTY-SIX

RYAN

I awoke, stretching. The aroma coming from the kitchen was making my mouth water. Smelled like eggs and coffee. And that sounded great.

I sat up and looked around.

Ruby was over by the dresser, staring at her phone. She was wearing my black cotton shirt, and oh my God...she couldn't have looked more delectable in sapphire silk and lace. My cock hardened, but before I called her over, I stopped myself. Something was wrong. Her body looked tight, and not in a good way.

"Everything okay, baby?" I asked.

She cleared her throat. "Yes. Fine. I made breakfast."

"So I smelled." I smiled.

"I let the dog out and fed him too." Her voice was stilted. "I'll go out in the kitchen and get the food ready for you."

I got up, used the bathroom, and then put my jeans on. I wandered out to the kitchen barefoot.

Ruby was seated already, and two plates and two cups of coffee sat on the table.

"Looks great," I said, taking a seat.

"Mmm," she said, taking a sip of coffee.

The omelet was lukewarm but was still delicious and

perfectly made. She had said she'd been cooking forever. Not everyone could make an omelet. God knew I couldn't. I screwed it up every time.

I was nearly done before I realized she hadn't touched hers.

"Not hungry?"

She looked up as if startled. "Not really. Hey, I'm sorry to do this to you, but I have to leave. Something has come up at work."

"Oh." I tried to keep the disappointment out of my voice. "If this is about last night..."

"No. I promise you it isn't. It's work related. Something I have to look into right away."

"All right. I'll miss you."

She smiled timidly. "I'll miss you too. I really will." She finally took a bite of her eggs and ate about half of the omelet before she stood. "I'll clean up in here. Then I need to get moving."

"Baby, don't worry about it. I have a housekeeper."

"Oh?" Her brows arched. "I keep forgetting how loaded you are."

"It does come with some benefits. So don't worry about the mess."

"All right. If you say so." She wandered down the hallway.

I got up, put our plates in the sink, and then went to the bedroom, thinking I might catch her in the shower. By the time I got there, though, she was nearly all the way dressed.

"No shower?" I asked.

"No. I mean, I already washed the world from my shoulders—or tried to, at least—in the middle of the night. I figured I could skip it this morning. I'm in a hurry anyway."

I pulled her to me. "You're not getting out of here without giving me a kiss." I smashed my lips down onto hers.

She struggled for a bit but then opened for me.

What was wrong?

Surely this still wasn't about last night.

I drew her out with the kiss, and the old Ruby seemed to be returning, until she pulled away abruptly.

"I'm sorry. This can't wait."

"All right. Can I see you tonight?"

"I'm afraid I'll have to play that by ear."

"Baby, what's going on? You can tell me."

"Official police business." She looked down at her feet.

Ruby wasn't one not to look me in the eye. Was she lying to me? I lifted her chin with my finger and forced her blue gaze to mine. "Official, huh?"

She looked downward. "Yeah."

"Look at me," I said.

She met my gaze.

"Don't lie to me again."

"I'm not—"

I shushed her with my fingers. "You're about to do it again. Look, if you need to leave, I get it. But don't lie to me."

She sighed. "All right. It's not official business. It's unofficial business." This time her gaze was not deterred.

"About your father?"

She looked down again.

"Hey," I said. "It's okay."

She cleared her throat. "Not exactly about my father, but he is definitely involved. I just have to look into some stuff. Get a few numbers traced."

"Do you have anyone in your office working with you?"

"No."

"Then how did this come up first thing in the morning?"

She pulled away and grabbed her purse and her jacket. "I don't have any more time to discuss this. Just...call me later. Okay?"

And without another word, she left.

★ ★ ★

I invited myself over to Talon and Jade's for lunch and then invited Joe and Melanie to join us. Marj was in the city for her cooking class and wouldn't be home until the evening. I wanted to pick their brains about Ruby and Theodore Mathias. I hadn't heard any news from Mills and Johnson since we'd gotten back from Jamaica, not even on the number I'd asked them to trace.

"That's odd," Melanie said, as we sat in the kitchen eating sandwiches Talon's housekeeper had prepared for us. "He got right back to me when I asked him to trace the number Jonah was getting those stalking texts from."

"I know," I said. "That's what's so troubling. I've left several voice mails for him and his partner, but nothing."

"Come to think of it, I haven't heard from them since before we left either," Talon said. "And he usually checks in every couple days, even if there's nothing new to report."

Talon was the one who'd originally hired Mills and Johnson to figure out who'd left the rose on Jade's pillow all those months ago. Turned out it had been Felicia, threatened into doing so by who we now thought had been Theodore Mathias. He'd been trying to frame both Larry Wade and Colin Morse, Jade's old boyfriend, for the break-in. Why?

Larry Wade was obvious. He was a scapegoat—and guilty as hell anyway, as one of the three who had abducted and abused Talon. We'd ended up catching him on our own. But Colin Morse—we hadn't figured out that part of the mystery yet. He was just some poor sap who'd left Jade at the altar.

Colin had ended up being kidnapped, raped, and tortured by Mathias and Tom Simpson, who was now dead. Joe had found him in the old house where they'd kept Talon all those years ago.

Colin had some part in this... Or his father did. Ted Morse had turned out to be some kind of mercenary who'd tried to extort money from us by claiming that Joe had been the one who raped and tortured Colin.

Some piece of work.

Would we ever find all the answers? Find the pieces to complete the puzzle?

I wasn't sure.

I'd been wondering lately if we'd be better off just letting it die. Talon was healing, Jonah was healing, and they were both happily married now. We'd brought two of the culprits to justice.

Why tempt fate?

But Ruby had changed my mind. The last of the three, Theodore Mathias, was Ruby's father. He had to be caught. Even if Talon no longer needed that closure, Ruby did.

So by God, I would see Mathias behind bars...or better yet, in his grave.

"That's not like them," Joe was saying.

Like what? Oh, right. We'd been talking about not hearing from Mills and Johnson for a while.

"We could go to their offices," I said.

"What offices?" Joe raked his fingers through his hair.

"You mean they don't have..."

Talon shook his head. "Nope. All they have is cell numbers, which change every now and then. Mills has changed his twice since we've been working with them. Johnson once."

"And it never occurred to either of you that that was a little, I don't know, weird?"

"Nah," Talon said. "They explained it when I first hired them. They work on the good side, but they have to break some rules to do it. The police know it. That's why they recommend them. They can do things the police can't, and they get away with it."

"So they break the law." I shook my head. "They're criminals."

"Yeah. And we're good with that, Ry," Joe said. "It's not like they commit murder. They hack into databases. They break into records. They don't assault people or hurt anyone in any way. Sometimes the end justifies the means."

Ruby would hate this. She was a cop, for God's sake. Then again, she wanted to bring her father to justice.

"I'm really sorry we didn't discuss all this with you at the time," Talon said. "It was your busy season. No one wanted to bother—"

"For fuck's sake! I'm your little brother. I've seen what all of this has done to both of you. You didn't think I'd let the fucking wine wait?" I shook my head. "I can't believe this. Why would you keep shit from me?"

"We didn't," Joe said, his voice calm. "We didn't keep anything big from you. Just that Mills and Johnson sometimes leave their scruples at home. What's the big deal, as long as they get the job done?"

"The big deal is that I would have liked to have known. You're springing this on me now, and..." I sighed. And what? I was pissy because Ruby was lying to me? Because my brothers had lied to me by omission?

"I'm just sick of the lies," I said. "All the goddamned lies."

"Ryan," Jonah said, "just what are you talking about here? We haven't lied to you. You know that."

No, they hadn't, although Joe's voice was a little off. I attributed it to him being a little miffed that he thought I was accusing him of lying to me. "I know that. But..."

"What is it?"

"I think Ruby is lying to me."

"About what?" Melanie piped in. "Are things getting serious between you two?"

"I don't know," I said truthfully. "I just know she's lying to me. She doesn't look me in the eye when she's lying. She left earlier today—"

"Wait a minute. You were with her last night?" Jonah said.

"Yeah, not that it's any of your business."

"That's great, bro," Talon said.

This was getting way off track. "It was just one night. Anyway, we were supposed to spend the weekend together, but she decided she needed to leave to handle something work related. Then she said it wasn't work related, but she wouldn't tell me what it was."

"Probably something to do with her father," Joe said.

"Then why wouldn't she tell me that? I, of all people, would understand. We want her father caught too."

"Maybe she was just in a hurry," Melanie suggested. Then her phone buzzed. She looked at it. "Sorry. I have to take this." She left the kitchen.

CHAPTER TWENTY-SEVEN

RUBY

I breathed a heavy sigh of relief when Melanie answered her phone.

"Hey," I said, "I'm sorry to bother you, but it's important."

"You're no bother. What's up, Ruby?"

"I got a weird text today. Freaked me out something awful, and in my line of work, I'm not easily freaked out."

"Who was it from?"

"That's just it. I don't know. But if I had to wager a guess, I'd say Wendy Madigan."

Silence. Then, "What did the text say?"

"It said, 'Stay the fuck away from my son, bitch.'"

"Wow."

"You know Marjorie contacted me, right?"

She sighed. "Yeah. Jade and I disagree with how they're handling this."

"She told me. I'm in your camp. Did you guys ever find out anything about the number that Ryan was getting calls from? You know, from the woman claiming to be his mother?"

"No. We've been trying to get in touch with Trevor Mills since we returned from Jamaica, but he hasn't been answering."

"I'm at the office now, running a check on this number. I'll forward it to you if you want to look into it."

"Yeah. Please do. Jonah and Talon will want to know about this."

"And Ryan?"

She sighed. "His siblings still think it's best to keep him in the dark. I don't agree, but what can I do?"

My clutch was burning a hole on my desk where it sat. I could almost see it pulse with the plastic bag containing Ryan's hair.

My heart raced.

I was a cop. I had made the truth my life. And here I was, holding a piece of evidence that could lead the Steel family to the truth.

But I couldn't betray Ryan.

I just couldn't.

But I could have the DNA extracted from the hair myself...

If I could get a hair from one of his brothers or from Marjorie, I could have them compared. That would show whether they were full-blooded siblings. Marjorie would gladly volunteer her hair.

God, what was I thinking?

"Ryan's here now, in the kitchen with the others," Melanie was saying. "He seems to be under the impression that you're lying to him."

"What? I didn't. Well, I did, but then I retracted it. I told him I needed to leave this morning for work. But he didn't believe me, so I said it was something unofficial. I could hardly tell him about the text. That would just worry him." And then I laughed out loud. "Christ, did I just say that? Here I am, trying to convince you to convince Jonah and Talon that the right thing to do is let Ryan in on all of this, yet I kept this text from him."

"You didn't want to hurt him or worry him," Melanie said. "Believe me, we all understand that. I've tried to convince them. Jade too. We just haven't been successful. He's their baby brother. They want to protect him, and I can't blame them for that."

The plastic bag containing Ryan's hair pulsed harder, almost with a heartbeat thud now.

Why had I taken that goddamned hair?

And I made a spur-of-the-moment decision. He already thought I was lying to him. What if the test proved he wasn't Wendy's son? Then he'd be spared any pain.

If I had the slightest chance of sparing Ryan pain, I would do it. I'd give Marjorie the strand of hair.

Even if it meant losing Ryan.

★ ★ ★

A half hour later, I had called Marjorie and asked her to meet me at the station. I had also traced the number of the text to a cell phone registered to a Mary Moon, who just happened to be an orderly at the psych lockup where Wendy Madigan was currently being held. Shocking.

Somehow, Wendy had stolen Ms. Moon's phone and sent the text. I made a quick call to the detention center and alerted them that Wendy was stealing phones and that they needed to up their security.

I wouldn't hold my breath, though. The facility was underfunded, and the staff was mostly apathetic. I sighed. From what I knew, apathy was not a good match for Wendy Madigan. Melanie had told me that she was some kind of genius, according to Larry Wade. Cunning and shrewd. Crazy as a loon, but brilliant. A lethal combination.

Whether it was true or not, she thought she was Ryan Steel's mother.

And a mother always protected her young.

I shook my head. I'd get to the bottom of this one way or another. I just hoped it wouldn't cost me—

My phone vibrated. Marjorie was downstairs. I buzzed her up.

She brought with her the hair Jonah had taken from Wendy Madigan's head and also hairs from her, Talon, and Jonah for comparison. "We decided we want to find out once and for all who is who," she said. "Here's hoping Tal, Joe, and I have the same mother. I know I'm her daughter. I'm the only one who looks anything like her."

"The lab is closed on the weekends," I said, "but I'll call the tech I use. He's usually agreeable to coming in and getting things done."

"Be sure to tell him we'll make it worth his while." She patted her purse. "I brought ten grand in cash if he can get results in twelve hours."

I stopped my eyes from widening. "It may take some more time. Blood or saliva is the best."

"Unfortunately, there was no way to get any of Wendy's blood or saliva. Though I'm sure Talon and Joe would have liked to get her blood."

That actually made me smile. I gave my tech a quick call, and as usual he was eager to do the extra work and make some extra money. And the Steels were offering a pretty penny.

We drove over and met him at the lab.

Tucker Madden was a science geek. Genius, but never had it together enough to actually do anything with his microbiology degree. So he worked as a lab tech. Which was good for the station. He was a wizard with DNA. He could pick out strands from samples that other techs couldn't make heads or tails of. The DA used him as an expert witness frequently, and we detectives always wanted him doing our tests.

He was wearing his white lab coat and black-rimmed glasses when we got there, his blondish hair in disarray.

"Hey, Tucker," I said. "Thanks for coming in on such short notice. This is Marjorie Steel."

"Good to meet you." He took her hand. "So let's see the samples you have."

Marjorie and I both handed him our samples. "We've got them all clearly labeled," I said. "And I know I don't have to say this, but this is completely confidential."

"Of course. Always."

Tucker's word was as good as gold.

"I have to tell you though. Hair isn't the best sample from which to extract DNA. Are the roots intact?"

"Yes, yes," I said. "You know me better than that, Tuck."

"True, Roo." He glanced at the samples in their clear plastic bags. "These look good so far as the naked eye can tell. I'll be able to tell more once I get them under the scope. So let me make sure I've got this right. You want to find out if the sample marked RS is a match to be the child of the sample marked WM."

"Yeah," I said.

"And the samples marked TS, JS, and MS should be compared to RS to see if they're full-blooded siblings, just as an extra precaution."

"Yeah," I said again.

"Good enough. I'll get started. You'll hear from me in

twelve."

"The sooner the better," Marjorie said.

"Oh? You willing to—"

"For God's sake, Tuck. Is ten K not enough for you?"

"Sure. But I'm good at this, as you know. I can shave several hours off for, say, another five?"

"Done," Marjorie said. "We're good for it. I only have ten with me now."

I rolled my eyes. "He's a genius, but he doesn't work for free."

Marjorie laughed. "I don't know anyone with great skills who does." She pulled an envelope out of her purse and handed it to Tucker. "Here you go."

"Just so you know, if the samples aren't viable..."

"Don't worry. You still keep the cash," Marjorie said.

He smiled. "Just so we're clear."

"Thanks, Tuck," I said. "You're the best."

Marjorie and I left. As we drove back to my office, I was silent.

"What's going on in that head of yours, Ruby?" she asked. "How are things with Ryan?"

Oh, great. I'm in love with him, in fact. But I wasn't ready to say that to anyone. Not yet. Especially since, if this test turned out positive, I would probably lose him.

So I said simply, "He's great. Really great."

"Yeah, he is," she agreed. "He's a great brother. I really hope this test shows that Wendy is not his mother."

I nodded, staring at the road as she drove.

Hoping I hadn't just made the biggest mistake of my life.

CHAPTER TWENTY-EIGHT

RYAN

"What gives, guys?" I asked. "The two of you go into your bedroom with Melanie for ten minutes, and then she leaves. What aren't you telling me now?"

I was alone with my brothers, and we had retreated out to the deck. Joe's dog, Lucy, was out with Jade chasing a ball.

Talon cleared his throat. "Maybe we should just—"

Talon stopped abruptly. Had Joe nudged him? I wasn't sure, but he could have.

"What is it, Tal?" I asked.

"It's nothing," he said.

"It's not nothing. I'm sick of feeling like the odd man out around here. What's going on?"

"You know everything we know," Joe said soothingly. "And right now, I'm really concerned that we haven't heard from Mills."

"I am too," Talon agreed. "Mathias has proved he can get to anyone. Look at poor Colin. I admit he's an asshole for what he did to Jade—though I'm glad he did, or I wouldn't have her. Still, he didn't deserve what he got at Mathias's hand."

"You think Mathias has done something to Mills and Johnson?" I said.

"I wouldn't put it past him," Talon said. "Nothing is off

limits to him, and if he found out that Mills and Johnson were working for us..."

"Mills and Johnson can no doubt take care of themselves," Joe said. "At least I hope they can."

"I do too," Talon said. "We don't need any more casualties because of me."

I tensed. I didn't like when Talon put this all on himself. He was the least guilty of all of us, and he'd been through the most. "None of this is your fault, Tal."

He raked his fingers through is hair. "If I'd just left it alone. Let sleeping dogs lie."

"Then you wouldn't be happily married now," Joe said. "You deserve happiness, Tal. You deserve healing. Don't take this on your shoulders."

"Yeah, please don't," I agreed. "We all want you to be happy." I gestured out to the green grass where Jade was playing with Lucy. "Look at all you have to live for now."

"I know." He nodded. "I know. Thanks, guys."

"So," Joe began. "We need to talk about the elephant in the room."

I was pretty sure they were talking about Ruby and me. So I started to open my mouth to speak, but Joe continued.

"Dad. We need to figure out how Dad was involved in all of this."

Good save. Of course. We'd recently found out that our father, Bradford Steel, former lover of Wendy Madigan, had been a member of the future lawmakers club at Tejon Prep School, along with Wade, Mathias, Simpson, Wendy, and Rodney Cates, Gina Cates's father. In addition, he had been the financial backer for the club's activities, which, as far as we knew, were masterminded by Theodore Mathias, Tom

Simpson, and Larry Wade—Talon's three abductors. Tom was dead and gone, and Larry wasn't talking.

"I agree," I said. "But how?"

"We go back to Larry Wade, for starters," Joe said.

Tal rubbed at his forehead. "I can't, Joe. I'm sorry."

"You already faced him. That's all you have to do. We understand you can't do it again, don't we, Ry?"

"Of course," I said.

"But I do need someone to go with me. I'll see if Melanie—"

"What about me?" I interjected.

Joe's face went white. "I'm not sure that's a good idea."

"Why the hell not? I'm just as much invested in this as you are. Maybe I want to face one of the motherfuckers who tortured my brother. Maybe I want to give him a fucking piece of my mind."

"Ry—" Talon began.

"You want to stop me too? Really? What the hell is going on here, guys?"

"Nothing," Joe said.

"Bullshit. You give me one good reason why I shouldn't go confront our uncle. Just one reason that has merit, and I'll consider it. Otherwise, I'm going."

Joe and Talon exchanged a look. What kind of look, I wasn't sure.

"You were there that day," Joe said. "It could have been you."

"So?" Could I face one of the men who'd tortured and raped my brother? Who would have tortured and raped me if not for Talon?

I'd do it. Joe had already faced our half uncle several times. He'd faced Tom Simpson. But Joe was strong. He'd always been the strongest of us.

"So...this might affect you more than you think," Talon said.

"I don't fucking care. You two have left me out of this long enough. I'm going."

Joe sighed. "Since there's no talking you out of it, how about this afternoon?"

"On a Saturday?"

He laughed. "There are no weekends in prison. Besides, I know the guards there. They'll let us in."

My stomach dropped. I was about to come face-to-face with one of the men who'd raped my brother.

Who would have raped me.

I swallowed. "Count me in."

★ ★ ★

Larry Wade didn't look anything like our mother, but then they were only half siblings. My mother had been dark-haired, dark-eyed, and gorgeous. Larry was graying-blond, balding, blue-eyed...and pretty far from gorgeous.

I stared at him. He didn't look so scary.

Of course, as a ten-year-old boy, and with Larry wearing a black ski mask, Talon had no doubt seen him as a menace.

I cringed as acid slid up my throat like hot lava. I had to get hold of myself. I'd wanted to do this, after all.

Larry was gaunt, his cheeks hollow. One eye was blackened. Joe had prepared me, but still, his appearance shocked me.

He sat down with a plunk and looked at me. "You must be the other one."

"I'm Ryan," I said shakily.

"Great. Another Steel. Perfect." He looked me over. "You have your mother's nose."

I did? No one had ever said that to me before. Marjorie was the only one of us who resembled our mother in the slightest.

"Enough, Uncle Larry," Joe said. "We're here for answers."

"Then you'll be disappointed, as always," Wade said.

"Maybe. Maybe not," Joe said. "You already know how difficult I can make your life when I don't get what I'm looking for."

"I'm not talking about Wendy Madigan," he said.

Wendy Madigan? Why would he bring her up? I looked to Joe, but he didn't meet my gaze. "We are not going to talk about Wendy Madigan. Not at all." He rolled his eyes toward me for a second. "Do you get my meaning?"

Wade arched his brow just a touch. "Sure. I get it."

I didn't. But whatever. I'd let Joe take the lead here.

"We're here to talk about our father," Joe continued. "We have reason to believe that he backed you, Simpson, and Mathias in your business—and I use the term loosely—dealings. I want to know how much money he gave you and what that business was."

"This could take a while."

"I don't have anywhere to be. Do you?"

Wade sighed. "I was about to go there with you last time. Are you sure you want to do it now?"

Joe looked at me. Was *I* sure? Hell, no, I wasn't sure. But we needed to figure out the role our father had played with these three. The role he might have played in Talon's abduction.

Just the thought nauseated me. Our father might have

played a role in our brother's abduction.

What kind of a man had Bradford Steel been? Truly?

I'd known him as a strict disciplinarian but loving in his own way. He taught all his children the value of a job well done and of a dollar earned. He taught us the business of ranching and to not take our fortune for granted. He was tough on us. But he was fair.

Never had I imagined there might be more to him than met the eye.

He was a good man. A good father.

How could he have gotten involved with three psychopaths?

"Find Simpson or Mathias. They can tell you more about your father than I can."

Joe scoffed. "You don't know? Tom Simpson is dead."

Larry jerked backward, his eyes wide, forehead wrinkled. "How?"

"Shot himself in the head, rather than face what he'd done."

Wade shook his head. "Lucky bastard."

Jonah went rigid, and I knew why. If Larry killed himself or was killed in prison by another inmate, we couldn't use him to get information. Not that he'd been overly forthcoming so far, but he had led us to the future lawmakers club and our father's involvement.

"Lucky? Maybe. Mostly he was a coward. After all was said and done, the iceman couldn't face the music," Joe said. "At least you're facing it."

Buttering Uncle Larry up? Interesting move, Joe.

"Look, we're going to figure this out with or without you," I said. "With would be easier. I know Joe has offered to get you legal counsel. That offer still stands. Why won't you roll over? One of the guys is dead. What does Mathias have on you?"

"You have no idea what he's capable of. What they're all capable of."

"All?" I asked. "Who do you mean?"

"The future lawmakers, of course."

"Oh, we know," Joe said. "An innocent woman is dead because she got us the yearbooks we needed. Yearbooks that had been erased from the online database and stolen from the school library. She stole them from the archives, and she paid with her life."

For a moment, Larry Wade almost looked like he felt something akin to sorrow, but it faded away seconds later. "It went too far. All of it went too far."

"What?" Joe said through clenched teeth. "What went too far, Larry?"

Wade shook his head. "I can't do it. I can't. Not even for the children of my sister. I barely knew her, you know."

"For God's sake," Joe said. "We mean nothing to you. Don't try to play the sister card."

"Besides, Simpson is dead," I said. "He can't get to you."

"Mathias isn't dead. And he isn't even the most dangerous."

"Then who is?" I asked.

He stared at me eerily. "You have your mother's nose," he said again. Then he stood and motioned to the guard. "We're done here."

CHAPTER TWENTY-NINE

RUBY

Marjorie and I ended up at a small café for a late lunch. Melanie joined us. She had driven into the city with Jonah and Ryan, who were visiting Larry Wade. I was nervous, waiting for a call from Tuck. I knew we probably wouldn't hear anything for a while, but Tuck could be speedy sometimes, especially where a lot of money was involved.

I'd rather he take his time and get it right.

"I'm thinking..." Melanie began.

"Yeah?" I took a bite of my BLT. Tasted like sawdust with mayo.

"We're not too far from that psych place where they're holding Wendy Madigan. Would you be willing to go speak to her?"

I nearly jumped off my chair. Go talk to the woman who might be my lover's mother? A woman who was batshit crazy? A woman who knew my father a hell of a lot better than I did? "Hell, yeah."

"Would they let us in?" Marjorie asked.

I pulled my clutch open and pulled out my badge. "This will."

Melanie nodded. "I was hoping you'd agree. I just want to talk to her. I'm not looking for any specific information. Just want to get a feeling, you know?"

"Actually, with your psychological expertise and my investigative training, we might be able to get somewhere."

"If you two don't mind, I'm going to bow out of that one," Marjorie said. "I'll do some shopping. I'm afraid I might just kick the shit out of the bitch."

I felt Marjorie's pain. "I understand."

"Me too," Melanie said. "We'll text you when we're done, and we can meet up later."

I shuddered. This would be another betrayal of Ryan. But I was all in already. I'd given Marjorie his hair and arranged to have the DNA testing done.

God, I hoped it was negative and we could all go our merry ways. Still, that in itself would be a lie. What had I gotten into?

Didn't matter. The test would be positive.

In the depths of my marrow, I already knew the truth.

Wendy Madigan was Ryan's mother.

And she was going to answer to me.

★ ★ ★

Wendy Madigan had medium-dark hair with gray roots. Her eyes were a dull blue. She might have been quite pretty in her day, but now, her hair was slicked back on her head and she wore hospital scrubs.

Did she know my face? Did she know I was the person she had texted? Two orderlies escorted her to our table, one male and one female. The female's nametag read "Mary." Perhaps this was Mary Moon, whose phone Wendy had stolen.

"Are you Mary Moon?" I asked.

"Yeah." She nodded.

"Keep better track of your phone," I said.

She arched her eyebrows at me and patted her pocket. "It's right here."

I said nothing more as Wendy sat down, an orderly on each side of her.

"Detective Lee," Wendy said, staring straight into my eyes. "How nice to see you."

Okay. Question answered. Wendy Madigan had eyes in all places. Time to figure out who was seeing for her and why.

"Nice to see you too, Ms. Madigan," I said with as much nonchalance as I could muster.

Melanie looked understandably confused. "Do you two know each other?"

"Oh, we go way back," Wendy said.

"Hardly," I said. "But you obviously know I've been seeing Ryan Steel. I'd suggest you quit stealing your orderlies' cell phones. That can get you put in solitary lockup." I didn't know if there was such a thing as solitary in psych, but I didn't much care at the moment.

"And aren't you a lovely thing," Wendy said to Melanie. "You're Joe's new wife. What a lucky woman you are. Jonah looks so much like his father, so dark and dominant." Wendy closed her eyes. "How I miss him."

I could tell Melanie was agitated. Truthfully, so was I. We'd both have to do a better job of covering it up.

"How do you know who I am?" Melanie asked.

"I keep tabs on all my boys," Wendy said.

All her boys? This wasn't sounding good.

"We're here for some answers, Ms. Madigan," I said. "Just exactly what do you mean when you say 'all my boys?'"

"Brad and his sons, of course."

"You told Jonah and Talon that you were Ryan's mother," Melanie said. "Is that true?"

She squirmed. "Oh, that? I was just teasing them. Of course I'm not Ryan's mother."

A sigh of relief escaped me. *Thank God!* Ryan would never have to know about the DNA test now. He'd never have to know how I'd betrayed him by giving his hair to Melanie and keeping this secret from him. That feeling I'd had earlier? In the marrow of my bones? It was just my fears getting the best of me.

That was what I wanted to be true. But Wendy Madigan was a known liar. I swallowed a lump in my throat.

Melanie wasn't convinced either. "Why would you lie to them about that? This is killing them."

"I never wanted to hurt Brad or any of his children, but some things can't be avoided."

"Meaning?" Melanie said.

"It's so sad about the middle one. What those men did to him."

"Look, Ms. Madigan," I said.

"Call me Wendy, dear."

"Fine. Wendy, dear." I fake-smiled. "One of those sick men is my father, and we need to find him. Larry Wade is in prison, and Tom Simpson is dead."

"Yes, so sad."

"What? That he's dead?"

"Any end of life is sad, don't you think?"

"No, not really. At least not that one." She was trying to get me off track. I recognized her tactic, and I was sure Melanie did too. "We need your help finding Theodore Mathias, my father."

"It is unfortunate that Theo is your father, dear. But that is precisely"—her voice went lower, darker—"why you need to stay the fuck away from my son."

My skin chilled as goose bumps erupted on my arms. "What? You just said—"

My phone buzzed. It was a text from Tucker.

I have the results.

CHAPTER THIRTY

RYAN

"You okay?" Joe asked as we were driving back to the ranch.

"Yeah. I'm good. I just didn't expect it to affect me quite so much."

"I know. I felt the same way the first time I met Larry. It's hard to believe he's my uncle. He doesn't look anything like any of us."

"Well, just a half uncle," I said.

"True. Still..." He sighed, watching the road. "Thanks for coming along."

"I should have done it before now. I should have been there for Tal." I shook my head. "My work is important to me. I live for the harvest and the winemaking season, but I put it ahead of my brother. I'm sorry, man."

"You have nothing to be sorry for. Believe me," Joe said.

I appreciated his sentiment, but I didn't believe him for a minute. Right now, I felt like the lowest of the low.

"Hey," he continued. "We'll all appreciate it when we taste that amazing wine."

"That wine won't be ready for several years." I sighed. "No, I'm feeling pretty fucking bad, Joe."

"Don't. Please."

Please? That wasn't like Joe.

He continued, "We've all been through enough, and it's not over yet. Don't invent reasons to feel bad, okay? We have enough real reasons."

"True enough." Though I got the feeling there was something Jonah wasn't saying.

I'd been getting that feeling around my brothers since before we went to Jamaica. I'd shrugged it off as pre-wedding jitters, although they were both so head over heels in love with their wives that I had a hard time believing either of them were the least bit jittery.

We were quiet the rest of the way home. Joe asked if I wanted to come over for a drink, but I declined. I wanted to be alone.

Why? I wasn't sure.

For some reason, I felt the need to think. About what? Again, I wasn't sure. "Hey," I said. "Do you have those yearbooks at your place?"

"No, they're at Tal's."

"Okay." No problem. I lived in Talon's guest house. I'd walk over and borrow the yearbooks.

I wanted to get a good look at the future lawmakers.

One way or another, I was going to unravel the mystery of my father's involvement with those men who'd tortured my brother...and who probably had wanted to torture me as well.

★ ★ ★

Armed with the yearbooks, I poured myself a glass of my aged cab and sat down in my leather recliner.

I hadn't spent enough time in this chair lately, and God, it felt good. I flipped on the massager and closed my eyes.

And then shot them open.

Now wasn't the time to relax. I didn't want to associate combing through my father's old yearbooks with my favorite chair. So I turned off the massager, got up, and sat at my bar where I could spread out the books.

First, I took a sip of my wine and let it linger on my tongue. The cab could use another year, but damn, it was good now too. Nice and dry with soft tannins and a blackberry finish.

But now wasn't the time to pat myself on the back for making great wine, either.

I grabbed the book where my father was a junior. That was the only one that showed the future lawmakers club with all six of its members. Simpson and Mathias were seniors and had graduated after this book, and Wendy Madigan, a sophomore in this book, had moved after that year. Rodney Cates, Uncle Larry Wade, and my father were juniors.

I stared at my father's photograph. It could have been my brother Joe staring back at me. The resemblance was uncanny. Jonah definitely favored our father the most of all of us. But Tal and I looked like him too, just a little less so. Not one of the three of us looked anything like our mother, other than our coloring. She was dark-haired and dark-eyed also. Marjorie had her face shape and nose, but none of us guys did.

Wait. Larry Wade had said I had her nose.

I touched my face. That wasn't my mother's nose. What the hell had he been thinking?

My nose was more like my brothers' noses, although it was a little smaller. I had finer features than they had. It had bugged me when I was little. I didn't like being a pretty boy. Now it didn't bother me so much. In fact, it was kind of cool to be considered the best looking of the Steel brothers, since both Joe and Tal were great-looking in their own right.

Looking at Theodore Mathias made me cringe. This man had fathered Ruby. Other than the dark hair, she didn't resemble him. He had a dark and Mediterranean look about him. Mathias was a Greek name, so that explained the look.

He was handsome. They all were. Tom Simpson looked exactly like his son, Bryce, had in high school, and while Larry Wade was graying and balding now, in high school he was good-looking and muscular. Rodney Cates was probably the least handsome of the lot, and even he looked good. Wendy Madigan was cheerleader-pretty with brown hair in the "big" style that was common back then. They hardly looked like the demons they'd turned out to be.

But my father wasn't a demon.

He couldn't be.

So why had he hung around these people? Why did he give them money? And what the hell did they do with it?

Future lawmakers? I scoffed. More like future law*breakers*.

I broke out in a chill.

Had I just stumbled onto something? Ice filled my veins. Was this what it felt like to have a premonition? Shit, I didn't believe in that voodoo...but God, I sure felt like I'd come to some kind of correct conclusion.

Was the future lawmakers a deliberate misnomer?

Had my father broken the law?

No. Not possible. His integrity had been legendary.

But why had he swept Talon's abduction under the rug, never allowing any of us to deal with the fallout?

The reason was out there.

And damn it, I was going to find it.

CHAPTER THIRTY-ONE

RUBY

My nerves did a jig under my skin as Melanie and I sat across from Tucker at the lab. Marjorie had elected to continue shopping and not join us. She was afraid she couldn't take hearing the results for the first time.

I wasn't sure I could either.

"This is Dr. Melanie Carmichael," I said to Tucker.

"Steel," Melanie said.

"Yeah, of course. Sorry. Dr. Melanie Steel."

"We appreciate you getting these results so quickly," Melanie said, her voice stiff.

"Not a problem. Turned out all the samples were great. Very viable. This is a first for me. I'm normally asked to test for paternity. I've never been asked to test for maternity, though I've heard it's becoming more common these days with surrogacy and egg donation."

"Let's get to it," I said, biting my lip. "I can't stand the suspense."

"I'm getting there. As you know, a child inherits half of his DNA from his father, half from his mother, so his DNA should show similarities to half of his mother's DNA. We look at twenty-five different genetic markers."

"Tuck, I know how DNA testing works, and Melanie is a

doctor, for God's sake. Just tell us. Is WM the mother of RS or not? I can't stand this anymore."

Tucker nodded. "She is his mother."

My heart dropped into my stomach.

Melanie let out a heavy sigh. "I don't think anyone will be surprised."

"No one but Ryan," I said. God help him.

"As to the other samples, JS, TS, and MS are full-blooded siblings. The RS sample contains roughly half of the same genetic markers as the siblings' samples, which means the four all share one parent—in this case, the father, since the DNA sample matching RS's other markers is from a female."

Thank God. I had allowed my thoughts to go a little crazy after Wendy had called the Steels "all of her boys." It wouldn't have surprised me if Tuck had said all three of them were Wendy's kids. In fact, I'd actually hoped in some crazy way that would be the case. At least then, Ryan wouldn't be alone.

He wouldn't be alone now. His family wouldn't desert him because he was only their half brother. I knew that. And I wouldn't desert him, even though he might desert me.

But in his mind, he'd be alone. Oddly, though I hadn't known him long, I knew that was how he'd see it. I couldn't bear it.

"Thank you for doing this so quickly," Melanie said again.

"I have a printout showing the results," Tuck said, handing it to Melanie. "This explains everything. Roo knows how to read it, and I'm sure you do too, Doctor."

"Yes," Melanie said, "though I wish it said something completely different."

"I'm sorry this isn't the result you were hoping for," Tuck said.

"It is what it is," I said. "In my business, results are always a crapshoot." But in my business, I wasn't usually personally involved. "Thanks again, Tuck. You're a lifesaver."

Though he had probably just ended any life I might have had with Ryan.

Melanie and I left the lab.

"What now?" I asked.

"I take this to Jonah and Talon, and they decide."

I turned and looked Melanie straight in the eye. "No, I'm going with you. I'm in up to my eyeballs now. I care about Ryan as much as the rest of you do. Whatever goes down is going down with me involved."

She sighed. "Fair enough. Let's go."

★ ★ ★

Sitting in Jonah's kitchen with the two brothers, Marjorie, Melanie, and Jade wasn't what I'd imagined for this Saturday evening. I was supposed to spend the weekend with Ryan. Of course, I'd been the one to bail. None of this was Ryan's fault.

"I'm the oldest," Jonah said. "I'll handle this."

"No, that's not fair," Talon said. "You and I should both tell him."

"Look," I said. "I'm about the farthest thing from a Steel family member sitting here, but I got the hair and I gave it to the lab. This involves me just as much as it involves any of you."

"Are you saying you want to tell him, Ruby?" Melanie asked.

Shit, no. I didn't want to tell him. "What I'm saying is—do we really have to tell him at all?" As soon as the words left my mouth, I knew they were crap. "I'm sorry. Of course we have to tell him. I just don't want..."

"What?" Jonah asked.

I closed my eyes and then opened them. "I don't want to lose him, damn it."

"None of us want you to lose him," Jonah said. "You're the best thing that has happened to Ry in a long time. And we appreciate you getting the sample. Melanie told us how terrible you felt about it, how you refused at first. In fact, Melanie and Jade both thought we should have told Ryan before we even did the test."

"I agree with them," I said.

"Then why did you get the hair?"

I sighed. "Because I didn't want him to get hurt. I thought maybe the test would be negative, and then he'd never have to know. If my involvement could have saved him being hurt at all, I wanted to do it."

"What are your feelings for Ryan?" Jonah asked.

"Jonah..." Melanie began.

"It's a fair question," Jonah said.

"It *is* a fair question," I agreed. "But I'm not going to tell you anything about my feelings before I tell Ryan. That's what's unfair about it."

"She's right," Jade said, "and both of you guys know it."

"Yeah, I know," Jonah said. "I'm being overprotective of Ryan, I guess."

"Look, the last thing I ever wanted to do was hurt Ryan. That's why I gave Melanie the hair, if that makes any sense."

"It makes perfect sense," Melanie said. "Don't let these guys rattle you, Roo." She smiled.

Only Tuck ever called me Roo. It sounded good coming from Melanie, as if we were old friends.

"No one's rattling me. I just don't want my involvement in this to be construed the wrong way. If I have a chance of Ryan forgiving me, I need to make it clear that I was trying to avoid hurting him."

"We'll make that clear."

"Yes, you will. And I'll see to it."

"What does that mean?" Talon asked.

"It means I want to be with you when you talk to Ryan. I want to tell him I got the hair—" I stopped abruptly. I'd gotten it by accident. It was on my neck after our sweaty encounter. I didn't really want to explain that to his brothers. "You know what? Never mind. You two talk to him."

"We don't have to tell him you gave us the hair, Ruby," Jonah said. "One of us could have easily gotten it."

I stood. "No, damn it. No more lies. Tell him where you got it, but tell him why I gave it to you. With the hopes that he could avoid being hurt. Please."

"We will," Talon said. "Absolutely."

"Yes, absolutcly," Jonah echoed. His phone buzzed. "I'll be damned. It's Ry."

CHAPTER THIRTY-TWO

RYAN

"Hey, Joe," I said when he answered. "If you're not busy, would you mind coming over? I'm looking at these yearbooks, and I've come across something that intrigues me."

My brother cleared his throat. "Yeah. No problem. Talon's here with me. I'll bring him along."

"Great. See you soon." I ended the call.

I looked again at the photograph of the future lawmakers club. Damn. The magnifying glass I'd been using sat on the bar next to my now empty glass of wine. Okay, now empty *second* glass of wine.

In less than fifteen minutes, my brothers arrived. Joe carried a manila folder. "What's that?" I asked.

"Some stuff we need to discuss," he said stiffly.

"You sound like you could use a drink," I said. "What's going on?"

"No drink, Ry," Jonah said. "We need to talk."

"Yeah, we do. I need to show you guys something." I grabbed the yearbook showing the photo of the future lawmakers club, all six members. "Check this out." I picked up the magnifying glass. "Look at the fingers on their right hands. They're all wearing identical rings. At least Dad, Simpson, and Mathias are. I can't see the others' hands."

"Let me see." Jonah took the yearbook and the magnifying glass and stared at the photo. "Yeah. They are. That's weird."

"That's what I thought. There's some kind of strange design on the ring that I can't make out. Do you remember Dad ever wearing a ring like this?"

"The only ring Dad ever wore was his wedding ring," Talon said.

"That's what I thought too," I agreed. "Maybe we should look through his old stuff and see if we can find this ring. We should talk to Bryce too. Maybe he can find Tom's. There might be some clues there."

"Definitely. Good call, Ry. What made you think of looking at the photo with a magnifying glass?"

"I don't know. I just felt like we had to be missing something that was right under our noses." The word "nose" hurled me back to the meeting with Larry. *You have your mother's nose.* I still couldn't get that out of my mind.

"Did you find anything else?" Talon asked.

"No. Not yet. But I'm just getting started. I plan to go through these with a fine-tooth comb. I've been AWOL on this stuff for too long. I know it was my busy season, but that's no excuse."

"Ry—" Talon began.

"No, Tal. It's no excuse. You saved me all those years ago, and I should have been here with you, figuring this out. You can count on me from now on. I swear it." I turned to the back of the book. "The only other thing I noticed so far is that Wendy Madigan's parents are listed in the sponsor section for the yearbook. I thought it was weird that Grandma and Grandpa weren't. After all, they had more money than anyone else's parents could have."

I pointed to the entry. *Mr. and Mrs. Warren G. Madigan, parents of Wendy Madigan, sophomore.*

"What about Simpson or Mathias? Are their parents listed?" Jonah asked.

"Nope. Just Wendy's. Probably not anything big. What was most noticeable is that our grandparents weren't listed."

"That is weird," Talon said. "Of course, no weirder than Dad lying to us that he went to Snow Creek High School."

Jonah shook his head. "I'm afraid Dad wasn't the man we remember him to be. This is only the beginning, unfortunately."

"What do you mean?" I asked. Joe had been acting strange since before we left for Jamaica. I was going to find out why. "I've had the feeling you've been keeping something from me for a while now. Both of you. I didn't want to screw up your wedding, so I kept quiet. But now I want to know what's going on."

"This isn't going to be easy," Joe said.

My nerves jumped. "Okay. Now you're freaking me out."

"Let me say something, first," Talon said.

"Of course." I'd always listen to Talon. He was my hero, my savior.

"You're our brother, Ryan. Always. In every way that matters. I love you, man."

Now I was really freaked out. "Tal...I'm not sure you've ever said that before."

"It's not what guys say," Talon said. "But I love you."

"I do too," Joe said.

Jonah had said he loved me recently, and now Talon? Very odd. "I love you guys too, but you know that. What the fuck is going on?"

Jonah grabbed the manila folder he'd brought with

him and took out some documents. "We came into some information recently. Information we were hoping would be proved false."

"Yeah?" Icy fingers crept up my spine.

Joe cleared his throat. "You know Wendy Madigan?"

"Of course."

"While I was with her, after she kidnapped me, she made a claim. About you."

"What about me?"

"God, Joe, how can we do this?" Talon asked.

"We're going to rip the Band-Aid off," Joe said, and then looked me straight in the eyes. "These documents prove something. Something we hoped wasn't true, but is." He cleared his throat. "I wish I didn't have to tell you this."

"Tell me what? Jesus Christ, Joe. What the fuck is going on?"

Jonah exhaled. "Ryan, Wendy Madigan is your mother."

CHAPTER THIRTY-THREE

RUBY

I jolted as fists pounded on my door.

"Damn it, Ruby. Open up!"

God. Ryan. They must have told him. Why would he have come here?

I opened the door, but what greeted me wasn't the Ryan Steel I knew. His hair was unruly, his shirt untucked. He had a feral and crazed gleam in his dark eyes.

"How could you?" he said. "How could you not tell me?"

"I..." I had no words. He was right. I should have told him everything. "We didn't know each other very well. We didn't—"

"Fuck that noise, Ruby. We had something special."

Had? Was it over? Probably. He had every right to end it. Every right to hate me. "Well...you know now." What a stupid thing to say.

"*I know.* What innocuous words those should be. Knowledge should be a good thing, shouldn't it?" He waved the DNA test papers at me. "This is knowledge. Knowledge I never wanted."

"Ryan, come in and sit down. Let's talk about this."

"I didn't come here to talk." He grabbed me and pulled me into him.

"What are you doing?"

"This." He crushed his lips to mine.

I'd kissed Ryan many times before. Sometimes the kisses were passionate with ferocity, sometimes gentle and loving. This was neither.

This kiss was punishing.

While his urgency and physical manner scared me, I couldn't pull away. Not now. Not after I was partially responsible for how he was feeling right now.

After a few seconds, he was the one to pull away. "Goddamnit, Ruby, kiss me back."

Hadn't I been?

No, I'd been cowering, trying to release the tension, trying to resist the urge to pull away. Being forced into something did not sit well with me, given my history. Probably even not given my history.

But this was Ryan Steel. The man I loved, though he didn't know that yet. In my heart, I knew he wouldn't hurt me.

So I opened to him, let him plow into my mouth with his tongue.

Yes, this was punishment, as sure as if he were taking me over his knee and spanking me. He was blaming me for what he knew. Blaming me for my part in it.

And he was right.

I'd take his punishment. Endure what he had in store for me. And hope like hell we'd be okay afterward.

He deepened the kiss, groaning into my mouth. It was primal, driven solely by instinct, and a few minutes later, when he broke the kiss with a loud smack, we were both breathless.

"Bedroom?" he rasped.

I pointed to the closed door off my living room. He pushed me toward it and opened the door. My double bed wasn't made.

I wasn't much of a housekeeper, and my tiny apartment was smaller than his bedroom. But in Ryan's current mood, he no doubt wouldn't mind.

He pushed me onto the bed. "Take off your clothes."

Rattling commenced in my nerves. I didn't move.

Show Daddy how much you love him. Now take off those clothes.

"Did you hear me? I said take off your clothes."

I closed my eyes and exhaled. *He's not your father, Ruby. He's the man you love. He's hurting. He needs you. He won't hurt you.*

I began to unbutton my crisp cotton shirt, my fingers shaking. *You can say no, Ruby. You can stop this at any time.*

But did I want to? I could say no, and I felt sure he would stop.

Sad truth.

I didn't want to say no.

I wanted this as much as he did, maybe even for the same reasons. Anger. Punishment.

I was angry at this outcome too, that Ryan Steel had been misled his whole life about his true parentage. I was angry at myself for not insisting he be told ahead of time.

I was angry at my father for making me afraid of men for so long.

Ryan Steel was not a man I was afraid of. He was a man I loved, and I would give him anything—*anything*—within my power if he needed it.

Right now, he needed my body.

I'd give it willingly, and I'd show him just how willingly.

Instead of going to the next button, I pulled the two sides of my shirt apart, ripping the buttons and sending them flying through the air, clattering to the hardwood floor.

Ryan's eyes burned darker.

I had pleased him.

And that fact thrilled me.

"Now the bra. Let me see those tits."

I couldn't rip off my bra, but I unclasped it as quickly as I could, throwing it to the floor as my breasts bounced gently against my chest.

Ryan sucked in a breath. "Your shoes. Your pants."

My sensible shoes were loafers, and I kicked them off and then removed my socks. As I began to work the button on my pants, I realized something.

My pussy was throbbing. Throbbing in anticipation of being taken forcefully by Ryan Steel.

It wasn't just that I was in love with him, that I was attracted to him. It was the anger that was fueling our passion, our desire.

I wasn't sure what to make of that, but it didn't matter. I was all in. I'd been all in since I'd given Marjorie that hair sample.

I slid my pants over my hips, following with my cotton panties. When all my garments were strewn on the floor, I sat in front of the man I loved, naked and vulnerable.

Was I frightened?

Hell, yes.

But also turned on as hell.

"Spread your legs. Let me see your cunt."

I resisted the urge to shudder at his graphic word. Instead, I obeyed, and he knelt at my bedside.

He stuck his face in my pussy and inhaled. "I'm going to eat you out, baby. I'm going to suck you dry and make you come and come and then come again. You're going to come so many times that you'll be begging me to stop. But I won't stop. I won't stop until you can't take it anymore. Until your body is so sated that you go limp. You got that?"

I nodded, shivering...waiting. Waiting for his tongue, his fingers...whatever he wanted to put into me. I was up for it.

"Do you know what a turn on it is?" he said. "That I'm the only one who's been inside this luscious pussy? That I'm the only man who's taken you?"

I nodded, not sure what else to do.

"No one else will ever taste this pussy," he said. "Not while I live."

What? I couldn't make sense of the words. I was too busy waiting for him to lick me. I was on edge, so ready to come. It wouldn't take much.

"Tell me," he said. "Tell me no one else will taste this pussy."

"What?"

"Damn it, Ruby. Say it." His eyes were dark, feral.

"No one... No one else will taste..."

"This pussy. Say it."

"Th-This pussy." Though I'd thought it, I wasn't sure I'd ever said that word aloud before.

"Good. Now lie back. Get ready. You're going to come."

And as soon as his tongue hit my clit, I did.

CHAPTER THIRTY-FOUR

RYAN

She tasted different. Even more delicious than usual. Or maybe it was the passion our emotion had aroused. I didn't know, but I had to have her. Didn't know what I'd have done if she'd sent me away.

Thank God she hadn't.

Her climax happened quickly, more quickly than I'd expected. I shoved two fingers into her heat and rubbed at her G-spot, milking more and more orgasm out of her. She moaned, cried my name, and with each "Ryan" that came from her lips, my cock grew harder and my passion grew more intense.

And the anger, the need to punish, subsided.

I wouldn't punish her. I would fuck her. I'd eat her and fuck her until I passed out next to her.

I'd lose myself in her tight little body, her tight little cunt, and maybe she could take the nightmare away.

I'd deal with the fallout later.

I removed my fingers from her pussy and replaced them with my tongue, alternating between sucking her slick folds and tonguing her clit. I pushed her thighs farther apart, attempting to go deeper and deeper into her heat. Wanted—no *needed*—to get closer. To taste the deepest parts of her.

Her pussy had never tasted so sweet. I devoured her as

if she were my last meal, and when she claimed her second orgasm, I was rewarded with sweet nectar all over my lips and chin. Her moisture fueled my passions further, and I dived back into her heat.

She cried out, another climax imminent, and I smiled against her folds as I sucked at them. *Again*, I said inside my head. *Again. Come again.*

As if she'd read my mind, she shattered around me, and I forced my two fingers back inside, scissoring them, rubbing her anterior wall, trying to touch every part of her channel. Needed more. So much more.

"Again," I said against her wetness. "Again, goddamnit. Come again." I nipped at her clit.

"God!" she screamed. "No. Too soon. I can't."

"You can," I said. "Come. Now."

And again she unraveled, drenching me in her sweet cream. I lapped it up like a feline, still finger fucking her, still trying to touch her innermost parts.

But my fingers weren't long enough. I needed my cock now.

But not until she came once more.

I sucked at her, ate at her, drove her to the edge until she tumbled over the precipice, her cries a sweet symphony to my ears.

I was still fully clothed, but I couldn't take the time to undress. I unbuckled my belt, undid my jeans, and pushed them and my boxers over my hips. My cock jutted out, as erect as it had ever been. I shoved it into her swollen pink cunt.

Ah, God, sweet suction.

She cried out, her eyes squeezed shut.

I wanted to milk another climax out of her, but I couldn't.

Not now. Not when I needed my release so badly. A release inside her tight body.

A salvation.

I thrust and I thrust. I fucked her and I fucked her.

And when my balls tightened and I shot my semen into her, the freedom flowed through my veins into every cell of my body.

I collapsed on top of her.

Sated.

★ ★ ★

I awoke the next morning alone in a strange bed.

Ruby's bed. It was Sunday, so she wouldn't have gone to work.

A clock radio on the nightstand said ten o'clock. Ten? I'd slept until ten? That was unheard of.

And then everything came crashing down again. What I'd learned yesterday, and how the world had tumbled down around me. My whole fucking world. My identity. How Joe and Talon had tried to talk to me, to bring me down from my rage. How I'd run out on them. How I'd come to Ruby's, intent on having it out with her for her involvement.

Instead, I'd nearly raped her.

I raked my fingers through my hair. God, I was still sweaty.

Why hadn't she stopped me?

Another reason to hate my life.

I still had my jeans and boxers around my thighs. My shirt was still on. Only my boots had been taken off.

Had Ruby even slept here?

I got up and pulled my pants back up. I walked out into

her small living area. She was seated on the couch, typing on her laptop and sipping a cup of coffee. I opened my mouth, but no words emerged. What could I say to her?

I hadn't wanted to hurt her. But I'd been so angry. Still was angry.

I cleared my throat.

She looked up. "Good morning," she said.

"Good...morning."

"Coffee's in the kitchen."

The kitchen was two steps away, so I helped myself to a cup and then went back to her. "May I sit down?"

"Sure." She scooted over a bit.

The couch was more like a loveseat. This apartment was so damned small.

"I need to..." I stopped and cleared my throat again. "I need to...apologize."

"For what?"

"For...taking advantage of you last night."

"No need. I don't do anything I don't want to do. Trust me."

Thank God. "I was just so..."

"So what? Angry? I get that, Ryan. I'm angry too. I'm angry at this whole thing."

I rolled my eyes. "*You're* angry? You're not the one whose life just shattered around him."

Then she glared at me with those intense blue eyes. "Really? My whole life has been like that, Ryan."

"I just mean..."

"Look. I wish I could take all this away for you. That's what last night was about. You know it as well as I do. You once told me you didn't want to be my escape. I never wanted to be yours either, but last night I was. You needed it. I needed it. It was a momentary reprieve. But we're back to real life now, and you and I both have to deal with this. The question is—do you want to deal with it with me or without me?"

The million-dollar question. She'd been a part of this whole thing—of keeping the truth from me. I wasn't just angry with her. I was angry with all of them. Mostly I was angry with my father. I was angry with a dead man.

A fucking dead man.

Who the hell *was* Bradford Steel?

And now, to find out that I grew in the uterus of a crazy woman...

"You should have told me," I said.

"Yes, I should have. I was hoping the test would be negative and you'd never have to know. Then I could have saved you this pain."

"I know. My brothers explained that. Still, they should have told me."

"I agree. So do Jade and Melanie. But they felt the same way I did. They didn't want to hurt you if it could be avoided."

"You gave them my hair."

She nodded. "I did."

"You're just going to admit it?"

"Why not? You want me to try to blame the whole thing on someone else? What good would that do? Yes, I gave them your hair. What I didn't tell them is that I came upon the hair by accident. I didn't pull it out of your head or go searching through your brush. The hair was on my neck that morning... after..."

He nodded. "Okay. Still, you didn't have to give it to them."

"You're absolutely right. I didn't have to. In fact, I thought a lot about whether I would. In the end, I decided to, on the chance that the test might be negative. That way, you wouldn't be hurt."

"Fuck, Ruby. You should have come to me."

"I won't deny it."

"So you're just going to sit there and agree with everything I say? Fight me, goddamnit! I need a fucking fight!"

"Sorry. You won't get one from me. You want to walk out that door? Say good-bye to me and anything we could have? I won't stop you, Ryan. I've lost a lot in my life. One more thing won't kill me."

Her eyes softened a bit then.

"Won't it? Could you really say good-bye to me?" I asked.

And then her eyes turned blue as the morning sky. "Could you say good-bye to *me*?"

CHAPTER THIRTY-FIVE

RUBY

I couldn't believe those words had left my lips.

Of course he could say good-bye to me. This was Ryan Steel, a man who could have any woman he wanted.

"I'm mad as hell," he said.

"I know that. I don't blame you."

"You're not making this easy."

"You're looking for a fight. Go to the fight club and box a few rounds. You won't get a fight here. I did what I thought was the best thing at the time. You may disagree with my reasons."

"Why didn't you just tell me what was going on?"

"I couldn't. That was your brothers' call. Not mine."

"But you're the woman I..."

"The woman you what?"

"Nothing. Never mind."

I'd been hoping he'd say I was the woman he loved. But he'd never love me. Not now. That didn't change the fact that I loved him. I didn't regret last night. If I'd been able to ease his pain for only a second, it would have been worth it.

"Why did you let me...last night?" he asked.

"I already explained that. You needed it. And frankly, so did I."

"You did?"

"Like I said, I'm as angry as you are. I'm angry at this whole situation."

"I don't know what to do." He sank his head into his hands.

I stroked his upper arm, hoping it was a comfort to him. "I don't know either. But I'll help in any way I can."

He turned, his eyes sunken and sad. "Would you go with me to see my mother?"

★ ★ ★

For the second time in two days, I sat in psych lockup facing Wendy Madigan, this time with Ryan at my side. He was stiff, and so far he hadn't said a word. Neither had Wendy. She was staring at him with a look in her eyes I couldn't identify.

It was a pleasant look...and then I realized. I *did* know what it was.

It was a look I hadn't seen since I'd lost my mother.

It was love. A mother's love. This woman, as nuts as she was, loved this man. Loved her son, and had lived her whole life never able to tell him that or even to let him know she existed.

No. I wasn't going to feel sorry for Wendy Madigan. There was definitely more to her than any of us knew.

Finally, she turned to me and said her first words. "Thank you for bringing me my son."

I cleared my throat. "He came of his own volition. He asked me to come along."

She turned to Ryan. "Then thank you. For coming." She shook her head. "Is it any wonder your father and I created such magnificence? You are truly beautiful. I bet you're the smartest of his children too. Such regal features."

Ryan touched his nose, which was odd. I couldn't tell

what he might be thinking.

She turned back to me. "Thank you again."

"Yesterday you told me to stay away from him."

"Did I?" She sniffed. "I don't think so. I couldn't possibly have said that."

Man, she was one piece of work. "You did." I turned to Ryan. I'd told him about my visit with Wendy on our drive here. "Melanie was here. She can back me up."

"I don't think you're lying," he said.

"I'm your mother," Wendy said. "I wouldn't lie to you."

Then Ryan scoffed. "You've been lying to me for thirty-two years. Why didn't you tell me you were my mother?"

"It was a secret." She giggled like a little girl.

I wanted to tell Ryan not to take anything she said seriously, that she was crazy as a loon, but this was his mother. He was already upset enough. Eventually, he'd start worrying about having half of her genes. It was a worry I was familiar with, being the daughter of Theodore Mathias.

"The cat's out of the bag now," Ryan said, looking at his hands.

"You mean you aren't questioning it?" Wendy asked.

"No. My brothers did a DNA test. You are my mother. But in a biological sense only. I want nothing to do with you."

"Then why did you come see me today?"

It was a fair question on Wendy's part. I was wondering the same thing.

"I want to know the truth. The truth about you and my father. The truth about Talon's abduction. The truth about... everything."

"I'm afraid we don't have that much time," she said.

"Fine, then. We'll start with my mother. Er...my father's

wife." He shook his head. "No. I don't want to talk about her. We'll start with you. Why did you give me up?"

"For your father. I did everything for your father."

"Oh?"

"Haven't your brothers told you how much we loved each other?"

"They've told me you loved him. Were obsessed with him. So obsessed that you kidnapped Jonah because you were convinced he was my father."

"Lies. I would never hurt any of Brad's children."

"You're the liar. You basically told Talon and Joe that you were responsible for Tal's abduction. That you orchestrated it to punish our father."

I stiffened. What Jonah and Talon might not have told Ryan was that *he* was let go because he was Wendy's son. At least that was Wendy's story. Larry Wade's was different. He still maintained that Talon was never meant to be taken.

From my limited dealings with Wendy so far, I knew she couldn't be trusted.

"Brad knew not to cross me," Wendy said, an eerie smile on her face.

This was getting nowhere fast. Wendy wasn't yielding any information, and Ryan was just getting upset. I touched his arm. "Ryan..."

"What?"

"We should go."

"No. I haven't gotten anything I came for yet."

"What do you need?" Wendy asked. "Anything. And it's yours."

He looked her straight in the eye. "The truth."

CHAPTER THIRTY-SIX

RYAN

Wendy was beautiful in her own way. Not drop-dead gorgeous like my mo— Daphne Steel. But even in a hospital gown, her gray roots showing through her brown hair, her blue eyes sparkled with something I couldn't quite identify.

And her nose.

I did have her nose.

I didn't expect to have any feelings for her, but looking at her, I couldn't help but feel something. This woman had given birth to me. I had grown inside her body.

Funny that I was accepting that so freely. My world had been shattered twenty-four hours ago. Shattered by this woman.

But not by her.

By the truth.

The truth she—and my father—had kept from me for thirty-two years. For what purpose?

She'd probably done me a great favor. Growing up on the ranch with my brothers and sister had been wonderful, even with the troubling times. I'd learned so much from all of them.

"The truth." She sighed.

"Ryan"—Ruby rubbed my arm again—"I don't think this woman would know the truth if it hit her upside the head."

Wendy ignored Ruby's comment. "I'll tell you anything you want to know."

"Did you love my father?"

"With all my heart. I still do."

"Did he love you?"

"Of course. He gave me his child."

"That only means he fucked you," I said crudely. "I want to know if he loved you."

"I was his true love. His only love."

"If that's true, why didn't you get together with him after my mother died?"

"Your mother is right here." She smiled. A strange smile. A plastic smile.

"You know what I mean. After...Daphne died." Calling the woman I'd known as my mother by her first name felt all kinds of wrong.

"Circumstances," she said.

"What kind of circumstances?"

She smiled the plastic smile again. "Nothing that would make any sense to you."

"None of this makes any sense to me. So what? I want to know anyway. You said you'd tell me the truth...Mother."

"I told Brad to stay away from the rest of them. I knew they were bad news."

"Stay away from who?"

"Simpson, Wade." She nodded to Ruby. "Her father."

Ruby visibly tensed. I wanted to comfort her, but I was in no shape to offer comfort to anyone at the moment.

"The future lawmakers," I said. "Tell me about them. Why did my father join their club? Why did *you* join their club?"

"I joined because I wanted to be near your father. As for

why he joined, you'd have to ask him."

Perfect. "You know very well that I can't do that."

"Why not?"

"He's dead."

"That's ridiculous. I just talked to him this morning."

Ruby rubbed my arm again. "This isn't getting us anywhere. She's delusional, like Jonah and Talon said."

Still, I wasn't ready to go yet. "What did he say to you this morning?"

"He said he missed all of you kids. He said he missed me."

"Really?"

"He said he'd come home as soon as he could. As soon as it was safe."

Ruby rubbed my arm again. I pulled it away from her, not gently.

"What about the ring all the future lawmakers wore? I saw it in their yearbook picture. What was that for?"

"Oh that? I didn't get one. I was only in the club for a year because we moved before my junior year in high school."

"But the guys are wearing the rings in the photo you're in."

"Are they?" She closed her eyes. "I'm almost sure I didn't have one."

"What were the rings for?"

"Just a symbol."

"A symbol of what?"

"Of their commitment to the club. And to each other."

My blood ran cold. "My father financed their activities."

"Yes, he did."

"What were those activities?"

"They started out small. They formed a secret corporation to buy and sell certain goods for profit."

"What kind of goods?"

"Goods that were difficult to get. Goods they could mark up substantially and sell to the highest bidder."

"Illegal goods?"

"Not at first."

Someone had kicked my stomach in. At least that's what it felt like. She'd just basically confirmed that my father had been financing something illegal.

"What did they start out with?"

"They'd buy up certain toys that were popular with kids at the time and then sell them on the secondhand market for double the price. Later they got into gaming systems. With your father backing them, they could buy in bulk. They made a ton of money."

All right. So far so good. Nothing illegal about that. At least not that I knew of. I made a mental note to ask Jade about it.

"Then they got greedy."

Ruby nudged me. She'd told me about the talk with her uncle, Rodney Cates. He'd said the future lawmakers got greedy.

"And...?"

"Selling illegal stuff yielded much higher profit margins. So they started dabbling in firearms. Then drugs."

I let out a breath I hadn't realized I'd been holding. "Drugs," I repeated.

"Yes. First just marijuana. Later cocaine. Then they got into narcotics."

"God..."

"But even drugs didn't make as much money as something else."

I wanted to puke. "What?"
She smiled her plastic smile once more. "People."

CHAPTER THIRTY-SEVEN

RUBY

I nearly heaved up my breakfast. Wendy was hardly a reliable source, but if she was telling the truth, my gut instinct had been correct.

My father and his cohorts were in the business of human trafficking. No wonder Juliet and Lisa's plight had affected me so deeply. This shit happened in the Caribbean and countless other foreign places, but it also happened right here at home.

I was going to lose my lunch. I stood. "I'm sorry. Please excuse me."

Ryan grabbed my hand. "Don't go. Please."

I swallowed. "You don't understand. I'm seriously going to be sick. Now."

"Take a deep breath. Please. I need you."

Wendy went on as if nothing else were happening. "People, you see, are a dime a dozen. They're easy to get. Much easier than drugs. And you don't have to pay up front."

God, she was talking like this was something normal! So matter of fact. I swallowed again to hold back the acid that was lodged in my throat. Ryan needed me. I'd stay. I'd hold it back.

"Easy to get?" Ryan said. "How can you say that?"

"The homeless. Runaways. Kids walking to school. Sometimes their own children."

I clamped my hand over my mouth. *Sometimes their own children.* This would have been my fate. Gina's fate.

Ryan turned to me. I must have looked green, because he said, "Go ahead. I got this."

I stood and ran out of the room. I looked around for the restroom but couldn't find it, so I headed for the nearest trash can and emptied my stomach.

I continued heaving once nothing was coming up. Sweat poured from my brow. Tears poured from my eyes. I shook, my stomach cramping. After what seemed like hours but was only a few minutes, I was finally able to stand.

An orderly came to me with a basin. "Are you all right?"

I took the basin from him. "I'll be fine. Thank you."

But fine was something I'd never be again. Something maybe I hadn't been in a long time.

Pull yourself together, Ruby. I was a cop, for God's sake. I'd seen worse in my lifetime.

But this was...personal.

So deeply fucking personal.

Wendy could easily be lying. She was certainly not a reliable source.

But she wasn't lying. I'd already formulated a similar theory in my mind. I just never actually thought it could be true.

Yet it all made sense.

Sense in a world that was hell on earth, especially for my father's victims.

Now more than ever, I had to find my father and bring him to justice.

★ ★ ★

I didn't know how much longer Ryan talked to Wendy. Time became a hazy thing, and I sat in the hallway, clutching my basin, but I didn't throw up again. Whether that was because nothing was left in my stomach or because I was holding it together, I didn't know. I didn't feel like I was holding anything together, that was for sure.

Ryan finally came walking out, his expression unreadable.

"You okay?" he asked when he came to me.

I nodded. Which was a big lie, but he had enough problems.

"Let's go. I can't take any more of this." He raked his fingers through his hair. "I can't believe my father would be involved in such a thing."

"Your father probably wasn't," I said. "But my father was. *Is.*"

He pulled me into a stand. "I'm sorry. That was thoughtless of me." He hugged me quickly. It wasn't intimate at all. "Let me take you home. I need to be alone for a while."

I nodded. That was understandable. "Just promise me that..."

He stopped my lips with his finger. "I won't do anything stupid," he said.

I hoped he was telling me the truth. His whole world had just been shattered. He was eerily calm right now...and I had the feeling it was the calm before the storm.

It was on the tip of my tongue to tell him no, I wasn't going home. I was staying with him. But I couldn't get the words out.

And it hit me. I needed to be alone too.

I needed to think this through, figure out what to do next.

Because doing nothing was not an option.

The drive to my apartment took only ten minutes. He gave me a hasty kiss good-bye and said he'd call me.

That was all. And I didn't expect anything else.

I flipped on the light switch and poured myself a glass of cold water but didn't drink it. Then I looked at my phone. I'd turned the ringer off while we were talking to Wendy. No calls, no texts.

I slid down the side of the wall to sit on the floor of my small kitchen.

My thoughts were jumbled. What next?

What next for Ryan and me? Could we even have a future now?

If only I hadn't fallen in love with him.

Clearly he wasn't in love with me, and right now he had way more to deal with than anyone should have. Bothering him about our "relationship" was not something I'd do.

What *could* I do?

More research on the future lawmakers. Another visit to my uncle, maybe. Another visit to Larry Wade. At least the two of them seemed less crazy than Wendy. Still crazy, though.

It all seemed so futile now. No matter how hard I worked, I never seemed to get anywhere. Questions didn't turn up answers. Only more questions.

What would make me feel better?

Being with Ryan, but that wasn't in the cards.

Then it hit me. I'd call Shayna. Just check up on her to see how she was doing. Maybe she'd heard something about Juliet and Lisa.

I searched my contacts and pulled up her number. It rang a few times, and then a female voice answered.

"Hello, Shayna? It's Ruby Lee, from Jamaica."

"Ruby? I don't know any Ruby."

"This is Shayna Thomas, right?"

"Yes."

"We met in Jamaica. Remember? When your...friends and you went off on those Jet Skis?"

"I'm afraid I don't know what you're talking about. Please don't call me again."

The line went dead.

What?

I called the number again. This time I got no answer. It went straight to voice mail. "Listen, Shayna," I said. "I'm not sure what's going on, but I assure you there's nothing to fear from me. I'm a friend. I want to help. I want to—" The line went dead.

I called again. No voice mail. She had blocked me.

Why?

What was she afraid of?

I shook my head, eyeing my glass of water on the counter above me. I wasn't thirsty. I wasn't hungry.

I wasn't...anything.

And then my phone rang. A number I didn't recognize.

Shayna! Perhaps she'd been afraid someone was listening in, and she'd tried a different phone.

"Shayna?" I said into the phone.

"No," a male voice said.

"Oh, I'm sorry. Who is this, please?"

"Ruby," the voice said, "this is your father."

CHAPTER THIRTY-EIGHT

RYAN

I'd saddled up my horse, Sergio, and gotten ready to go for a run, when I realized Sergio, as fast as he was, wouldn't be able to give me the speed I was craving.

I patted him down. "Another time, boy," I said.

Then I wandered back up to the detached garage at the guest house where I kept my pride and joy—my Porsche 911 Turbo. Sleek navy blue—custom paint job—and posh leather seats, the convertible sat under its chamois cover. His name was Jake.

I removed the cover and stared at it in all its glory.

Neither of my brothers were into cars. They were more comfortable in their pickups than in the luxury sedans they both owned. Me? I loved them, though I didn't take Jake out as often as I would have liked to.

Right now? I needed speed. I needed the wind blowing through my hair as I sped a hundred twenty miles an hour down deserted country roads.

My life was in shambles.

The woman I—

The woman I what?

Loved?

Fuck. I shoved my fingers through my hair.

I fucking loved her.

Ruby. Ruby who'd kept a secret from me. She'd taken my punishment for that. A woman who had only recently opened her body and mind to sex had let me take what I needed from her.

Damn.

My life was a mess.

I couldn't have a relationship, and I had no idea if she felt the same way anyway.

So for now, I'd get Jake out onto the open road and scream through the next couple hours at top speeds.

My phone buzzed.

Shit. It was Joe.

"Yeah?" I said into the phone.

"Hey, Ry. Tal and I just wanted to..."

"What, Joe? What the fuck do you want?"

"To make sure you're all right."

"All right? Of course I'm not all right. My life has been shattered, and I just spent the last hour listening to my biological mother spin all kinds of tales."

"You went to see Wendy?"

"Yeah. You got a problem with that?"

"No. Of course not. But we should have been there with you."

"Ruby went with me."

"Good. Then you weren't alone."

"Alone? I got news for you, Joe. I'm fucking alone. I have no idea who I am anymore. I have no idea who my brothers are anymore. It doesn't get much more alone than that." I ended the call, furious.

I got into the Porsche, put the top down, and backed out of

the garage. "Let's go, Jake," I said. "Show me what you can do."

I drove through the private roads and off our property and then headed into the deserted country roads. Route 78 was straight and narrow with the ups and downs of the foothills.

Perfect.

The first one hundred miles an hour came easy. Jake's engine roared with power, promising me more speed, more thrill. The sound of his tires screaming along the road began to disappear as I eased him toward one forty. The rubber clawed at the road.

I resisted the urge to close my eyes and drift away with Jake.

Closing one's eyes at a hundred forty miles an hour was never a good idea.

I edged toward one fifty, and Jake drove as smooth as a gazelle running across the savanna. One fifty-five. One sixty.

Oh, yeah.

Lift. I felt the oxygen tunneling under the engine. Much more speed and I'd get into the air like a fucking plane.

Of course not, but I felt it. Truly felt it.

Jake's engine had now drowned out all road noise, what little there'd been.

My blood thumped in my ears in time with my heartbeat.

One sixty-five.

One seventy.

Vibrations. Vibrations against my thigh.

Just the engine. Just me flying through the goddamned air.

No.

It was my phone.

Answering the phone at a hundred seventy miles an hour?

Not a good idea. But what the fuck did I care?
I put the phone to my ear, a smile on my face. "Hello?"
"Ryan," a male voice said. "This is your father."

Continue The Steel Brothers Saga with book eight

Twisted

Coming December 26th, 2017

MESSAGE FROM HELEN HARDT

Dear Reader,

Thank you for reading *Shattered*. If you want to find out about my current backlist and future releases, please like my Facebook page: **www.facebook.com/HelenHardt** and join my mailing list: **www.helenhardt.com/signup/**. I often do giveaways. If you're a fan and would like to join my street team to help spread the word about my books, you can do so here: **www.facebook.com/groups/hardtandsoul/**. I regularly do awesome giveaways for my street team members.

If you enjoyed the story, please take the time to leave a review on a site like Amazon or Goodreads. I welcome all feedback.

I wish you all the best!
Helen

ALSO BY HELEN HARDT

The Sex and the Season Series:
Lily and the Duke
Rose in Bloom
Lady Alexandra's Lover
Sophie's Voice
The Perils of Patricia (Coming Soon)

The Temptation Saga:
Tempting Dusty
Teasing Annie
Taking Catie
Taming Angelina
Treasuring Amber
Trusting Sydney
Tantalizing Maria

The Steel Brothers Saga:
Craving
Obsession
Possession
Melt
Burn
Surrender
Shattered
Twisted (December 26th, 2017)
Unraveled (February 13th, 2018)

Daughters of the Prairie:
The Outlaw's Angel
Lessons of the Heart
Song of the Raven

Anthologies:
Her Two Lovers
Destination Desire

DISCUSSION QUESTIONS

1. The theme of a story is its central idea or ideas. To put it simply, it's what the story *means*. How would you characterize the theme of *Shattered*?

2. Discuss the differences among the Steel brothers—specifically, how Ryan is different from Jonah and Talon.

3. Ryan talks about the "darkness" that shrouds both Jonah and Talon, but not himself. What might this darkness be, and why doesn't Ryan share it?

4. Discuss the contradiction in Ruby's character. On the one hand, she's a competent police detective and knows how to take care of herself. On the other hand, she's scared to death of men.

5. Both older Steel brothers are very dominant in the bedroom. Do you see this happening with Ryan? Why or why not?

6. Where do you think Mills and Johnson are?

7. Discuss literary devices used in the story. Any foreshadowing? Other devices? What is the significance of the story's title?

8. What do you think really happened to Juliet and Lisa?

9. What new things do we learn about Wendy Madigan in *Shattered*?

10. Discuss the future lawmakers club. What more do we know now? What might their rings signify?

11. Was it fair of Marjorie to ask Ruby to get a strand of Ryan's hair? Why or why not?

12. How did you feel to watch Jonah and Melanie and Talon and Jade exchange vows?

13. Do you think Bradford Steel is alive? Why or why not? What might his story be?

14. How do you think Wendy got pregnant with Ryan? Did she trap Brad? Did she use in vitro fertilization?

ACKNOWLEDGEMENTS

While *Shattered* begins the story of Ryan and Ruby, I hope all of you were happy to see the previous two couples exchange their wedding vows. Jonah, Melanie, Talon, and Jade certainly deserve their happily ever after.

Ryan is different from his brothers. Though he does possess some of the Steel darkness, he's more optimistic and jovial than either Jonah or Talon. We learn things in *Shattered* that might begin to explain this, but there are more secrets to come... As for Ruby, I had so much fun easing her out of her shell. She and Ryan made a splash together, and I hope you all loved reading it as much as I loved writing it.

Thanks so much to my amazing editors, Celina Summers and Michele Hamner Moore. Your guidance and suggestions were, as always, invaluable. Thank you to my line editor, Scott Saunders, and my proofreaders, Jenny Rarden, Chrissie Saunders, and Amy Grishman. Thank you to all the great people at Waterhouse Press—Meredith, David, Kurt, Shayla, Jon, Yvonne, Jeanne, Renee, Dave, and Robyn. The cover art for this series is beyond perfect, thanks to Meredith and Yvonne.

Many thanks to my assistant, Amy Denim, for taking care of business so I can write. I couldn't do it without you!

Thank you to the members of my street team, Hardt and Soul. HS members got the first look at *Shattered*, and I appreciate all your support, reviews, and general good vibes.

You all mean more to me than you can possibly know.

Thanks to my always supportive family and friends and to all of the fans who eagerly waited for *Shattered*. I hope you love it.

Thanks to my local writing groups, Colorado Romance Writers and Heart of Denver Romance Writers, for their love and support.

You all know I can't resist a cliffhanger. I hope you're excited as I am to continue Ryan and Ruby's journey!

ABOUT THE AUTHOR

#1 *New York Times,* #1 *USA Today,* and *#1 Wall Street Journal* Bestselling author Helen Hardt's passion for the written word began with the books her mother read to her at bedtime. She wrote her first story at age six and hasn't stopped since. In addition to being an award winning author of contemporary and historical romance and erotica, she's a mother, a black belt in Taekwondo, a grammar geek, an appreciator of fine red wine, and a lover of Ben and Jerry's ice cream. She writes from her home in Colorado, where she lives with her family. Helen loves to hear from readers.

Visit her here:
www.facebook.com/HelenHardt

ALSO AVAILABLE FROM
WATERHOUSE PRESS

MISADVENTURES OF A GOOD WIFE

#1 *NEW YORK TIMES* BESTSELLING AUTHOR
MEREDITH WILD

#1 *NEW YORK TIMES* BESTSELLING AUTHOR
HELEN HARDT

Kate and Price Lewis had the perfect marriage—love, fulfilling careers, and a great apartment in the city. But when Price's work takes him overseas and his plane goes down, their happily-ever-after goes down with it.

A year later, Kate is still trying to cope. She's tied to her grief as tightly as she was bound to Price. When her sister-in-law coaxes her into an extended girls' trip—three weeks on a remote Caribbean island—Kate agrees. At a villa as secluded as the island, they're the only people in sight, until Kate sees a ghost walking toward them on the beach. Price is alive.

Their reunion is anything but picture perfect. Kate has been loyal to the husband she thought was dead, but she needs answers. What she gets instead is a cryptic proposal—go back home in three weeks, or disappear with Price...forever.

Emotions run high, passions burn bright, and Kate faces an impossible choice. Can Price win back his wife? Or will his secrets tear them apart?

Visit Misadventures.com for more information!

ALSO AVAILABLE FROM
HELEN HARDT

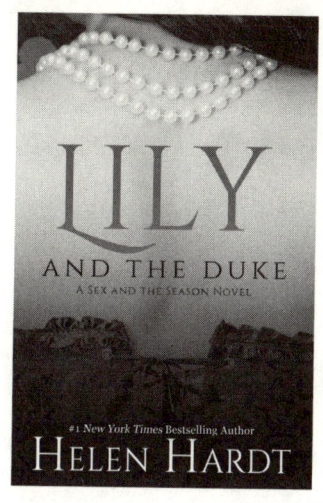

Lady Lily Jameson is thrilled to attend a house party given by Daniel Farnsworth, the Duke of Lybrook, but not because he's the most eligible bachelor in the peerage. Her only interest is his famous art collection, which reputedly includes a painting by her favorite artist, Jan Vermeer.

Daniel, duke only by virtue of the untimely deaths of his father and older brother, wants nothing to do with his new duties. He'd rather continue his rakish ways. When he finds the lovely Lily sneaking around the property in search of his art collection, sparks fly.

Despite her father's wishes, Lily has no intention of marrying. She wants to travel the world to gain real life inspiration for her painting and writing. And what could be better worldly experience than a passionate affair with the notorious Duke of Lybrook?

But circumstances may change the game and the players...and danger lurks, as well.

Visit HelenHardt.com for more information!

ALSO AVAILABLE FROM
WATERHOUSE PRESS

MISADVENTURES OF A CITY GIRL

#1 *NEW YORK TIMES* BESTSELLING AUTHOR
MEREDITH WILD

USA TODAY BESTSELLING AUTHOR
CHELLE BLISS

Fresh off a divorce from a Hollywood hotshot, Madison Atwood needs an escape. With the paparazzi fresh on her heels and her love life splashed on every tabloid, she runs away to a swanky retreat in Northern California. Avalon Springs is the mountainside haven she needs to find herself again.

Luke Dawson lives off the grid, preferring solitude to society. When he finds a beautiful woman soaking in the hot springs on his property, he can't stop himself from watching her. She captures his attention, but she's just a city girl—a beautiful distraction disturbing the peace he's settled here to find.

When Madison discovers Luke's secluded cabin, he can't turn her away again. They make no promises. Madison needs to feel wanted again, and Luke misses the touch of a woman. But when mother nature has other plans, they're forced to spend more than a night of passion together. Can Luke say goodbye to the only woman who's made him feel anything in years, and can Madison leave behind the man who brought her back to life?

Visit Misadventures.com for more information!